I0805906

A DEATH IN ARCADIA

Also by Mike Papantonio

Novels

The Middleman—A Legal Thriller (2025)
Suspicious Activity—A Legal Thriller (2024; with Christopher Paulos)
Inhuman Trafficking—A Legal Thriller (2021; with Alan Russell)
Law and Addiction—A Legal Thriller (2019)
Law and Vengeance—A Legal Thriller (2017)
Law and Disorder—A Legal Thriller (2016)

Nonfiction

Closing Arguments—The Last Battle (2003; with Fred Levin)
Resurrecting AESOP—Fables Lawyers Should Remember (2000)
Clarence Darrow, the Journeyman—Lessons for the Modern Lawyer (1997)
In Search of Atticus Finch—A Motivational Book for Lawyers (1996)

A DEATH IN ARCADIA

A LEGAL THRILLER

MIKE PAPANTONIO

Arcade Publishing • New York

Copyright © 2026 by Mike Papantonio

All rights reserved. No part of this book may be reproduced in any manner without the express written consent of the publisher, except in the case of brief excerpts in critical reviews or articles. All inquiries should be addressed to Arcade Publishing, 307 Fifth Avenue, 4th Floor, New York, NY 10016.

Arcade Publishing books may be purchased in bulk at special discounts for sales promotion, corporate gifts, fundraising, or educational purposes. Special editions can also be created to specifications. For details, contact the Special Sales Department, Arcade Publishing, 307 Fifth Avenue, 4th Floor, New York, NY 10016 or arcade@skyhorsepublishing.com.

Arcade Publishing® is a registered trademark of Skyhorse Publishing, Inc.®, a Delaware corporation.

Visit our website at www.arcadepub.com.

Please follow our publisher Tony Lyons on Instagram @tonylyonsisuncertain.

10 9 8 7 6 5 4 3 2 1

Library of Congress Cataloging-in-Publication Data is available on file.

Cover design by Erin Seaward-Hiatt
Cover image from Getty Images

Print ISBN: 978-1-64821-170-6
Ebook ISBN: 978-1-64821-171-3

Printed in the United States of America

ACKNOWLEDGMENTS

The author wishes to thank the following individuals for their help in the preparation of this novel: Raymond Benson, Cynthia Manson, Kim Lim, and my colleagues at Levin-Papantonio Law Firm.

This is a work of fiction but it is inspired by true events.

1

1970. Late Summer.

Fight Night.

Bucky Carlton was pitted against Logan Manring.

Both of them seventeen-years-old.

Both of them incarcerated in the reform school known as Sandbury Housing for Boys. SHB.

Of course, SHB wasn't much of a school. Sure, they provided classes in English, Spanish, math, science, geography, and history. But since the facility housed boys aged thirteen to seventeen, the in-depth levels of these courses differed.

Very few of the boys paid much attention in classes. Most of them just wanted out. Most of them just wanted to survive.

For all intents and purposes, Sandbury Housing for Boys was a juvenile prison. A detention center. A place meant for reform, but that rarely occurred.

Most of the population, when they aged out of SHB, simply transitioned to an adult prison, depending on what brought them to the school in the first place. If they were released to public life, odds were that they would commit worse infractions and end up in an adult prison anyway.

There were, though, a handful of boys who did not belong in SHB. They wound up there due to some stupid mistake they might have made, parental neglect or maliciousness, an incompetent lawyer, an overzealous prosecutor, or a corrupt judge. These individuals were more often than not "good boys" who took a wrong turn somewhere or made a bad decision. Or they were simply cast away by an uncaring family or a dysfunctional system.

Bucky Carlton was one of the good boys.

His crime? Having a deceased mother and a deadbeat father who was missing in action.

Sentenced to SHB until he was eighteen. All because he had been caught squatting in an empty vacation home near Peace River. A trespassing charge and no guardians to keep him "in line."

Unfortunately, Bucky had also made the mistake of attempting to escape and run away. He was caught in the act, a serious violation.

The boys' camp guards had a routine of punishing runaways or any of their wards they thought were troublemakers.

Fight Night was one of the tools.

Boy against boy in an Anything Goes fight to exhaustion.

Bucky had mostly kept to himself in the camp, but he had developed the reputation as a badass in the time he'd already spent there. Thus, the boy he was pitted against had to be not only big but also psycho quality violent.

Logan Manring fit that bill. He outweighed Bucky by fifty pounds, was taller by ten inches, and he played dirty.

Fight Night always happened hours after dinnertime, when the boys would normally be going to sleep. The guards put out the word to the various kids who the administration called "helpers," but the rest of SHB's population called "rats."

"Fight Night tonight!"

The message traveled through the system, eliciting excitement—and fear—among the boys. It meant that at ten o'clock, they would all be called to the gymnasium to witness the fight. Sometimes more than one, but usually it was a single bout featuring a boy who had committed some camp infringement against someone who would beat the crap out of him. Occasionally both boys had been caught disobeying a camp rule, in which case the odds were more or less even.

Bets were taken by all the guards on which boy would disable the other first or who would cry soonest.

Once he had been told he was participating in Fight Night, Bucky knew it was not going to go well for him. The butterflies in his stomach made him ill for most of the day. Nevertheless, he was the type of kid who put up a good front. He never let his fear show. He put up the bravado that he was going to beat Logan Manring's butt.

Two beefy guards brought him to the gymnasium right on time. The rest of the population sat on bleachers on both sides of the gym floor. A large mat covered the space where ordinarily the boys played basketball. The rules were that neither boy could exit the mat's boundaries by choice. Sometimes a boy might be thrown *out, but that was all right. But if either fighter moved off the mat to escape his opponent, even worse punishment might be inflicted on the offender.*

Bucky took his place at one end of the mat and faced Logan, who stood confidently on the other side. Neither boy wore boxing gloves. Fight Night was always a bare-knuckle ordeal. It was meant to be old-fashioned boxing, but if one of the kids happened to know martial arts, that was permitted. In fact, nothing was off limits.

A guard served as the referee, but all he really did was shout, "Fight!" There were no rounds. No breaks. The boys were to fight until the referee felt like calling it finished.

Most of the time, the boys observing the fight did so in silence. They all knew that Fight Night was a terrible thing. Only a few of the more aggressive residents shouted or cheered on a favored fighter.

Logan lumbered toward Bucky like a tank. Bucky stood his ground, his fists properly raised and in position. He had been in fights before. He knew how to box. Unfortunately, he didn't know how to stop a battering ram.

Logan swung. Bucky blocked the blow, but Logan swiftly punched hard with his other fist. Bucky fell to the mat, dazed. Logan then kicked Bucky in the ribs and moved away.

"Get up, loser!" Logan shouted.

After a moment, Bucky managed to rise on all fours. He finally stood, blood pouring from his mouth. He spit on the mat and then charged.

For the next four minutes, Bucky gave the fight everything he had. He succeeded in landing many blows, even knocking Logan down once. But by the sixth minute of the fight, Bucky was tiring and weakening. Logan's size and weight mattered, and it wasn't long before the heavy artillery aspects of his attacks multiplied. Bucky fell again . . . and again . . . but he repeatedly stood and shakily kept going.

When Logan broke Bucky's nose in minute nine, it was all over. Bucky dropped to his knees, barely hanging on to consciousness. Logan moved around behind his opponent, got on his own knees, and wrapped a heavy forearm around Bucky's neck.

The guard referee negligently stopped the fight a few seconds too late.

Bucky Carlton did not survive Fight Night. Logan had crushed his neck after a brutal ordeal.

It was too common a story for juvenile detention centers in Florida and elsewhere in the United States. One of many tales that were swept under the rug by employees of the facility and by management.

It was the kind of thing that still occurred over fifty years later.

TODAY

Trayvon sat at his table alone.

Being solitary was what he desired the most, and it was what he had been used to.

The fifteen-year-old boy wasn't really by himself, though. At least thirty other boys of varying ages sat at a dozen tables eating lunch in the small cafeteria of B Camp School for Boys.

Trayvon remembered that when he had attended kindergarten—an eternity ago—the teacher had played soothing music on a stereo system while the kids ate lunch, did arts and crafts, or simply played together. Here, the only sounds were plastic spoons scraping plastic plates and the occasional soft whispers.

The guards insisted on quiet. No noise. The walls in the place tended to reverberate the slightest hums, thuds, and chatter. Trayvon would have liked to shout "Hey!" just to hear his voice echo in the cold room. Instead, though, the boys were conditioned to display calmness and composure.

This outward appearance of serenity was a far cry from the terrifying reality that Trayvon had witnessed in his twenty-five days at B Camp in Sweeton, Florida.

Why had his mother allowed that "health services" person to bring him there? He knew the answer, of course. His mother was a junkie, a woman who went from man to man just to survive. The most recent boyfriend was also her dealer. Trayvon hated him. Bruno.

When his mother and Bruno were saying their goodbyes just before he was driven off to B Camp, she told Trayvon that she loved him "very much."

Right.

Trayvon kept his head down as close to the lunch plate as possible. The few times he felt brave enough to look up and scan the room only resulted in magnifying the fear, making it difficult to breathe. He would lose his ability to feel his arms or his legs. It was like staring down a dark tunnel, something that recurred in his nightmares.

What was the so-called food on the plate? Some kind of meat-mash that reminded Trayvon of dog food. Oh, look, there were a few bits of macaroni noodles that weren't fully cooked! And was that supposed to be broccoli? It was brown and yellow! At least the apple juice tasted somewhat normal.

Trayvon felt unsafe among the other boys. Many were bullies who sucked up to the guards. Being of small stature, Trayvon's instincts told him that he needed to make a move that would land him back into the protective walls of a solitary confinement cell. He had felt somewhat secure there when he'd done something wrong on his fourth day and was placed into one. Trayvon wasn't sure exactly what his transgression had been, but the burly guard known as Perkins had simply grabbed him from behind, growled, "Shouldn't have done that, kid," and thrown him into solitary. It might have been for three days, but Trayvon wasn't sure. It turned out to be a blessing. No one bothered him. He could really *be* alone.

Maybe he could go back.

Staying in the general population of B Camp was unpleasant and dangerous. The big boys picked on the smaller ones. Guards turned blind eyes away from horrible things that happened. Especially at night.

He hated confrontation, he hated his inclination to cower, he hated that he was a target. It's as if he'd had a bullseye drawn on his back from the moment he had stepped foot in B Camp.

Trayvon couldn't understand why he was there. He knew he hadn't done anything wrong. He was a good kid. His teachers had said so, that is, when his mother had stuck around one place long enough to enroll him in school. Trayvon often got compliments on his drawings. At least B Camp allowed him to have a sketchbook. He loved to draw cartoons and superhero figures. And he also documented things that went on in the camp. He had to be careful that none of the guards actually *looked* at his sketchbook. That would be bad.

Yes, he had been sickly as a younger child. His mother hadn't put up with that, as if it were his fault that his health was poor. She couldn't fathom that it was their transient lifestyle and the squalor in which they often found themselves that contributed to his illnesses. Live with disease and you get diseased. Made sense.

It was true that for the past couple of years Trayvon desperately wanted to be free from his mother. It would have been the best thing for him, to get away from her and Bruno. But not like this. Not here.

He didn't think he could survive in B Camp. Some of the older boys had let him know that it was *his* turn that night. He didn't know what would be worse. Nighttime with the older boys or being sent to the Little Red House. Where *special* punishments occurred. The horror stories about *that* place were enough to give him nightmares for life.

The safest place in the facility was solitary confinement. No one could bother him there.

Do it!

It was now or never. Trayvon stood, turned, screamed at the restraint guard, Perkins, who was standing at the door directly behind him, and threw his plate of food at the man's feet. The last images Trayvon registered were not what he had expected.

Perkins smiled and gave a nod as if he were sending a kind of hidden message to someone behind Trayvon.

The fifteen-year-old boy's legs folded. Something snapped. As he hit the ground, the immediate pain made it clear that his left knee had been broken by the same boot that was now kicking him in the side, stomach, and head. Repeatedly. Then Perkins dropped onto Trayvon's chest with the full weight of both knees. As the boy struggled to breathe, the man's bulk pushed harder onto the sternum and throat.

The boy's struggle for air was almost over. As the bright lights in the room became total blackness, for a mere second Trayvon smiled.

He was about to be free at last.

2

Deke was running late.

His before-work, four-mile morning walk around his Spanish Trace neighborhood had taken longer than usual. Eighteen-minute miles had become thirty-five-minute miles because of all the distractions he encountered as he struggled to get through his morning routine. Mr. and Mrs. Peacock wanted the name of a good estate lawyer. Mrs. Bradford needed help rolling her garbage can down the driveway by herself for the Tuesday morning pickup. The Proctor dog had to be cornered, picked up, and returned to its home that Deke had already passed three houses behind him. It was clear to Deke that this had the potential to be one of those days completely controlled by gremlins.

After checking his wristwatch, Deke knew he should pick up the pace. That wasn't too much of an effort, even at his seventy-one years of age. It seemed as if he had hit the big Seven-O only yesterday, but an entire year and more had passed in the blink of an eye. The daily walk, though, kept him fit, and it was also good therapy after the injuries he had suffered a year earlier in Chicago while on a case. He had retained his weight of approximately 178 pounds, which was darned good for a tall man of six-foot-one. His sandy brown hair was much greyer now, but as his wife Teri liked to say, the color complimented his greenish-blue eyes.

He had one mile to go as he reflected again on his age and if and when retirement would ever be on his radar. It wouldn't be easy. Not only was he married to Teri, his wife of four decades, but he was also wed to his work.

The Bergman-Deketomis law firm had built its reputation on lawsuits with broad national reach. In the prior twenty-five years, the company had launched cases ranging in significance from the national tobacco to the national opioid litigation. It was a firm that had taken the lead in eighty of the largest pharmaceutical injury cases in the nation as well as dozens of complex and far-reaching ones against Wall Street, corporate toxic polluters, and even the human trafficking cartels. This was no 1-800-Car Crash outfit that rarely chose to use bar licenses to confront mega corporations that killed and injured US citizens by the thousands. Nicholas "Deke" Deketomis could often be heard giving speeches to lawyer groups where his themes centered around the idea of how easy it was to just be average, but how scary it was to take chances and put everything on the line for a greater good. Everyone who ever worked with him could recognize that he walked the walk.

He was on the last quarter stretch of his walk when his phone rang. Pulling it out of his shorts pocket, he saw that it was one of the few numbers that he ever took time to answer on his walk.

"Yes, Diana?"

"Sorry to call right now, Deke, but I thought you'd want to know. A communication from Judge Ashworth's court came in that you need to see. Peter and Jeff wanted me to interrupt your walk. I'm sorry."

Diana Fernandez, the Bergman-Deketomis law firm's office administrator—and Deke's administrative assistant for more than thirty-five years—knew that this was supposed to be his sacred time alone, but Deke suspected that his colleagues, Peter Voss and Jeff Grandy, were reacting to something that he and they were expecting might happen.

"It's not good news, is it, Diana?"

"Uh . . ."

"Got it. Say no more. I'm running late right now, Diana, but if I bypassed all the niceties like a shower and dressing in my lawyer costume with a jacket and tie, I can be there in about a half hour. Do you get the impression it warrants that?"

Diana didn't hesitate. "My Spidey senses tell me 'yes' to that. However, you're not going to want to go home to shower and change later. So go ahead and do that now. This can wait. Don't worry. I'll tell Jeff and Peter."

Deke got the message. Diana wanted to spare him some bad news, even though his teammates wanted his input immediately. She was right to do so. He knew exactly what was coming anyway. Might as well face it fresh and smelling like roses.

Nope, retirement was definitely not on the radar.

* * *

The Kaplan family had become a target for Nicholas Deketomis.

They had been instrumental in causing the death of more than 150 people a day for more than a decade from drug overdose. The product the Kaplan family claimed was nonaddictive actually had such a high dependency rate that the number of fatalities it generated was staggering. They didn't like to call it an opioid, but that's what it was. For almost a year, Deke and his team had been uncovering a level of corruption that by most standards would have been described as rank criminal conduct. The family's billions of dollars had allowed the Kaplans to creatively buy a pass from prosecution from America's mostly dysfunctional criminal justice system, and, to an even larger degree, America's civil justice system.

Deke and two of his best trial lawyers were on the hunt, but so was the Kaplan family.

The bad news that Diana had hinted at was a recently delivered communication from the court handling the case. Deke examined it and then dropped it on his desk as if it were poison ivy. He then pushed the button on the intercom.

"Yes, Deke?"

"Diana, see if the Kaplan case trial team can meet me in the conference room in about fifteen minutes. As you know, I just got notice that I'm in line to be sanctioned by Judge Ashworth for something I said in the media about those very special bottom-feeders."

"Got it. Do you want the investigators and the lawyers, Deke?"

"Yeah, better have the whole team there. Looks like I might have let my mouth overload my butt on this one."

They assembled in the conference room where the law firm's most important decisions and strategy meetings took place. It was what Gina Romano, one of the company's lead partners, had described as California-casual when she convinced her colleagues to do away with all the traditional heavy oak and cherry wood that dominated the fifty-by-thirty-foot space and replace it with white, grey, and silver decorative furnishings. There were large windows that wrapped around the room, but the twelve-foot ceiling provided enough wall real estate to hang a mixture of photographic and painted art amidst the most technically sophisticated audio and visual technology available.

Deke sat at the end of a twenty-foot table and delivered a big smile at Peter Voss as he entered through the two large double doors. Voss waved a paper as if it were a fan in front of his face. Deke had huge respect for the opioid trial team he had assembled for the litigation against the Kaplans, and Voss had been a lead lawyer in one of the most important mass tort cases ever filed against all the opioid manufacturers and distributors in the country. Deke regarded Voss as one of the key players in that case and was generally amazed at the level of commitment and innovation the high-energy lawyer brought to the project.

Now, though, Voss's typical trial lawyer composure had apparently unraveled. "What I'm reading here is a sign of the times, Deke," he coughed, nearing the edge of a scream. "Even the most disgusting conduct by sociopath corporations is blessed and damn near forgiven by some judges these days, but when a lawyer uncovering that conduct actually comments about it, God have mercy on his soul. I'm sorry you even have to contend with this regressive order, Deke, but let's deal with it."

The paper in Voss's hand was the court order in question. It required Deke to appear in front of the judge and defend himself for making a statement on television. He had called the Kaplan family a "marginal criminal enterprise that should possibly be tried for manslaughter."

Jeff Grandy, who was also part of the National Opioid Trial Team, added, "Deke, what we continue to uncover about the Kaplans needs to be made public. This is another example of an out-of-touch judge putting hundreds of thousands of potential opioid users at risk of death in order to protect what the Kaplans claim is confidential proprietary information. There should not be a proprietary right to murder 150 opioid users a day. Peter and I realize it's your butt on the line, but we should test this kind of order as far up the appellate line as possible. We cannot fall on our swords on this, and I promise we won't let this go bad, but we have got to push back hard on this judicial half-wit. Judge *Assworth*, if you ask me."

Deke sighed. "Look, I'll bow to whatever you fellas recommend I do. I've had it with this judge, too, but let's not sink to sophomoric name-calling. The judge is a *she*, remember."

"Yeah, I know, sorry," Jeff said. "I'll bet I'm not the first person to refer to her with that name, though."

"Well, it's her husband's surname, right? He probably had a hell of a time in grade school. All right, let's talk strategy."

3

It was only a half hour after the meeting that Diana buzzed Deke at his desk.

"Sorry to call right now, Deke, but there is a husband-and-wife couple here in the lobby. They're demanding to see you this morning with a threat to quote 'go down the road with the biggest case in Florida' unless they can talk to you today."

"Geez, what about?"

"All I know at this point is that it involves a child who was allegedly beaten to death, and they won't tell me any more beyond that." She lowered her voice. "The man is full-body tattooed, and the woman has bright blue hair. They're angry, they're pacing the lobby, and they're a bit intimidating."

"I'm a little busy with this sanction business, but okay. Show them into the conference room, and I'll be there in a minute."

He actually kept them waiting seven minutes. When Diana walked him into the room where the couple was waiting, she said, "Deke, this is Claudia Clapper and Bruno Williams."

Deke took one look at the man and woman, turned back to Diana in the doorway and said, "Please ask Michael to join us, would you?" He then stepped inside and addressed the couple. "Good morning, I'm Nicholas Deketomis, but you can call me Deke."

He figured the woman to be in her thirties, but it was impossible to tell if she was closer to her twenties or forties. She did indeed have blue streaks in what might have been blonde hair, paper white skin with red sores around her forehead and mouth, and three metal rings that pierced her nose, eyebrow, and lower lip. She wore a ragged Disney World T-shirt featuring Minnie Mouse and cutoff blue jean shorts. Bruno was Black, had a shaved head, and indeed sported tattoos over his neck and arms. He wore a soiled tank top and sweatpants with grease stains on them.

Deke immediately suspected they were wasting his time, but he sat in one of the chairs and asked, "What can I do for you?"

"My son was murdered," Claudia said with venom. She then launched into an incoherent rant about her boy, Trayvon, who was killed in a protective services facility called B Camp. She paused only when Michael Carey, one of the law firm's most accomplished attorneys and former Air Force pararescueman, entered the room. His six-foot-three, 190-pound, perfect athletic frame projected a street fighter's attributes. His bright red shoulder length hair and small tuft below his bottom lip, ice blue eyes, and a nose that might have been attached to an eagle collectively commanded that all eyes focus on him. To Deke, Michael was a young warrior lawyer whose results-oriented drive often pushed the limits of acceptable lawyer conduct. Michael's fists had been used a few times to convince players on the opposite side that they needed to proceed with caution if they ever made threats to anyone associated with Deke's firm.

Deke quickly introduced him, the handshakes were repeated, and Michael sat. Deke noticed that Bruno immediately adjusted his posture and demeanor, his eyes wide at Michael's imposing physique. That had been Deke's intent.

Deke began, "Mrs. Clapper—"

"Miss. Bruno and I are not church married but we've been common law married for three years."

Michael spoke up. "Florida doesn't recognize common law marriages. Did you know that?"

"What?" Bruno uttered.

"It's true," Deke said. "You say you've been together three years?"

"That's right," Claudia answered. "We've been living as man and wife."

"I know it's not why you're here, but since it came up, you might want to know. You don't have legal spousal rights, such as the right to inherit from each other or make medical decisions for each other."

Claudia and Bruno looked at each other with jaws open.

"But you came in here about your son, right?" Deke asked.

"Yes!" Claudia snapped, getting back to the business at hand.

"How did Trayvon end up at B Camp?"

"Some sheriff's deputy in Miami put him there," she said with spite. "He had run away, was living on the street. It was supposed to have been for his own good, but obviously it wasn't!"

Deke then knew there was much more to the story than deadly negligence on the part of B Camp, although he was aware that child confinement facilities, also known as reform schools, did very little to *protect* their wards.

In fact, he knew this truth all too well. An involuntary shiver went up his spine.

Bucky Carlton . . .

Michael said, "The deputy didn't put Trayvon there, surely. It was likely HRS."

Bruno said, "That's right. HRS." With sarcastic bitterness, he added, "The Florida Department of *Health and Rehabilitative Services*. What a joke."

Claudia said, "Look, Mr. Deketomis, or Deke, or whatever you want us to call you, we need a lawyer who can sue the hell out of B Camp and HRS and anyone else you can think of who had something to do with Trayvon's murder. What do you think we could get? Ten million? Fifty million?"

Michael noted that Deke sat silently, unmoving, staring across the room.

"Deke?"

"I'm sorry, what was that?" Deke's head had shivered, as if he were waking from a bad dream or trying to escape from an unpleasant thought.

"You okay?" Michael asked.

"Yeah, maybe I got overheated on my walk this morning."

"I want to know how many millions we could get," Claudia repeated.

Deke held up his hands. "Hold on, Miss Clapper. Let's not get ahead of ourselves."

With the mention of HRS being involved, it became clear that Trayvon's mother had lost custody of her child, possibly several times. She had also been stripped of privileges as a parent because of dereliction of responsibility to Trayvon. Now she and her "common law" husband were simply vultures circling the boy's dead body.

He continued with a sudden fervor. "Claudia, to give you our best evaluation, we really need to know a lot more about Trayvon. His whole life story. And yours. And Bruno's. Any documentation you have about Trayvon's confinement at B Camp, all court papers, medical records, and anything else that could be relevant sure would be helpful. My team will need to do at least a preliminary investigation and interview you both in a little more depth to give you the best advice we can if there's a case here."

"Oh, there's a case," she said. "There's definitely a case."

Michael interjected, "Let us make that judgement after we look much closer, Miss Clapper."

"Call me Claudia."

Deke continued, "Claudia, I'm very sorry for your loss. Losing a child can be horrendous. Especially in circumstances like this. But I will need you and Bruno to take a step back, approach the situation with level heads, and try not to be impatient. If we go forward with this, and I'm not saying we can or will, it might take years before you see any kind of settlement."

"*Years*?" Bruno gasped.

Deke shrugged. "The justice system often moves at a snail's pace. But it does move. Now, Claudia, knowing that, if you still want us to do everything we can to pursue this, I'm going to turn you over to one of my partners, Gina Romano. She will spend some extended time reviewing with you what kinds of documents you now have in your possession and get as much detail as possible from you about everything that has occurred surrounding Trayvon's life and tragic death. You will appreciate her thoroughness."

Gina had secured three of the largest child wrongful death jury verdicts in the state of Florida. If the facts were what Deke had already imagined, he knew that B Camp was going to have its world rocked with Gina on the case.

"How much will this cost?" Bruno asked.

"Don't worry about that now. This preliminary work we are going to do is on the house. If we can't help you, there is no charge."

After a few minutes of niceties and goodbyes-for-now, Deke and Michael went into the hallway and spoke before fetching Gina. Michael shook his head. "Deke, are you really thinking about taking on their case with all the huge projects this firm is already dealing with? Really? Bruno uses heroin. I saw the track marks on his arms. The sores on Claudia's forehead and the rotting teeth in her mouth clearly indicate serious meth use. You can bet that child has been kicked to the curb most of his life by these two and now they want to cash in a lottery ticket with his dead body."

Deke nodded. "I saw all that, but my inclination is to dive right into this. I'm going to tell Gina to get Cara to work with her on it. Just from the preliminary details, I think I know what happened to this poor kid. I want to go after B Camp, and you can bet the facts are there to do it."

Michael stepped back and looked at his friend and colleague. "Deke, are you all right? I could swear your whole body is trembling a bit. Did those two get you—"

"It wasn't them, Michael. Maybe I've got a bugaboo about so-called child protection services. It's a dismal, failed system that I know about firsthand. I'm thinking more about the son, not that couple. I'm thinking more about what probably happened at B Camp. I'm thinking of . . . well, never mind, let's go talk to Gina and get her motivated about this case."

"You're the boss, my friend."

As Michael walked away toward Gina's office, Deke knew that it wasn't just the few facts he had just heard about Trayvon or B Camp that had both his mind and body tied up in knots.

The trembling Michael had witnessed was about lingering ghosts from the past.

4

Cara Deketomis, Deke and Teri's twenty-nine-year-old daughter, finished the hurried lunch down the street from the Bergman-Deketomis law firm and began the walk back to the office. She took her time, though, for the rendezvous with a law school colleague was demanding her thoughtful attention.

Zach Morrison had been an on-again, off-again beau during school, and the two of them were still good friends. He was in Pensacola on business and had asked to see her. Cara gladly appeared at the hole-in-the-wall no-name "Diner" that had been a favorite haunt during their younger days. He was a lawyer, too, already a partner at Dunlop and Markle in Boulder, Colorado, a place known as a "mover and shaker" full of young, bold attorneys.

"Cara," Zach had said, "do you ever think about leaving Florida and your father's firm . . . and working someplace else? Another state?"

"No, not really," she had responded.

"Didn't you tell me once that you weren't sure about working under your dad's 'shadow?' That you wanted to quote-unquote 'spread your wings and establish yourself on your own?'"

"I guess so. Why?"

"Well . . . we're expanding our offices in nine months, and we're going to be looking to hire some new, bright attorneys. I can tell you right now that we would love to have you on our team."

"What?"

"I mean it, Cara. We want you to come join our firm in Colorado."

He had thrown out a compensation figure that was competitive and tempting.

Working in her father's practice had its perks, to be sure, but Cara was well aware of the drawbacks. After she had finished law school, Cara had considered taking an entry-level position somewhere far away from Florida. New York, perhaps, or California. Illinois or Massachusetts. She had the transcripts and ability. She had taken the national bar exam and aced it; she would just need to take any exam specific to whatever state she chose. Graduating with a heavy emphasis on trial skills and ending up in the top two percent of her class made for an impressive start to job interviews. A nationally known federal prosecutor had called her "one of the true up-and-coming rising stars in the legal world."

But when her father offered the entry-level job for a much higher salary and the opportunity to get into the weeds of *real* cases rather than as a typical associate grunt to some senior partner with the tasks of endlessly writing memos and exclusively doing research—Cara decided that it might not be so bad to join the family business. Would she be accused of nepotism? It wouldn't be the first time that a child of someone famous had been so. In the end—who cared?

In the four years since joining the firm, Cara had worked her way up from not quite the bottom of the ladder to a member of the firm's complex case trial team. So far, the work had been engaging and far from "routine." Becoming a partner at the firm was clearly just ahead, not because of any special treatment by her father, but because of the reputation she was building as a respected young trial lawyer.

But now this temptation.

"I could put in a good word to get you into the courtroom as quickly as possible," Zach had said. It was a chance to get away from the Deketomis name and influence over her career—not that this was anything negative.

Cara wondered . . . shouldn't she try it? Go out into the legal world and, as Zach had put it, make it on her own?

Zach had said they weren't in a hurry. Cara really didn't have to make the decision immediately. But in lawyer-speak that meant she should know the answer "soon."

What a way to scramble her day.

When she arrived back at the office, she found a note on her desk from Gina Romano. Of all the partners at Bergman-Deketomis, Cara admired Gina the most. A woman in her forties, Gina was one of the firm's most valuable assets. Cara was always thankful when she was able to work with her. In many ways, Gina had served as a mentor to Cara over the four years of her tenure.

CARA—TAKE A LOOK AT THESE MATERIALS
AND COME SEE ME.—G.

* * *

"I don't get it," Cara said as they sat across the desk from each other in Gina's office. She held up Gina's note and documents that had indicated the two of them were assigned to the Trayvon Clapper case. "Why would my father take his focus off one of the most high-profile and lucrative cases in the firm to take on this wrongful death thing? I saw the mother and her husband when they were leaving the building. They would both be a walking horror story in front of a jury."

"I agree with you, Cara," Gina said, "but we can't judge people purely on how they look. Trust me when I tell you we will have them looking like they came directly off the cover of *Home and Garden* magazine before we walk into court with them. You know that."

"Oh, I know, and I didn't mean it that way. Forgive me. It's just . . . I don't know. You have to admit those two reeked of drug abuse and a lifetime of really bad decisions. Any jury is going to see that, no matter how much paint you put on them."

"Maybe that could be a task in your bailiwick. Do a makeover of Claudia Clapper."

"What? Me?" Cara found the idea ludicrous.

"Well, think about it. We haven't signed onto the case yet."

"Well, it seems Dad is just jumping in as if his pants were on fire rather than focusing on the Kaplan family case like he needs to. That's where you, me, Dad, and every lawyer in this firm needs to be concentrating. Why doesn't he see that?"

"Well, Cara, I think I might have a clue."

Cara cocked her head. "Do you know something I don't?"

"What do *you* know about your father's childhood?"

"Would you believe . . . not a lot? I haven't been privy to, well, very much at all. He never talked about it. Just bits and pieces. All the time my brother Andy and I lived under the same roof with Dad and Mom that's a topic that hardly ever came up."

"I'm not surprised."

"I think there were two things we didn't talk about in the household. One was that Mom, Andy, and I laid down the law to Dad that he had to leave his work at the office. The world of 'Nick Deketomis,' the respected lawyer, had to stay at the law firm. The second one was, I suppose, something he imposed on *us*—that his past was a mysterious thing kept in a locked diary buried somewhere inside his soul that he rarely, if at all, cared to open. You probably know more than we do!"

Gina raised her eyebrows. "Well, maybe I do, maybe I don't. I can tell you what I do know. Maybe I know why he wants to jump on this case. A few of us here in the firm are aware of some things that he's let drip over the years. You are so right that your father is normally very private about his past."

"It's downright ridiculous. My brother and I used to joke about the possibility that he's an alien without any earthly origins."

"Your father is not taking on the Clapper case because he wants to help the boy's mother and step-whatever-he-is. It goes back to his own childhood. You know your father was kind of on his own as a boy?"

Cara sat back in her chair. "Yeah, but mostly he's always said it was a positive experience for him."

"I think it was, for the most part. But something else happened that wasn't so positive."

"What?"

"Well, Cara, that I don't know. *Something* happened. Your father has intimated a few things here and there, but not much. I remember one time he mentioned knowing someone who had a bad outcome with Florida's childcare system, or something similar."

"And you're saying this was when my dad was a boy, too?"

"Yes. I know about this only because Deke opened up to me about it once when we were out of town on some case. He had read about a high-profile case in which several boys had been abused and, well, tortured, while in the supposed *care* of a reform school."

"Keep talking, please. I know Dad lived with a lot of different families when he was a kid, but I don't think Andy and I ever knew much more. Dad never talked about it."

"I don't know. You'll have to ask him. Look, he wasn't exactly in the foster care system."

"What do you mean?"

"I'll give you as many of the details that I've picked up when we could actually get him to talk. Cara, I'll tell you this because I'm going to consider it to be background to the case and you need to have your mind right about what we're doing, all right?"

"That's fine with me."

"Okay." Gina took a sip of coffee and began. "Well, as far as I know, your father came dangerously close to being sent to a place called the Sandbury Housing for Boys, but an influential family he worked for interceded on his behalf and took him in. But for the most part, the story I know is that he avoided both the camps and the ugly side of the foster care system. Basically, families were willing to take him in and provide homes that were far removed from the disastrous foster care system that was in place in Florida while he was growing up."

Cara nodded. "The only thing he ever said was that his mom and dad were faced with hard times and couldn't make things work. His dad, in fact, pretty much disappeared. I met my grandmother but not my grandfather. I know Dad had a very positive home in his later teens, before he went off to college. But I don't know much about the kinds of boys' camps where this Trayvon Clapper was. Are those camps just for boys who get in trouble with the law?"

Gina explained, "Not at all. These boys' camps, then and now, are part of a nasty process that still exists today in most states. Many of them are owned and operated by churches or small businesses that are paid money by the state to house not only serious criminal offenders but also kids that are just minor offenders. Kids can end up in one of those horror homes for running away, missing too much school, or any number of extremely marginal offenses. It's big business and big income for the folks who own and operate them. In some instances, county judges actually get big kickbacks for sending even the most minor offending kids to those homes."

"So how does Dad's experience fit into all this?"

"I don't know. But there's something. Like I said, someone he knew."

"Should I ask him about it?"

Gina shrugged. "You're his daughter. But, frankly, I think it's an off-limits spot with your dad. Something very painful. I think I just wanted you to know that if you and I are going to work on this case together, you needed to understand that something from the past is driving your father in this Trayvon incident. As we work on this case we might be able to shine a light on that history your dad hides so well."

5

Congressman Bob Minds had been reelected two times by the voters in Massachusetts.

It wasn't surprising. After all, he had movie star good looks and charisma in spades. A tabloid once likened him to a "stunt double for a young Robert Redford." Housewives fawned over him when he appeared on television. Men appreciated his "tell it like it is" persona. He was intelligent, confident, and brash. His status as a divorced man was not an issue, and his reputation as a playboy was, oddly, a feature. Men wanted to be him. Women wanted to be *with* him. This may have gone against the grain for what is admired about or expected of politicians, but the world was in a different mindset these days.

He got things done.

At least, he went to great lengths to make it appear that way.

Anyone paying close attention might have figured out that most of Congressman Minds's time in Washington was devoted more toward serving his own personal interests. He had typically won his reelection efforts with catchy jingles like "My Mind is Always on You" or "Bob is Always Minding the Store." But the truth was that the congressman typically only paid attention to Massachusetts voters who could best increase the amount of money he had in his political war chest and the dirty money he could put away in his personal bank accounts, under his bed, or hidden in his closet.

Very few people knew that Bob also had a secret weapon.

Her name was Skyler Bannock.

A woman half his age, Skyler knew how to squeeze every possible penny out of any donors' pockets, legally and illegally.

They were indeed a team. Bob had a knack for politically strong-arming anyone who stood in the way of profiteering. Skyler had mastered the art of charm and seduction. She had learned all the tricks of persuasion in her late teens and early twenties, dancing on poles at the very place where Bob had introduced himself as a big tipper. There was an immediate attraction that could never be described as actual love. They occasionally played the "friends with benefits" card with each other, but usually their sexual proclivities were directed elsewhere.

Their arrangement was more of a long-term business plan that Congressman Minds had been developing during the ten years he had served as the CPA for the Massachusetts mob, a shady organization with which both Bob and Skyler still did business. This was a long-standing "family" that generated multimillions of dollars each year in everything ranging from prostitution to drug distribution. Both Bob and Skyler were highly skilled in keeping their relationship with the mob—and with themselves—a secret from the public and, more importantly, from Congress.

From the outside looking in, though, the congressman appeared to be more of a squeaky-clean handsome Rotarian president than a politician almost totally reliant on graft to pay the exorbitant bills of the extravagant lifestyle to which Skyler was drawn like a winged insect circling a flame.

The congressman's major money sources ranged from the pharmaceutical industry to the weapons industry, but the most predictable money for more than four years had flowed from a multi-international business called Phoenix Industries, a company that controlled almost one quarter of all private prison corporations and troubled teen housing institutions.

Congressman Minds was what Phoenix executives regarded as one of their many problem solvers and fixers. One of the biggest demands they made of Congressman Minds was that he would always show up and be available on quick notice when the Phoenix organization encountered troubles that could best be solved by a corrupt politician.

Today was one of those days.

The rock and roll team of Bob and Skyler had been called upon to work more of their dark arts magic.

As Bob entered the Grand King Room of the Boston Raffles Hotel, he sensed the tension emanating from the three Phoenix executives sitting around the large, expensive Scandinavian antique table. Bob immediately knew what was going on. Two years before, things had gone sideways with a payoff attempt to one of the hundreds of supervisors in charge of an agency from which Phoenix needed help. Bob was required to step in and smooth the situation. Apply the grease. Make the bureaucracy work for Phoenix and solve its problem.

This kind of thing was never easy, but Bob had a knack for applying charm, money, or strong-arm tactics to produce the desired results. The aid of his mobster friends also helped immensely.

Could this kind of stuff become known and ruin his status in Congress? It was a risk of doing business, to be sure, but Bob seemed to have Teflon armor that couldn't be pierced. And besides, whenever there were problems with his "clients" like Phoenix, that meant more income into his coffers.

He thrived on business crises. They gave him visions of dollar signs.

Even the quiet butler efficiently moving around the elegant table pouring wine seemed nervous. There was a palpable edginess generated by the three intense characters huddled together, carrying on a conversation in whispered tones.

Paul Baker, Phoenix's CEO, was the only one of the three men at the table to stand when Bob and Skyler entered the suite. His cliché close-cropped silver hair, his five-thousand-dollar Armani suit, and his six-foot-five towering frame all added to an almost made-for-a-movie-set specimen of a man. After a quick handshake, an almost demeaning slap on the back and a less than friendly hello for the congressman, Paul moved immediately to Skyler. He gave her an embrace that lasted far beyond a time that would have been appropriate to most observers. Bob didn't care. Skyler and her much-heralded special talents had saved the couple's bacon with their relationship to Paul after a screwup in the past that was no fault of Bob's. Something he referred to as the

"Alabama debacle." The CEO was no doubt looking for more in the way of apologies.

Bob remained silent, but there was an edgy smirk on his face that only Skyler could have detected. A hint of laughter came from the other two executives at the table as they observed the undeniable chemistry between Paul and Skyler. To everyone in the room, the congressman might have seemed indifferent as Paul put his arm around his companion's waist and escorted her to the blue silk sofa in the corner of the expansive room. The other two executives, who had barely acknowledged Bob, followed behind Paul and pointed to the three large comfortable chairs arranged in front of the couch, indicating where Bob should sit. Paul pulled Skyler closer to him as both of them reclined with hugs and smiles as if they were the only two people in the room.

Bob remained silent but his eyes and body language told Skyler all she needed to know about what he was thinking. She and the congressman exchanged knowing glances clearly missed by the three Phoenix executives.

Then it was time to begin the meeting. Paul released Skyler, sat forward on the couch, and cleared his throat. He adjusted his tie and collar and then stared at the congressman for a full thirty seconds.

"Paul?" Bob cocked his head. "You have something to say?"

"What the hell, Mr. Minds?" Paul exhibited one of those well-practiced executive smiles they taught in MBA School. "One of my contacts with the Administration for Children and Families gave me a call two weeks ago. She told me some nobody lawyer in North Florida is snooping around and asking questions about our Sweeton, Florida incident. More importantly, she said she phoned you about it, and you haven't bothered to return the call to get involved with what might be going on. Does that sound like money well spent on you and your, er, partner here?"

Skyler was the first to speak as Bob bought a moment to think, guzzling some of the bottled water he had carried into the room with him. With the voice of a seasoned courtesan, she purred, "First of all, sweetie, you aren't the only group we work hard to protect. And let me point—"

Bob jumped in mid-sentence. "And, secondly, don't ever, ever show me the disrespect you and these two Harvard monkeys of yours have displayed in the last five minutes. Who the hell do you think you're dealing with?"

Paul's mouth opened but he said nothing. He turned to look at his colleagues, who also had similar expressions on their faces.

"Don't expect any advice from your pantywaist Ivy League lightweight pissants you brought to this meeting," Bob continued. "I will gobble up all three of you and every part of your teetering business with three phone calls, and some of what I talk about will involve that great State of Alabama."

With a kneejerk response, Paul stood. Stunned, he realized he had no viable collection of words with which to respond.

But in that moment the uncouth congressman, who incongruously wore a TJ Maxx discount clothing combination, was in full control of the room. "Well, Mr. Princeton Phi Beta Kappa, are you going to say something or just wish like hell that Skyler and I would just go away? And oh, by the way, the next time you and your lightweight team come to town to play Mr. Big with me, your wife and five children will get pictures of you doing the nasty in this very suite. My memory is that Skyler here was riding you around the room on all fours like a dog for most of the night. Hell, we've even had the films and pictures enhanced so we can post them on porn sites."

Paul swallowed, his pallor growing pale. The other two men froze, their bulging eyes and jaws on the floor.

Bob exhibited sincere ferocity, but in truth he was only enjoying his performance. "No, this is how things are going to go with you, your company, and Skyler and me going forward. That marginal money you deposit in my Caribbean holiday bank just increased by fifty percent. We will refer to that as apology cash for these last ten minutes Skyler and I have had to endure being treated like the help. The other fifty percent you will deposit in the banks of my choice we will consider a down payment for the serious problems you and the half-ass American side of your business are now facing. You see, while I was taking a pass on returning the call from that insignificant idiot you referred to as your ACF contact, I was actually doing what you pay me for."

Paul, still standing but exhibiting far less arrogant self-importance, managed to reply, "Congressman, let's start this conversation again. Maybe my friends and I were out of—"

Bob snapped. "Out of line? Were you going to say, 'out of line?' No, you and your ass clown friends are out of room to negotiate. So first let me hear a big yes that we understand each other with the finances going forward."

"The finances will be no problem," Paul answered as he took a seat on the opposite end of the couch from Skyler.

"Wonderful." Bob turned to Skyler and winked. Back to Paul, he said, rather matter-of-factly, "I will need at least two hundred thousand dollars to spread around to a few low-end players in the ACF bureaucracy. They should be able to clean up a few of the field reports that show exactly how half-ass your operation is when it comes to actually doing your job and protecting kids that are placed in this joke of an operation you call starter facilities. As I'm sure you already know, the number of reports showing everything from abuse to nothing short of child manslaughter have increased fourteen percent, even after the Alabama incident. Just as a reminder, in case you dumb shits have forgotten, the folks at the ACF pay attention to numbers like that. Shake your head yes if you understand how serious that is, Paul."

The CEO held up both hands. "Congressman, needless to say we get that and we're trying to bring those numbers down. That's part of what we wanted to talk to you about today. We wanted to know, given your position on the ACF congressional subcommittee, if you can find the right people within the ACF to make those statistics perhaps look not quite so bad. That would keep us from being put on the non-referral list because of the Sweeton incident. The non-referral list would be a problem for all of our eight US facilities."

"Problem? Well, that's a damn sure nice way to put it, Paul. The truth is, if I can't get a few of the incident reviewers and statisticians to go my way on this Sweeton disaster, the ACF could shut you down for a long time." Bob stood and took a few steps away from the group. "As far as the folks you describe as insignificant lawyers, the ones out of Florida that are on your trail, you need to know that they are the real deal." He turned back to the group. "These are the folks who caused the tobacco industry to cough up $265 billion for killing mostly adults. Hell, you're killing *kids* here. You might also want to know that as rare as it is, they actually saw to it that two or three peckerwood CEOs just like yourself found themselves picking up shower soap in federal penitentiaries for far less serious conduct than what I'm seeing with Phoenix. To put it in terms you might understand, they don't play around; they are serious people, Paul."

"Okay, I hear how you might be able to help us stay off the non-referral list, but you know, and I know, that didn't work out so well before. Your plan almost put my entire company into a bribery investigation. What happened in Alabama can't happen again."

Bob delivered a weird giggle that sounded more like it had come from a teenage girl. "You ever heard that overused statement, 'I know a guy who knows a guy?' Well, I really do know a lot of guys. I will see what they can do."

Paul and the other two Phoenix executives stood when Bob Minds signaled that the meeting was over by asking Skyler, "My dear, would you like to spend the night in the suite? Mr. Baker was ever so kind, once again, to book us this marvelous suite for our personal use after our most productive meeting!"

"Congressman, you will never regret trying to hel—"

"Shut up, Paul, and pour me and my colleague a couple of glasses of that wine you were drinking when we came in." He then took Skyler's hand as she stood. They headed to the suite's master bedroom, but before entering, Bob turned, winked, and barked a loud, "Arf arf!"

Paul Baker had little doubt that the congressman, in his position on the ACF House Subcommittee, could do major damage to Phoenix. The company had experienced a difficult time wielding any influence over the organization that had complete control over national children's health and safety issues. The ACF was a part of the US Department of Health and Human Services. Their marching orders were to make sure that economic, social, and health programs designed to protect America's children worked as flawlessly as possible. That included both direct and indirect oversight of every children's confinement institution in the country.

Phoenix had built most of its business around the lucrative launching and maintaining of private adult prisons. In the last ten years, they had also initiated their children's confinement centers referred to as "starter facilities." The big payday government contracts that were directed by ACF had grown exponentially three years in a row primarily because of rapid expansion of refugee resettlement housing needed for unaccompanied immigrant children crossing the border. Federal contracts, together with state-funded contracts, had allowed Phoenix to operate in the black, and those numbers were moving higher by the month. A non-referral status that resulted generally from failures by Phoenix to provide adequate safety, medical care, or general oversight protection could dry up millions of dollars almost overnight. Any trends surfacing in mandatory incident reports, such as lack of control over health, safety, possible abuse, or injuries, had the capacity to initiate detailed investigations by the ACF. Phoenix could not possibly weather something like that.

Paul knew that Bob Minds had the juice to have adverse reports sanitized. Trends that were clearly showing serious failure on day one could disappear on day two. Bob had played everything close to the vest as to who his two or three go-to fixers were in the ranks of ACF. That sly secretiveness had prevented Paul from dealing directly with the source. But what weighed on Paul's mind was that a motivated trial lawyer could dig deep enough to follow the money Bob had been spreading around for two years.

For days he would mull over which would be worse, the expansive criminal investigation that had the potential to emerge, or the thought of having his wife of twenty years and his five children seeing their naked father crawl around the floor, led by a naked woman with a damn belt around his neck.

Bob Minds's send-off had a serious subtext that Paul couldn't forget. *Arf, arf* indeed!

6

When Deke held a strategy meeting, there was mandatory attendance for key players involved in what he quantified as the firm's most important cases; but most of the folks in the conference room were puzzled how a single death claim would fall into the realm of the firm's more serious cases. It wasn't the kind of litigation they were used to working on. They certainly considered the death of a fifteen-year-old boy more than tragic, but single event cases such as this were rarely on the firm's radar.

Deke stood and addressed the room. "I want to begin by explaining why the entire complex litigation staff was asked to attend this meeting. Gina and Cara have prepared a bullet point presentation with as much material as they had access to, so let's get right to it."

He pointed a remote control toward an eight-by-six-foot screen and a picture of a mixed race boy of about thirteen. "Trayvon Clapper is a child I want all of you to get to know. For most of his fifteen years, this child was shoved around between a parent who admittedly was hopelessly addicted to meth, and foster homes that were so substandard that he had to repeatedly be reprocessed through the system and either placed back with his mother or another foster care home. The court system removed Trayvon from Claudia, his mother, on three separate occasions."

Deke again pointed the remote toward the screen and quickly scanned through a series of documents as he spoke. "Claudia never married, but for three of Trayvon's years, she invited Bruno Williams to live with Trayvon and herself in public housing when she could get it." Large pictures of a woman and a man appeared on the screen. The woman was clearly posing for a criminal mug shot. She looked much the same as she had when she had visited the offices. "The man on the screen is Bruno. He had been reported by school officials and hospital staff several times for what appeared to most as clear abuse of Trayvon. Unfortunately, each time Child Services believed it was a great idea to return Trayvon to his mother."

Deke took a seat for a moment and briefly sat silent.

Again, Michael noted that his boss went away somewhere for an instance.

Eventually Deke stood again and continued as if nothing had happened. "When Trayvon was not living with his meth-addicted mother, Claudia, and his heroin-addicted live-in wannabe father, he was living in foster care homes. At age fourteen, Trayvon had had enough abuse in barely subsistent living conditions. He tried to make a break from an unstable mother, from his mother's brutal boyfriend, and generally from the children's dumping grounds we call Florida's foster care system."

He hesitated again and walked across the room to get a bottle of water from where a coffee service was set up with a large ice bucket and drinks. The people in the room sat motionless. There were no whispers. It was evident to anyone who knew Deke that he was having difficulty talking about the case.

Pointing the remote back at the screen from where he was standing, Deke unveiled another picture. One side of Trayvon's face was badly bruised. Both of his eyes were bloodshot red, and his hair was almost shoulder length with patches of hair missing.

"Trayvon was on the street. Thankfully he avoided having to survive through all the horrors that we learned about during the human trafficking litigation. But you can see from the picture that he must have run into some kind of trouble. He was vulnerable there, for sure. A sheriff's deputy in Miami, Florida had the good sense to take Trayvon into protective custody and do what he believed would be best for Trayvon by urging a children's court judge to place Trayvon in a children's confinement institution. He simply didn't know better."

Again, Deke hesitated and remained silent, staring at the picture of Trayvon on the screen. The pause seemed to have no end until he said, "Gina, why don't you take it from here? Give us a rundown on the rest of Trayvon's life in that hellhole for children."

Deke handed Gina the remote and took a seat in the back of the room.

Cara knew her father well enough to understand that this was code for *I can't talk about this anymore.* She had a sudden flash of memory. One Christmas, her brother Andy had said something about feeling sorry for "kids who didn't have families." It was an innocent, well-meaning comment from a child. The smile on her father's face abruptly vanished. He slowly rose from the chair where he had been watching the kids open presents and left the room. Andy hadn't noticed, but Cara and her mother had. Nothing was said about it.

Unaware of his daughter's thoughts, Deke tried to shake off the cloud that had come over him. It helped to survey the team around the table. The Bergman-Deketomis law firm had built its reputation on assembling a group of trial lawyers who would easily be recognized as some of the best in the country. Gina Romano, Michael Carey, and a half dozen more of Deke's trial experts were considered "headline lawyers" because their names often appeared in the opening paragraphs of the most important legal news in the country. Each of these remarkable lawyers had cultivated their own effective styles throughout their careers. As for Gina, the press described her style as fierce, vehement, and intense. Deke was sure he would see all those descriptions repeated as Gina and her team focused on some semblance of justice for Trayvon Clapper.

She stood and pointed the remote at the screen. An enhanced autopsy report with key parts underlined appeared.

"Trayvon died of strangulation," Gina said. "Not only was the strangulation caused by his wind pipe being crushed by the three-hundred-and-twenty-pound ex-felon that sat on top of him with his knees placed on Trayvon's throat and stomach, but the strangulation was also enhanced by the food that regurgitated up his throat through his crushed windpipe. Fred Perkins, the freak that killed him, also had some help from what is called a 'guards gang' in teenage institutional dumpster facilities like this. Before he was strangled, three teenage psychopathic wannabes got him to the ground by breaking his knees with direct kicks from behind."

Deke spoke up. "Gina, tell them more about the guards gangs."

"Sure. Kids like the ones who helped kill Trayvon are usually the most violent in the institution. They are usually what they call 'long-timers' who get their violence training and reputation creds long before they typically end up in state or federal prison. Guards recruit these little psychos in training to help keep order, usually with violence." Gina went through the next several slides quickly as she narrated. "Since we're talking about it, here are a few headlines from newspapers around the country where they point out how normal it is to have really special relationships between selected kids and guards. Guards stage boxing matches right there in the facility, pitting the weakest and youngest children against the oldest and strongest long-timers in the institution. These articles discuss how the guards take bets on how long the weaker child will remain conscious or whether the weaker child will start crying or remain on his feet. One of these articles tells the story of a thirteen-year-old who is now living with permanent brain damage."

Diana walked into the conference room and went to Deke. She whispered, "Is this a good time to take a break? Peter and Jeff are in your office. They say they need to talk to you now, if possible."

Deke knew that for Diana to interrupt a major strategy meeting, it had to be something that needed his immediate attention. "Gina," he said, "I'm sorry, I would like to be here for the rest of your rundown on this. But would you mind if we reschedule to bring this all in for a landing?"

"That's fine," Gina answered. "Cara expects to talk to a couple of witnesses very soon. Also, I have all the details about the corporate ownership structure coming in bits and pieces. How about we reschedule until after we have all that?"

"Perfect."

Deke stood and hurriedly left the room.

* * *

Cara exited with Gina.

"That was disturbing," she said.

"There's a lot about Trayvon's case that is," Gina replied.

"That's not what I meant. I'm talking about my father."

Gina stopped and raised her eyebrows. "Go on."

"It's just . . . as I was listening to him laying out all the pivots to what I know will ultimately end up in some form as part of a closing argument at trial, I kept thinking about whatever it was he's hiding. I could see my father struggling like I never have before."

"Do you want to talk to him about it? Maybe you should."

"Well, not yet. I want to get into the weeds of the case, first. But this tale unfolding is obviously as much about my father as it is about Trayvon Clapper. He's carrying some kind of burden, Gina, like you guessed. Has he been carrying it around for most of his adult life? I sure don't know about it. From what I just saw, I want to go into his office and hug him. Tell him it's okay! Whatever it is, it's okay!"

Gina gently placed a hand on Cara's upper arm and smiled. "Now you're beginning to get the passion he has for this case. It will do you well as we move forward. Come on, let's grab a cup of coffee and get back to work."

Cara nodded and brought a hand up to her blonde hair in a salute. "Right. Lead on, sergeant."

It was the kind of welcome levity that made the two women a good team. If she left Bergman-Deketomis and joined Zach's firm in Colorado, would she find the same camaraderie there?

That thought was a reminder for Cara. She needed to seriously think about Zach's proposition.

What to do, what to do? Stay in Florida under her father's influence . . . or declare her independence cross-country and be a totally different *Deketomis?*

Given her father's unusual behavior lately, maybe it *was* time to bow out.

* * *

Peter was pacing like a tiger on the hunt when Deke walked into his office. He launched into it. "I'm sorry, Deke, but Judge Ashworth set an emergency hearing for two o'clock tomorrow afternoon. She obviously wants to take up the Motion for Sanctions against you. She demanded that you, Jeff, and I be present. She set it *sua sponte* without any request from the defense." That legal term referred to actions judges might take without first receiving a motion from any of the parties involved. It was the kind of hearing that rarely ended well for lawyers.

Jeff Grandy spoke as he sat on a couch in the middle of the large ultra-modern office. "I think we should immediately ask for a continuance. Not that she will grant it. She is clearly on a get-even-with-Deke mission, but I think it's critical to paper everything we do on this motion since we'll be running every decision she makes up through the appellate courts. She is a plague on the Civil Justice System, and I am convinced we have a responsibility to show that."

"Hell, I tried to make that fact as public as possible with her judge-malpractice on the Brynistan case," Deke said. "Yes, we might have gone a tad overboard with that full page ad. But by God, that was my right to get the word out to the public that Brynistan was a drug that could kill them. The case was over. She had done all the damage she could possibly do by dismissing the case with overwhelming proof that the company had basically committed nothing less than manslaughter."

Peter added, "And hundreds of women will continue to die from using that product that she dropped the ball on, but, Deke, let's focus on the here and now. Tomorrow we will have a judge with no talent yelling at us in a predictably childlike way. She recognizes that she has discretion enough to sanction you in some form to show you that she basically hates you."

"Well, I guess there's that." Deke laughed wryly. "Look, I get it and I'm sorry I put us all in this boat, but truth be told, this may be the perfect set of facts for us to try and end this criminal hide and seek that drug companies pull off on the consumer public. So, you're right about the strategy. Her position is that it was blasphemy to label the Kaplans as the criminals they are, but, damn it, I sure had the right to pose the question about why they have not been charged with manslaughter for killing all the folks they have around the world with their so-called 'addiction-free' narcotics and—"

Jeff interrupted, "Deke, listen. Let's not waste any more time. I will be up most of the night preparing the best setup pleading I can. We're going to ask for a continuance for a week. She will say no, and we will have the beginning of some strong elements to show just how biased this flying monkey judge really is. Is that a yes?"

"Yeah, yeah, yeah. I'm all in."

Deke had no false hope that Judge Ashworth would give him a pass and not render some type of sanction. The only question in his mind was how severe they would be. Just two years before, Deke had declared a very public war against Ashworth by spending a substantial amount of money attempting to get his friend, Nora Patterson, elected in a heated campaign against the judge. He had bought several full page ads in local newspapers describing how Ashworth had dismissed fifty cases all consolidated in front of her because, in the wording of the ad, she was not smart enough to actually understand the state law in complex product defect cases. All fifty women lived in the state of Florida, and they all had contracted urinary tract cancers from an anti-spermicidal gel called Brynistan. The drug posed health issues so severe that it was actually removed from the market in five European countries. Deke had hoped that social media would jump on Ashworth's name and begin calling her by the more profane nickname that was so easily used by people who didn't like her. His candidate, Nora Patterson, was polling five points ahead of Ashworth when she suffered a minor stroke and pulled out of the race.

Deke and his lawyers had been fortunate enough to work magic most of the time and avoid ever appearing in front of what was now an outwardly hostile judge. Bad luck reared its head and even after two separate motions demanding that Ashworth recuse herself from the case, she still was there in a black robe waiting for the opportunity to play a game of paybacks. Deke was pretty sure that regardless of how brilliant Jeff's research and pleadings were, he was going to feel the festering wrath of the judge the next day.

Weighing more heavily on Deke's mind at the moment, though, was how he had behaved during the PowerPoint presentation for the Trayvon case. Had the team noticed he had choked?

Ugly echoes from the past were clear and present.

7

1969. Late Fall.

"How old are you, kid?"

The boy stood in front of Deke, his hands on his hips, his boots planted squarely in the half-mud, half-grass. The stench of cattle dung wafted off of his overalls, but that was also the case for Deke.

"Fourteen," Deke replied.

"I thought so. A real tenderfoot."

Deke squinted at the teen who was not much bigger. Both of them were tall. He was tan, had dark hair that was a little long and shaggy, piercing brown eyes, and a crooked nose. Had he broken it in the past?

"How old are you?" Deke asked.

"I'm sixteen. Compared to you, I've already been around the world three times, visited a zillion foreign countries, and laid a hundred different girls!" He laughed at that.

Despite the crudeness of the remark, Deke laughed, too.

"What's your name?" the older kid asked.

"Deke."

"That's your real name?"

"No. It's Nicholas. Nicholas Deketomis. But friends call me Deke."

"I'm Bucky Carlton." He wiped his hand on his overalls and then stuck it out. Deke shook it. "Maybe you'll let me call you Deke."

"You already have."

Bucky smirked. "Touché."

The large cattle ranch where they worked had hired both boys to do odd jobs. Mostly grunt work that the men didn't want to do. Cleaning latrines and such. Shoveling dung. But also herding the cattle and learning how to do more complex ranching chores. The pay was practically nothing, and the younger boys on the ranch were essentially slave labor culled from families living on prayers and false hopes. Some of them were as young as twelve. Still, Deke considered himself lucky to have the job.

"So, Deke, how'd you get this lovely, spectacular job?"

"Through my parents."

Bucky cocked his head. "Your parents? I heard you were a foster kid."

Deke looked down and shuffled his own boots in the mud. "Well . . ."

"It's okay. I'm practically one. It's just me and my mother, but she's hardly around."

Deke looked up. "What about your dad?"

"Gone with the wind. And I don't mean the movie."

"My—well, the man of the house where I live—he knew someone here at the ranch. That's how I got in."

Bucky nodded. "I went in and asked for the job. I have experience with horses. It beats cleaning toilets at the city parks."

"You got that right."

"You haven't been in a shitty reform school, have you?" Bucky asked, turning his head sideways but keeping his eyes on Deke.

Shaking his head, the younger boy answered, "No, I've avoided that so far."

"Good for you. You need to stay out of those places. They're hellholes from what I hear. What did you mean? About the 'man of the house where you live.' Is he your foster dad?"

"No, no. Just a family I live with. You know the Nealies?"

"Sure. The Nealie boys come around here all the time."

"Yeah. Their father had a word with Jones, and I got the job. I've . . . I guess I've bounced around a bit. I'm on my own." Deke shrugged.

"I get it. Your mom and dad . . . gone?"

"Something like that."

"And these families aren't foster families?"

"Nope. I've been lucky to find some nice people that take me in. Like the Nealies. Don't know how long I can stay with them, though. It doesn't last forever. It's why I've moved around."

Bucky then pulled out a pack of Lucky Strikes. He tapped one out, stuck it in his mouth, and then offered the pack to Deke.

"Uh, no thanks."

Bucky shrugged and returned the pack to his pocket. He then lit the cigarette with a match from a book he'd also had in his pocket. Bucky then threw the used match on the ground. Bucky puffed a little, coughed, and puffed some more.

"You really like that?" Deke asked.

Bucky coughed again and managed to croak, "Hell, no. But it looks cool, don't it?"

That made Deke laugh. Then he asked, "Aren't you that bareback rider who was in some rodeo competitions?"

Bucky raised his eyebrows and grinned. "You heard about that?"

"Yeah. Some of the other ranch hands were talking about it. Are you any good?"

"I was in three junior rodeos in Central Florida. I didn't get no prizes, but I did all right. A 'respectable showing' was what they said. I got thrown in the first competition, but I wasn't hurt. I stayed on the horse in the next two. Didn't win, though." He shrugged. "But, hey. You don't win it unless you're in it. Someday I'll get my high school degree and move on to be the best damn bareback rider on the rodeo circuit. It's what I call the Big Dream. But I'm going to make it come true."

Deke had been afraid Bucky Carlton would be a bully like some of the older ranch hands. But he was beginning to like the guy, even though he felt some envy and a little jealousy that Bucky could see his future so clearly. That he had what seemed to be a truly achievable plan, something Deke didn't have. The guy's self-confidence was infectious. Deke liked Bucky's optimism.

That was a survival asset for anyone without a solid, steady home.

Jones, the foreman, blew a loud whistle over by the barn. "Uh, break's over," Deke said.

"Yeah, back to work. Back to herding cows and stepping in shit. Fun, ain't it?"

Deke laughed again.

Maybe the job on the Desmond Ranch wasn't going to be so bad after all.

TODAY

Teri Deketomis, Deke's wife of thirty years, pulled into the garage of their home in Spanish Trace and immediately noticed that her husband was sitting in his own car with the engine turned off. He was partially reclined in his seat gazing at nothing. Teri noted the time on the dashboard clock as only four o'clock. Pleased but surprised that the man she had lived with for so many years was home almost three hours earlier than usual on a Tuesday night, Teri was also concerned. Over the course of their marriage, she had come to know her husband's body language and recognize his unintentional messaging. It ranged from sad and worried to jubilant and peaceful. What she now saw was something not new, but indeed rare. Mysteriously pensive, as if he needed to talk to someone but was unwilling to start the conversation. In fact, he was so lost in thought that he hadn't noticed that she had parked her car beside his.

She stepped out and walked over to tap on Deke's driver side window. Startled, he jerked his head to her with wide eyes, and then they both laughed. Deke got out and greeted Teri with a full body embrace that lasted longer than she was accustomed to.

"How about we pour a tall glass of wine, sit on our bedroom balcony, and catch up with each other's life?" she suggested.

"Sounds like the perfect plan." Deke gave her upper arms a little squeeze, and then they went inside the house.

A granite topped table was the centerpiece on the spacious balcony directly outside the half dozen French doors that opened from the master bedroom. High-end stylish rattan furniture placed around the table created a comfortable setting that was frequently used for romantic sunset dinners or a late morning Saturday breakfast. Tropical plants thoughtfully arranged around the space added to the peaceful tranquility of the couple's balcony retreat. Escambia Bay was calm, taking on the appearance of twenty square miles of glass. The sun was gradually dropping out of the sky, reflecting magic light on the green-blue water.

It was in this peaceful environment that Teri wanted to promote an open conversation about whatever it was kicking around in Deke's head.

They sat together on the rattan chair made for two. Deke grabbed the bottle of Sauvignon Blanc sitting in the ice bucket that Teri had brought out and placed on the table. He poured one glass, then two, as she first told him about her day and they took a bit of time to enjoy the view. Then Teri decided it was time to peel back the layers of whatever had thrown Deke into this unusual mood.

"All right, big guy, I'm thinking we have been staring at this bay making small talk for about forty-five minutes now, and you have not even given me a hint about what those gremlins chasing you around today even look like. What's up?"

Deke sat silently, taking a swallow of wine and looking out at the bay. Finally, he answered, "It's one of those complicated, messy feelings I'm having about a case I'd rather not be working on. That said, I've convinced the team that it's an important one."

"Complicated and messy, as you know, is my specialty." Teri smiled as she sat cross-legged and put the glass of wine to her lips. Again, Deke was slow to respond but he knew the conversation was not one he had any chance of avoiding. Teri's eyes were locked on him.

"Aw, heck," he said. "It's not that I'm reluctant about the case. I think I'm scared of it, actually."

Teri reached over and lightly touched his left cheek. "Scared is not a word I usually hear from you. You want to talk about it?"

He finally asked, "Do you remember that time we made a drive down to the Keys with the kids for a small vacation, and we stopped in Arcadia so I could show all of you the homes where I lived down there as a boy?"

"How could I possibly forget?"

"Remember the graveyard I took you to and explained a few details about my friend Bucky Carlton?"

"Of course, Deke. He was your best friend when you were a teenager. I still think of what you told me from time to time. You said he'd died in a boys' camp."

Deke nodded. "He did. And I feel like I gave you the end of that story without filling in all the blanks."

"I'm here to listen, Deke, you know that."

Deke cleared his throat, stood, and walked to the balustrade of the balcony.

He still didn't think he could do it.

"Come on, Deke. Escape from the camp is a really bad idea."

Returning to his seat next to her, he quietly emptied the remaining wine into both of their glasses.

"You don't want to tell me, do you." It wasn't a question.

"Teri, this Trayvon Clapper case, the child murder case that you have seen a few headlines about, is a case that our firm has been asked to handle. Guilt can generate an echo. Every time I look at the facts that we're analyzing or look at the pictures together with the autopsy report, all I see and hear is the ghost of Bucky Carlton and . . ." He paused and shook his head.

Teri said, "Then great! Follow that ghost. Do what you do best and go after all the people who allowed that to happen. All I'm seeing is that you were made for a case like this, Deke. Life prepared you for it."

This made Deke smile for a second.

"Will you ever tell me the story?" she asked.

"Someday. Likely sooner rather than later. But not tonight."

"Fair enough." She clinked her glass against his and kissed his cheek.

8

Deke made his way to his office with an oversized cup of coffee to find Gina and her Trayvon trial team waiting at the conference table. His daughter, Cara, the firm's head of Safety and Security and Investigative Services, Carol Morris, and Michael Carey. Powerhouses all. Carol, a fifty-something, no-nonsense former law enforcement professional, along with Gina and Michael, were perhaps Deke's closest and most valuable colleagues at the firm.

"So much for a quiet cup of coffee. I'm thinking all of you have too much of a lean and hungry look for this early in the morning," he said, eyeing them all. "What's up?"

"Have a seat, boss," Gina said. He took his usual chair at the end of the table. "First off, we've learned that Bruno Williams has been arrested and extradited to California for an old manslaughter charge."

"Oh, great . . ." Deke muttered.

"Yeah. But on the positive side, we don't have to use him as a witness. Claudia Clapper, on the other hand . . ."

Deke shook his head. "She's important to us but I don't know if we'll ever be able to present her to a jury. One look at her, and you can see she's an addict. I think we have to write her off and simply use Trayvon's family history as background to why he was in B Camp in the first place."

Cara spoke up. "What about rehab?"

"What?"

"Let's put Claudia in rehab. It will be months before we go to trial, right?" She glanced at Gina, who subtly winked at her.

Carol said, "I have serious doubts that woman would be responsive to rehab."

"How about you let me try to work with her for a while?" Cara asked. "I mean, why not?"

Deke rubbed his chin and then looked around the room. "What does everyone else think?"

Michael answered, "Might be a long shot."

Gina said, "I'm for it. It'll be worth the expense . . . if it works."

Deke shrugged. "All right, Cara, give it a try. Find a place out of state, far from here. If Claudia resists or tries to run away or becomes a problem, we're closing that effort down. Clear?"

"Got it. I'm on it, Dad."

"What else, Gina?"

She turned a page of her notes and said, "We might have gotten the kind of early break that we almost never see this soon in a case like this. An angry whistleblower who actually sounds credible. Carol, give Deke the details."

Carol had been with the firm for two decades. During her law enforcement career she had received a meritorious service medal and two commendation medals for extraordinary achievements in the line of duty before her thirtieth birthday. At five-foot-six with an athlete's build and more energy than ten people, Carol was, in Deke's mind, indispensable to the firm.

She tucked her short, still natural blonde hair behind her right ear and began. "At this point, Michael and I have spent a solid three days on B Camp, the place where Trayvon was murdered. And I don't use the term 'murdered' lightly, Deke. We have certainly been involved in disturbing cases, but the facts surrounding this place called B Camp are chilling on many levels. Most of the folks that have worked there or work there now are either too terrified to talk or too indifferent and uncaring to give a damn about what happened to Trayvon. But a man named Dan Douglas gave me a call last night. He told me he didn't want to talk on the phone for very long, but my takeaway was that he knew the entire history of Trayvon from the day the boy walked into the facility, and he had all the details about the murder."

Deke asked, "Details that he would tell only us or details he would testify about?"

"At this point, I'm unsure. What is clear is that he is personally afraid and has not gone back to work since the murder. He told me he had worked at the facility for seven years and is aware of much more than just the Trayvon story. He is willing to talk to our lawyers, but if he does, he wants to know that we would protect him and his wife."

"Has he reported anything to the police?"

"When I asked him that, he laughed. He said when we get there we would understand that reaction. I wasn't sure what to take away from that other than the fact that the small community where the facility's setup is definitely proud of the place. It employs about a quarter of the folks who live in Sweeton. Also, I thought it was interesting that it's a large soybean farming area. A fair number of the boys from B Camp are 'given the choice' to work on those farms for below minimum wage. Or work around the facility as groundskeepers or janitors. It would be easy to see how their police team of four officers might intentionally look the other way. Deke, I don't need to tell you about the moving parts of a tiny, reasonably regressive backcountry community like Sweeton. To some degree, small town politics don't allow space or time to move at all. Sweeton exists in that kind of Southern time warp."

Cara spoke up. "Dad, what I found in my research is that about sixty miles from B Camp there was a facility called Dozier Boys Camp that was in business for almost seventy years. The parallels between what we are looking at now in Sweeton and what occurred at Dozier for decades are incredibly similar. The facts about Dozier are well-known; it was national news. There have been books, magazine articles, and even a documentary that tell the story about what occurred there for decades while every Florida governor, state legislature, and law enforcement agency knowingly ignored the truth about how badly the boys suffered there."

"Yes, I am familiar with Dozier," Deke said. "Those kinds of institutions were spread out all over the smallest towns in central Florida where I grew up and primarily in North Florida. Surely, we are not looking at a reemergence of those kinds of facilities?"

Gina answered, "Unfortunately, we are seeing that, Deke. Only it's worse. Now the boys' camp industry is being organized and financed by the predators on Wall Street. Cara hired a forensics team to give us every detail they could find about Phoenix Industries, the corporation that runs B Camp. To say that it's a complex labyrinth of corporate hide and seek would be a dramatic understatement. Their ownership interest in the private adult prison system, not only in the US but also in Europe and Asia, is disguised so completely that it even gave our forensics team migraines. Cara, why don't you give us all a ten-thousand-foot picture of what our folks have found so far?"

"Sure. When we get a little further along, I will chart all this for us because it's as complex as a Rubik's Cube. But I can explain the biggest points right now. Phoenix Industries moved into the adult private prison business with money that our people traced to three primary private investor groups. The money that's been used has come mostly from treasury money market funds and municipal securities that have originated with state and even local governments. That money, plus a huge amount of private equity money, is the engine for both the adult private prisons and the children's facilities."

"What was the methodology you used to get all this?" Deke asked.

"Dad, I know how AI freaks you out, but our people used the most sophisticated AI firm in existence to do what I will call a commonality search. That's where they plugged in questions about names, fund management organization, lobby groups, politicians, regulators, and about fifty other specific searches. This was after they created the extensive body of information they plugged into their AI program."

Deke asked, "So, are you saying we hired a whole forensics team to do a Google search?"

"No, Dad, it's nothing like a Google search. Google is an antiquated, broken-down car. What I'm talking about here is an Aston-Martin. If it's okay, you and I can spend some time with me explaining AI a little better at lunch. But let me continue. Our forensics people have a rating system I don't even understand. They identify 'trends that tell stories,' as they explained to me. One trend that they caught was the overlap between lobby groups, politicians, and political donations. I had asked them to pay particular attention to that. They came up with the name Skyler Bannock. She's linked somehow to none other than Congressman Bob Minds. You probably remember he was the Boston congressman who was the target in a monthlong trial for everything from bribery to fraud. The juror foreman mysteriously went missing after a hung jury result. The headline on that is that the other jurors believed the foreman had been bribed to hang the verdict, and then he disappeared to forever keep that a secret."

Deke rubbed his chin. "A couple of questions, Cara. First, how big are the congressman's footprints around the Phoenix group, and how much ownership does Phoenix have over the prison facilities and children's camps nationally?"

"As far as the congressman's involvement with Phoenix, it's big, at least according to what our people are describing to me. As far as how much of the industry Phoenix owns, it's somewhere in the neighborhood of thirty percent and growing. They're not making big profits in the children's facilities yet, but they are killing it in the private prison space. Our finance savvy experts tell me, though, that a couple of huge verdicts against them could have the potential to close down the children's facility piece of their business."

"Gina, let's see if your team can accomplish that. Michael, you've been way too quiet. Are you going to be able to jump into this case with what you already have on your plate right now?"

Michael Carey, as one of the firm's most effective litigators, brought to every complex case he had ever worked the same kind of intensity that helped him survive as special ops before he was seriously injured in Afghanistan. He had been trained as a pararescue operator, referred to as a 'PJ.' Performing a HALO jump forty thousand feet into a shark-infested ocean and swimming two miles to begin a rescue mission was a piece of cake for Michael. It was the challenge of coloring inside the lines with all the restrictions a lawyer faced that presented him with his biggest challenges.

"Deke, with the team of all-stars at this table, there is no chance of me sitting this one out," Michael replied. "I'm ready to dive in. Gina can direct me, you can direct me, anyone . . . I'm at your disposal wherever you want me to excavate."

Deke laughed. "Thanks, Michael, and I thank all of you for already pushing this case as hard as you are. I think I understand all the moving parts you've laid out for me so let me make a few requests. Gina, would you personally focus on understanding how the congressman specifically is connected to our Trayvon case, if at all? Probably need to make a few trips to Boston. Cara, why don't you go with her?"

"Glad to," his daughter acknowledged.

"Carol, if you could spend another few days in Sweeton digging much deeper, along with getting a sworn statement from Douglas this week, I'm pretty sure that will start building the bones of this case. Maybe take Jake with you." Jake Rutledge, an investigator with the firm, had been a key player working with Carol on some of its most prestigious—and dangerous—cases.

"I'll see what's on his plate," Carol said.

"Michael, all the dysfunction we uncover in Sweeton will no doubt be similar to what all these Phoenix child facilities are plagued with. Start building the case that highlights the issue of common corporate conduct and common management failures of all these facilities around the country. It will be a long list, I'm sure."

"Got it, boss."

"As for me, if I'm not in jail after the humiliation hearing this afternoon in front of that judicial abomination, I will be back diagramming strategies for attacking Phoenix with written discovery, depositions, and a lineup of experts. Let's take it to 'em, my friends."

As they filed out into the hallway, Cara touched her father's sleeve.

"Yes, Cara?"

She gently tugged him to the side and said, "I just wanted to make sure you're okay, Dad."

Deke blinked. "Why, sure. What makes you ask that?"

She gave him a smile and shook her head. "Nothing, never mind."

"Is there something you want to discuss in my office?"

"Maybe later. I better get with Gina so we can plan our trip."

When he was alone again, Deke sat at his desk and thought about his daughter's comment. He had to be careful and not exhibit to the team what he'd been feeling. To that end, though, he allowed himself to become lost in the memories that had kept coming, relentlessly, ever since he'd begun working on the Clapper case. The only thing he could do was to let them flow, embrace them somehow, even though they were like knives penetrating his soul.

9

Not a week later, Carol Morris and her associate investigator, Jake Rutledge, began the process of knocking on doors in Sweeton by first arranging to meet informally with Dan Douglas, who had indicated he might be willing to be a whistleblower. After entering the small town, she drove her white 2023 Toyota RAV4 to the fast food joint where Douglas agreed to see them.

Jake, a man in his late thirties with a linebacker build, had been a lawyer in West Virginia, where he involved Deke's law firm in the very first chapter of opioid litigation several years earlier. Unfortunately, he had released privileged information that he believed the public had a right to see. He was disbarred because of his disclosure, mostly because corrupt defense firms and the judges, who often did their bidding, loved to keep even the ugliest corporate conduct a secret. While that legal mess played out, he had become addicted to the very drugs over which he was litigating. Nevertheless, Deke helped him get clean and offered him a job as an investigator, a position in which he had proven his worth several times over.

They sat at a booth at McDonald's. Mid-afternoon, so it wasn't crowded. Just Douglas and Carol and Jake by themselves on one side of the dining area.

Dan Douglas was thin and had a full head of grey hair. His glasses were the Coke bottle type with very thick lenses, making his eyes appear unnaturally large behind them.

"I worked at B Camp for seven years," he said, somewhat bitterly. "Started off in the stockroom handling supplies—you know, toilet paper, towels, pencils, paper—you name it. Whatever the place considered a 'supply,' I handled it. I became the supervisor two years later. I just resigned, thank goodness. Couldn't handle it anymore."

Carol asked, "Why did you resign, Mr. Douglas?"

"It's a bad place. I, uh, also needed to help take care of my wife in our happy home. She's been under the weather as of late. To tell the truth, I simply didn't want to work there anymore." He shrugged. "The fifty hours a week I put in at one dollar over minimum wage did allow me and Florella—that's my wife—to make ends meet. I couldn't risk walking away until I could. I would like to find another position somewhere. Out of this godforsaken town."

"Can you tell us what happened to Trayvon Clapper?" Jake asked.

Douglas's eyes widened, and he furtively looked around the restaurant. "I'm not going to testify. No way. You said this was informal, right?"

The two investigators could see that the man was scared. "What are you afraid of, Mr. Douglas?" Carol asked.

"*Them.*"

"Can you elaborate?"

"The people who run B Camp! Phoenix Industries. Or, rather, their henchmen."

"What if we just had you do a sworn statement? Maybe a video interview?"

"I don't know . . ."

"Well, why don't you tell us what you know, Mr. Douglas?" Carol attempted to sound as if she understood perfectly where he was coming from.

"The truth is," he said, "I cared about the many Trayvons who passed through B Camp's doors over the last few years. I can't tell you how difficult it was for me, working in the supply room, to know exactly what took place inside those camp rooms and be unable to stop it."

"Stop what?" Jake asked.

"The bullying. By both the guards and the older boys. Once, I remember Trayvon . . ." The man's voice caught. He winced and took a sip of his coffee. The man was getting choked up.

"Take your time, Mr. Douglas," Carol said.

"Trayvon had to go to the supply room to get something, I don't remember what. One of the guards sent him. He . . . he asked me to help him get away. The kid broke down into tears, saying he was afraid of the Little Red House."

"What's that?" Jake asked.

"You don't know about the Little Red House? They have one at all the Phoenix facilities."

"Is that the same as solitary confinement?" Carol asked.

"*No*. It's much worse. My God, I'm so ashamed and disgusted with myself that I didn't make more of an attempt to learn what went on when those doors were closed and locked. All the boys, young and old, were terrified to talk about it."

Carol and Jake glanced at each other. They may have hit pay dirt.

* * *

When Deke's six o'clock alarm went off, he covered his head with a pillow. A wave of dread held him down like heavy chains. Being yelled at and preached to by judges who never had enough talent as lawyers to even carry his briefcase was not new to Deke. However, today was different. He was going to have to answer to a judge with so little talent that even a perfect argument with precise, on point legal briefing would be meaningless.

The phrase "throwing pearls to swine" popped into his mind as he forced himself to stand and keep his feet moving toward the master bath for a cold shower. Deke never had a tendency to feel sorry for himself, but as he emerged from the fog of sleep it struck him that he was at the bottom of the curvy wave line. It was a concept he had taught his kids when they were growing up. If one of them was going through some kind of crisis, he would draw what looked like an oscillating sound-wave line and convince them that whether you were a king, a queen, a superstar athlete, or just a regular person, sometimes life would feel like the pinnacle of the wave. Other times it would feel as if they'd hit the deepest bottom. The point he'd always made for them was that the oscillating wave always moved forward, up and down. And it was exactly the same for every living person on the planet. No exceptions. When they were at the bottom, it should be a comfort to them that the life wave would soon catapult them back to the top.

This morning, though, Deke felt like a life lecture fraud. He felt firmly attached to the bottom of the wave.

* * *

Deke was at the office by 7:30, ready to be briefed. He had confidence in the legal abilities of Peter and Jeff. He had not felt the need to question their plans. He had worked with them long enough to know that they had his back. They would be ready for Ashworth's payback hearing. Still, Deke had often half-jokingly posed the question about why judges were not regularly sued for judicial malpractice. Had that been a viable possibility, Judge Ashworth would have found it impossible to buy malpractice insurance.

Jeff had worked all night but was nevertheless clearly energized and ready for war. When Peter arrived right behind Deke, the three lawyers cranked up the coffee maker in the conference room. What was the strategy they would use in front of Ashworth? It would certainly center on laying groundwork for the appeal grounds. Make Ashworth look as bad as possible to the inevitable appellate court. One advantage they had was that she had been reversed more than other trial judges in North Florida. "Appellate decisions commonly used words that came just short of referring to Ashworth as an incompetent boob," Jeff had once quipped.

He led the conversation. "Deke, just so you know, Pete and I are going to come right at Ashworth by demanding that she recuse herself as judge in this case, as we have already done. But this time, it is not our intent to be as warm and fuzzy about the request as we've been in the past. There is some brand new case law that makes it much more difficult for her to thumb her nose at this recusal request."

Deke raised his eyebrows, a signal for Jeff to continue.

"She will predictably start her tirade at me immediately. What we're looking for is for her to be so caustic and so combative, on the record, that even without the court reporter's tape recordings, it will be apparent to the appellate court that she has gone totally batshit with anger."

Deke interrupted, "Jeff, should we all carry our toothbrushes over to court in case she asks the bailiff to escort us to the pokey?"

Jeff replied, "If it goes bad it will go bad for me, not you or Pete. I'll be the one doing the talking at that point."

Peter interjected, "Without going into too much detail, Deke, two areas I'm going to argue will center on your constitutional first amendment rights to speak out and the public health nightmare that Ashworth has become a part of by issuing a gag order in this case."

"It makes no sense for us to go into all the details about our arguments," Jeff added. "We are ready. You have trusted us for many years now, so trust us on this. We absolutely will not get a favorable ruling from this judge, but we may get a very quick expedited opinion out of the appellate court that, first, reverses whatever sanctions she hits you with and, secondly, applies the newest cases to the question about her recusal."

He took a deep breath before continuing. "Here's the tough part, Deke. We both want you to sit and not speak. Just be as invisible as you possibly can. We can accomplish more by simply making your arguments for you and precisely focusing on the law. She has the facts. She is keenly aware of the words you spoke and you don't have to repeat them. Let's allow clear case law to speak for us, Deke. You say as little as is humanly possible in that courtroom. Can you do that?"

Deke shook his head. "I would rather jam sticks in my eyes than sit there and endure her rantings, but yes, I will be good." He raised his hand in a "Scout's honor" gesture.

"Great, we have a plan then." Jeff and Peter grabbed their legal pads and shot out of the office.

There was nothing at all Deke liked about being relegated to being a third seat in any courtroom, but he understood the ramifications of what this judge could potentially do to cause harm to him and his law firm.

He had about six hours to imagine the worst that could happen.

10

At 2:30, Deke and the two lawyers who were intent on saving him from Judge Ashworth's wrath walked into the judge's open courtroom. Jeff and Peter began organizing boxes and files around their table. Both the court security guard and the bailiff approached Deke and extended their hands for a welcoming handshake. Deke had been instrumental in helping the guard, Derrick, get his job with the courthouse ten years earlier. In fact, Deke had tried many cases in front of both these men, and they had a strong respect for him. Nearly all the staff who waved and smiled at Deke had a pretty good idea why he was there.

Deke and Derrick walked to the back of the courtroom and traded whispers.

"Derrick, do you have any interest in changing places with me today? I've always had an interest in law enforcement, and I bet you'd make one heck of a lawyer."

Derrick smiled at that, but said, "Most days I'd say yes, Deke, but from what I can piece together just from her majesty's dark and annoyed look, I feel more secure behind this badge."

Deke quietly laughed. He appreciated the fact that Ashworth had in just a few years managed to alienate the majority of personnel working around the courthouse with her black robe sense of self-importance.

"What did you do to bring all this about, Deke?"

"Well, if I'm honest, I'd say I allowed my butt to overload my angry mouth. If I'm giving you a lawyer answer, I'd say I was exercising my

First Amendment right to call a spade a spade. So today I'm sticking with answer number two."

"Deke, I understand," Derrick said. "And I made a call to someone who might be able to help."

Before Deke could ask what he was talking about, the bailiff who had already made his way to the front of the courtroom spouted out his *Hear ye, hear ye* speech indicating that the judge was entering the room and the directive for everyone to stand. Deke moved to his seat between his two lawyers and stood as Ashworth stomped her short frame to the bench, never looking up to acknowledge that other human beings were standing in the courtroom. Her small, bleach blonde head, barely visible behind the enormous cherry wood judge's bench, might have promoted at least a giggle. The oversized, square, black-rimmed glasses that barely hung on the edge of her nose added to the overall cartoonish appearance, detracting from the wannabe scholarly judicial image she no doubt was desperate to project.

With a few vastly unnecessary strikes with her gavel, the judge called the court to order and instructed everyone to have a seat. At that moment, Tom Franklin, the defense attorney for the Kaplans, walked through the large courtroom doors and took his position at the defense table.

Ashworth eyed the newcomer. "Mr. Franklin, I'm not sure why you are here. I personally issued my rule to show cause motion *sua sponte*, and this hearing is one I intended to conduct with only the pertinent parties present. Unless you personally have also violated the rules of this court, like Mr. Deketomis, then the parties you represent would be unaffected. A trip over here from Tallahassee seems a bit wasteful."

Franklin stood and addressed the judge. "Your Honor, any ruling against Mr. Deketomis would potentially have impact on the resolution of the Kaplan case. When I heard that this hearing was taking place without notice given to the Kaplan defense team, it caused me concern since Mr. Deketomis and I are in serious discussion about a potential resolution."

Deke was hard-pressed not to allow his jaw to drop. There was nothing precisely accurate about what Franklin had stated to the court, although it could not be characterized as a lie. Two sophisticated opposing lawyers would always be working toward 'resolution.' Deke now understood that Franklin was there to help him in any way he could. Derrick's call had been to him, likely giving Franklin a heads-up that Deke was in trouble. It was a call that Derrick knew Deke would have been too proud to make.

Few people in the lawyer community knew the backstory regarding the two attorneys. Deke had helped Tom, a client—and friend—he'd had during his early days in the profession, not only get into law school, but he had also assisted in financing his first year. Franklin had done extremely well as a student and managed to graduate number two in his class. In the process of achieving excellence as a student, he had lost a battle with alcohol and drugs. The week after Tom's graduation, Deke showed up at the young man's Birmingham apartment and for two hours gave his best lawyer reasoning on why it was essential that they make a trip together to enroll Tom into an Atlanta rehab center for ninety days at Deke's expense. Tom was well aware that the trip had more than likely saved his life. When he hit the lawyer job market, one of the most prestigious corporate defense firms in the southeast hired him. For ten years he had steadily worked his way into a role as one of their key negotiators in complex cases.

Even if they worked on opposite sides in some of the country's most combative national cases or would not outwardly appear to be close friends, Tom Franklin had always felt a sense of indebtedness to Deke.

"I hear you, Mr. Franklin," the judge said, "but this matter is uniquely between the court and Mr. Deketomis."

Franklin pressed on without any outward signaling of defiance, but his attitude about Ashworth was not at all different from that of everyone else in the courtroom. "I understand this hearing centers around questions of inappropriate statements made about my client. I want it made clear on this record that those statements had no impact on our ability to proceed further with potentially productive negotiation. We want the record to reflect that this hearing is taking place even in light of the fact that neither I nor my client ever made any requests for any kind of sanctions against Mr. Deketomis. I also think it is significant,

Judge, that we were not even afforded notice of this hearing. We were relegated to finding out about it from random word on the street."

Ashworth's red face and obvious awkward effort to maintain control of her anger was palpable. "Are you through, Mr. Franklin, or would you care to double down on the unusual position you are taking as a defense lawyer in this case?"

"No, I simply thought it might be important to state our position on the record in case an appellate court had to review what occurs in this hearing. Thank you for allowing me to speak."

"Okay, Mr. Franklin, you had your opportunity to speak. Unless there is more you intend to add, let's say goodbye to you now," the judge said with an edge.

With that, Franklin turned and made his way out of the courtroom.

Ashworth didn't miss a beat addressing Deke and his defense team. "Also 'for the record' and as is detailed in the order to show cause document, Mr. Deketomis has made an attempt to try this case against the Kaplans in the media by stating on national television that their conduct was, let's see, let me read this exactly . . . Oh yes, 'borderline criminal and should be treated as nothing less than manslaughter for selling their poison to the public.' Mr. Deketomis chose to speak those words, notwithstanding the gag order I had entered in this case. Mr. Deketomis, how do you respond?"

Jeff stood. "Actually, Judge, Mr. Deketomis won't be responding. I will, since I'm one of the many lawyers who will be handling any interlocutory emergency hearing that might be necessary for any rulings of this court today. Secondly, we have provided you with the most recent case law that is dramatically unequivocal about your duty to recuse yourself from this case. In addition to that case law, you will see the list of public statements you made about my partner after he purchased that less-than-flattering full page ad about you during your last judicial race."

Everyone in the courtroom waited for the judge's head to explode as she gripped her gavel with both hands. Her now fire-engine-red face was comically contrasted against her bottle blonde hair. Her anger resulted in her making the mistake most talented judges avoided on an issue as important as a recusal motion.

She ruled from the bench. "Motion denied. Let's get to the big question about sanctioning your partner who now silently sits beside you."

Jeff continued, "First, let me point out that there was no gag order in place when my partner made the statements that you just recited. In fact, you didn't even sign a gag order until two days after those statements were made on CBS. So, I suppose we should address your position that my partner was trying this case in public and somehow would interfere with the orderly litigation of this case. To that question we provided the court this morning with a ten-page brief that lays out an easy-to-follow analysis of how a public policy of secret, behind-closed-doors court proceedings is very often dangerous for the consumer public. I suppose the operative fact that this court seems to be willing to ignore is that more than a hundred and fifty people are dying every day from the very kind of poison that the Kaplans are selling. I'm pretty sure that would seem significant to most people, and they certainly should have the right to know as even a most basic public policy concept."

"Yes, and I'm pretty sure I understand public policies and evolving law, Mr. Grandy. But why don't you, in less than two minutes, tell this apparently ignorant judge what I should focus on in your brief."

"Terrific. You might want to start with the constitutional First Amendment free speech analysis stating that even lawyers have the right to put the public on notice when conduct and safety issues being disclosed in an American courtroom might pose a life or death question for consumers. The public has a right to know, and lawyers have a duty to warn them. In other words, Judge, the kind of statements my partner made might actually save a few of those folks from dying a horrible death from drug overdose."

"Great, Mr. Grandy. I'll read your brief as if it is some profound emerging new concept in American jurisprudence, but to be clear, I know the law and, in my courtroom and in my jurisdiction, as far as I can see, your partner seems incapable of following that law."

Ashworth banged the gavel, stood, waddled to her chamber door entrance, turned, and let everyone know they would hear from her soon.

The eyes of Deke and his colleagues met. All three men thought the same thing. First, that it was the shortest hearing they had ever been involved with and, secondly, that it had taken place in front of a judge who was a judicial trainwreck.

Deke wondered if he'd reached the end of the line.

He felt a flood of disgust with himself, prompting once again the running of scene snippets in his head, much like celluloid film passing through an editing machine.

* * *

1970. Early Spring.

"She's dead, Deke."

It was the first and only time Deke had ever seen tears streaming down Bucky's cheeks.

The past few months had been ecstatic for the teen. Deke had never had a friend who had become like a brother to him. With all his moving around, he hadn't experienced that kind of companionship before. He and Bucky Carlton had become joined at the hip. They spent nearly every waking hour together. Working at Desmond Ranch and during their leisure time off. Deke was in school, of course, but the Nealies were fairly lenient in allowing him to carouse Arcadia with his newfound buddy.

Deke had been without a father or mother, one or the other, after the first ten years of his life. They had split up early on. His father disappeared with another woman, and his mother left for Chicago when Deke was twelve. Luckily, the Mortons, for whom he mowed the lawn, were kind enough to take him in, at least for a little while. The foster care system in Florida didn't know about Deke's homeless issue. Chip Morton taught Deke to drive, but the man was a hopeless, but happy, alcoholic. Deke had ended up driving Morton around to various bars in town. Eventually, though, the Mortons couldn't afford to "keep" Deke. Now he was with the Nealies, who had shown him tremendous kindness. Their two sons were a bit older than Deke, and they hung out together, but they were not close to him in the way Bucky was. At least Deke was still under the radar of the authorities.

Thus, Deke was used to being alone. It wasn't "loneliness." There was a difference. And that's why he and Bucky hit it off so well. Bucky's expertise on the ranch elevated his new friend to teacher and mentor, too, and Deke learned a lot from him. He became Robin to Bucky's Batman. In fact, they often joked about being one of the famous pairs in history for a day. One afternoon they were the Dynamic Duo, and on another, the Two Musketeers. They were Butch Cassidy and the Sundance Kid, Bud Abbott and Lou Costello, and Wyatt Earp and Doc Holliday, all rolled into two teenage boys on the verge of becoming men.

Bucky had just turned seventeen. Deke would be fifteen in the summer. The future was prime for taking.

Until today.

The boys were hauling bales of hay in the barn, and Bucky had been awfully quiet. Finally, Deke asked, "Hey, man, what's up? You okay?"

That's when he'd answered.

"She's dead, Deke."

"Dead? Who?"

"My mother."

"What?"

"It was a car accident." He bowed his head and shook it. "It was her fault, too. I think she was drunk."

"Oh, no. Bucky, I'm so sorry!"

Bucky wiped his face with his dirty sleeve. "They can't find my father. No one knows where he is. Bastard."

"Where are you going to live now?"

"Hell if I know. The damn state is getting involved. I have some kind of case worker who ain't worth shit. I'm probably going to be put into what they call the 'childcare system.' Hell, I ain't no child."

"No, you're not."

They continued to haul the hay, but the wheels in Deke's head were turning. After a while, he said, "So, look, Bucky . . ."

"Yeah?"

"You've got not quite a year until you're eighteen, right?"

"Yeah, so what?"

"When you're eighteen, you're an adult. You don't have to be in a 'child-care system.'"

Bucky laughed under his breath. "What am I supposed to do, hide until my next birthday?"

"Well . . . yeah!"

His friend gave him that sideways look that was so typical of Bucky. "What do you mean?"

"We just have to find you a place to live. If you drop out of school and take a GED program, you could probably disappear into the crowds of ranch hands that are constantly coming and going. Florida's got a big cattle business. I know a few families that might open their houses to you rather than allowing those state pinheads to get involved. I could pitch some of them on the idea of allowing you to live with them."

"Really? What makes you a professional social worker?"

"Well, I have been in a few homes like that myself. They are just decent people willing to help. I know how it works. And if it doesn't, I'll bet there are plenty of empty vacation homes in those winter resort areas along Peace River."

"Are you saying I should just stay in one of those empty houses? Isn't that illegal?"

"Bucky, the main thing is we've just got to let the clock run out. When you turn eighteen next year, you'll be emancipated!"

"That's a big word for a fifteen-year-old."

"I can help you, Bucky. You can be like the Man With No Name, *a nomad, squatting from place to place, one step ahead of the law. I've done it myself before for a month at a time. In the meantime, you work for the ranches. Hell, they pay cash, they don't care if you tell 'em your real name or not. As long as you can do the work, and you can! You're valuable. Jones knows you're good. He's promoted you twice to more responsible jobs. Bucky, we can do this."*

"We?"

"I'm your friend, ain't I? I'll help you through it."

Bucky finally smiled. "Yeah, maybe. Maybe it can work."

Deke clapped his pal on the upper arm. "Trust me!"

11

Midas McDonald always appreciated out of town jobs. He loved the sense of total freedom every time he was given the opportunity to drive long stretches in his huge diesel pickup truck.

It had taken Midas two years to perfect the *modus operandi* that provided everything he needed in his line of work. The oversized cargo bed in the pickup had been an expensive modification. Smooth, shiny stainless steel covered a false bottom that opened to a compartment containing the tools of his trade, as well as any items that needed transport after a successful job. Midas was thrilled with the ease of cleaning the stainless steel, as it left no trace of what his cargo might have been.

He had struggled most of his life to turn his obsessive-compulsive nature into a positive attribute. His years working in theater had trained him to be a consummate actor, makeup artist, and lithe, athletic dancer. These abilities also gave him strength, agility, and the ability to disguise himself with great skill.

His virtually spotless and glossy black truck made its way toward North Florida. The "Save the Whales" and "Adopt a Pet" stickers on the back windshield may have interfered with the overall perfect appearance of the vehicle, but like everything else in Midas's life, it was part of the disguise.

Earlier in his life, Midas had found it difficult to camouflage every detail about himself, but as an adult he had mastered the art of hiding his lack of compassion and empathy with a highly practiced superficial charm. Strangers bonded with him in a matter of minutes. It was that charisma that misdirected people from his eyes. They were so black that the pupils were nearly indistinguishable from the irises. Even the sharp incisors mixed with a mouthful of extremely tiny baby teeth were offset by magnetism when Midas smiled. His flawless, powder white skin, colored-in eyebrows, shoulder length jet black hair in a tight ponytail, and overly thin, towering stature typically mesmerized others. While Midas was recognizably male, he had an androgynous appearance akin to the likes of the late rock star David Bowie during his "Ziggy Stardust" era.

Midas was particularly excited today because there was nothing equivocal about his assignment. The "Slick Stick," as he liked to refer to his employer, had not sent him off to "spread terror" or to "make it painful" as was so often the code words for "let them live." Today, Midas was given full rights to "take them out," which allowed for creativity and, more importantly, pure fun. Always a bonus for any highly paid psychopath, and he had no qualms with self-deprecatingly describing himself as such. He liked to think he was a charter member of the Psychopath Country Club. Midas also delighted in the notion that he was paid the same amount for one quick job as what his ignorant half-ass old man had earned in a whole year as a school janitor.

A scenic drive, two hours of entertainment—depending on what the situation called for—and a boatload of Bitcoin deposited into his account . . . life was good for Midas.

* * *

"This place should be called Stepford Township," Jake said on the phone to Gina, referring to the classic Ira Levin horror novel. The fictional Stepford was also a place that was outwardly hostile to strangers because of a deep, ugly secret that no one was willing to discuss, especially with outsiders.

The secret in Sweeton seemed to center on the two boys' camps that were located in the area: B Camp, the one inside Sweeton itself, and the other less than sixty miles away, a place called Pemberton. But after a series of difficult interviews, a storyline was emerging for both camps. Jake frequently called in newly discovered facts as close to real time as possible to Gina. In-house researchers then followed up with deeper dives, no matter how seemingly insignificant the information might be.

"Pretty good day for just day three here," Jake continued. "Ninety-nine percent of all the stuff our whistleblower Dan Douglas disclosed is bearing out, even though we're getting only small drips of facts from the peculiar folks in this godforsaken town. I swear, Gina, you can see unhinged fear in the eyes of the people who have given us even the slightest bit of information."

"What do you think about Mr. Douglas?" Gina asked. "Will he ever agree to a deposition and maybe a trial appearance if needed?"

"Right now, he is so freaked out that all we might possibly get is a video interview of a sworn statement with a court reporter present. Not exactly a home run, but it's a start. He keeps telling us 'they' know about him, but he doesn't seem to know who 'they' are. He thinks his neighbor across the street is spying on him and has been asking who we are. He's telling them we're insurance salespeople, but he's terrified they're talking to someone."

"Has Carol worked out a place where he can live safely for a while?"

"Yes. Both he and his wife have family in Mississippi. Carol has been able to call in a major favor to get him a job there as a night guard. Trust me, he's ready to go tomorrow, but he still needs a few days to pull things together. We will have a company out of Tallahassee provide security for him starting in two days."

"Give me a few big picture items."

Gina was on speaker phone. Carol kept her eyes on the road and spoke. "Hey, Gina. Listen, the similarities with the shit show that went on at the Dozier facility back in the day are strong here in Sweeton. We're looking at it with the understanding that it's owned by Phoenix. Is that still verified information?"

"Absolutely. There's a subsidiary that works under a different name and license but it's joined at the hip with Phoenix."

"Then you're probably going to lose it when you hear these new facts. The Dozier facility had a place on campus that was nothing short of a damn torture room where they took kids, tied their hands and feet to bed posts, and beat their entire bodies, head to toe, with a phone book or heavy rolled-up towels. That would sometimes go on for an hour or more with short breaks in-between. That came from a boy—now a man—that lives in Utah who I ran down on a lead. It's consistent with facts we've been able to learn from Mr. Douglas about these two Phoenix facilities we're looking at. More importantly, a few people right here in Sweeton also refer to a place called the Little Red House at B Camp. Mr. Douglas told us about Trayvon's half dozen trips to that place. Gina, from what we're dragging out of these Sweeton folks, it's probably time to launch a national ad campaign and search for potential witnesses. We also need to start an immediate request for production specifically identifying the names of kids who have been housed in B Camp and Pemberton for the last five years."

"No problem. You should know that records show that the old Dozier camp was finally closed by the ACF after seventy years of business. I'll make a request to the ACF for the list you want on B Camp and Pemberton. My bet is that we'll get some early pushback from ACF because they will no doubt be legitimately humiliated by the legacy they've left there. Not exactly bureaucracy at its best. Fortunately, some of it is public record, so we'll dig in. Good luck over there."

"We're keeping our eyes peeled and ears open," Jake responded.

"Well, proceed with some semblance of caution, even though I know Carol won't want to!"

* * *

Cara was ten minutes late to Jaco's Bar and Grille. Her mother and father were already at a booth with a couple of glasses of wine.

"We started without you," Teri said with a smile as Cara slipped in the seat beside her mom.

"Sorry! I was down a rabbit hole with work on the case," she said, catching her breath.

"The Trayvon case?" Deke asked.

"What else? That's my main focus these days, Dad. You know that."

"Everything going okay with Gina?"

"Absolutely. Gina's great."

He nodded and continued to look at the menu in front of him. He seemed distracted.

"Well, relax, dear," Teri said. "We're glad you could make the time to join us."

Cara picked up the menu and started to browse. "Jaco's is always a treat. I couldn't miss our monthly family dinner!"

It had been a ritual for years. The Pensacola Bayfront restaurant was a popular joint serving a wide variety of fare from seafood to steaks to vegetarian dishes. Cara had fond memories of being there with her brother and parents. Whenever Andy was in town, they'd make it a point to go back to Jaco's. Sometimes they would invite family and friends to join them. Cara recalled that she had first met Gina Romano at Jaco's. The conversations at these gatherings had always been buoyant and covered any number of topics, except that politics, law, and religion were taboo. And, although the practice had ceased as of late, Cara had grown up with a game they would play at the table to get a lively discussion going. As corny as it sounded, someone would ask—

"So," she began, "What is the most important thing that has happened to you lately and what is the biggest challenge you've faced in the last few weeks?"

Teri laughed. "Ah, tradition returns!" She started to sing the chorus of the number from *Fiddler on the Roof.* "Traditioooon . . . tradition!"

That got Deke to laugh, too, just as their waiter appeared. "Well, Cara, we'll each take turns answering you, but first let's put in our order. Cara, did you want wine or a cocktail?"

"A margarita, please! I need it."

The waiter left and Cara said, "Speaking of Gina, I'll never forget her story at one of these dinners where she described in detail all the challenges she faced trying to find a man with enough confidence to just accept her for who she was. She said he didn't need to be a triathlete or an astronaut. She said she needed a man who was more of a wise, interesting, caring Golden Retriever."

Teri added, "And I remember that she ended it by saying she was still looking!" More giggles. Deke remained quiet. Teri spoke again. "How about I go first? Last week I stepped up my workout at the gym, and, yeah, it's a challenge. But what's life without a challenge, you know? And as far as the most important thing that's happened to me lately . . . hmm, how about the constant realization that our entire family, each one of us, you, Andy, me, Deke . . . we're all healthy and productive and doing what we love."

"Hear, hear," Cara said. "If I had my margarita we could clink glasses."

"Use your water glass, dear," Teri said.

They lifted their glasses, tapped them together, and took sips.

"Dad? Your turn."

"Hmpf," he said, rolling his eyes. "Well, as you can imagine, the most important thing to me right now is everything going on at the office. The Kaplan judge and what she's doing, this Trayvon Clapper case . . . You know, Cara, the Clapper case . . . well, it's tough and it's horrible. It's also the challenge part of your question. How are we going to bring down this corporation that supports the abuse of children? Because that's what it is. The more I look at the facts we've uncovered so far—and there's still a lot more we have to do—I just get . . . well, I'm not a violent man, but I'd like to wring some necks!"

As her father delivered what became a peculiar soliloquy, Cara and her mother sat and listened with growing consternation. Deke's face became flushed, his shoulders discernably tensed, and his voice grew louder and more intense.

"The child reform school system in this country is a *disgrace*! It was a disgrace fifty years ago, and it still is today. Corporations fund these things as a money making enterprise. They don't give a hoot about actually *helping* the boys that are in these places. I imagine the girls' schools are the same way, but I have no experience with those. I *do* have experience with places like B Camp. Back in my day there was Sandbury Housing for Boys. If I could have, I would have either sued the hell out of that place or burned it to the ground for what they did. It was eventually closed and bought out, and its facilities are now some other business, thank God, but it looks like B Camp is just a rinse-and-repeat operation!"

Teri reached out and gently shook his arm as if she were waking someone from a bad dream. "Deke."

"What?"

"We're in a public restaurant. And remember the rules, we don't talk law when we're at family dinner."

He let out a long exhale. "Sorry. You're right. I guess I'm a little enraged about this particular case."

At that moment, Cara's margarita showed up. She thanked the waiter, grabbed it, and took a long sip off the side of the rim. Then she said, "Well, Dad, I'd really like to know why you're so passionate about this case. Gina and I have noticed that you—"

"Gina and you? What? Noticed what?"

"Well, that you haven't been yourself. She thinks it's about something that happened to you. A long time ago."

"She does, huh?"

"Doesn't it?" Cara turned to her mother for backup, but Teri gave her a *Don't go there!* look.

Deke didn't answer. After an awkward moment, Cara said, "Never mind, Dad. Maybe you'll tell me when you're ready. Right now let's just enjoy a family night."

For the next few minutes, silence pervaded the table. Deke went into an odd sullen funk without saying anything. Cara eventually moved the conversation by asking her mother about her gym trainer and what books she was reading. The food eventually arrived, and they set about eating.

Finally, as they were finishing, Teri said, "Cara, you never answered the challenge-important thing question. Do you have something to say?"

Cara, exasperated by her father's reaction and his unwillingness to talk, decided that it was now or never. Her hands were folded on the table, and she looked at them for a moment.

"Cara?"

"Well, okay, here goes." She sighed and began. "The most important thing that's happened to me lately is, of course, collaborating with Gina on this case we're doing. It's hard work but I love it. So, I thank you, Dad, for bringing me onto the case and pairing me with her."

"You two work well together," Deke said, almost grudgingly. "But I sense you have something else to say."

"Yeah, it's the challenge part of the question." Cara took another deep breath. "I've been asked if I might want to go work at Dunlop and Markle in Boulder, Colorado."

Deke blinked. "You what?"

"You may remember my old boyfriend, Zach Morrison? Really great law student? Well, he turned out to be a great lawyer, too, and he's there. He was on a fast track to make partner, and he did. They're looking to expand the office with—quote unquote—young up-and-coming talent with some trial experience. Zach recommended me, and the partners liked what they saw. They want to make an offer if I show them I'm interested."

Deke just stared at her.

"Dad, you look a little pale."

His voice cracked a bit when he asked, "Are you going to do it?"

Cara looked over at her mother, who was staring with wide eyes. Then, back at her father, she said, "Well, that's the challenge. I don't know, Dad. I haven't made a decision. You know I love working for you. But we had this conversation back when I got out of law school before you hired me. I raised the issue . . . Will it forever put me under your shadow? Dad, I've lived in Florida my whole life. I think part of growing as a person is to experience other places, other people . . . getting away from home."

"Sounds like you've made up your mind."

"No, I haven't. I just wanted to tell you about the possibility, that's all. And, yes, I'm considering it. But I was hoping for some guidance from you. Don't you agree I should maybe get out from under your wing at some point?"

"That's what you think of me as? A mother hen?"

"Dad!"

"Cara, look, do what you need to do. If you want to go to Colorado and work at another firm, do it." He raised his hand and got the attention of the waiter. "Excuse me, check please!"

Aw geez, Cara thought. *That went well.*

* * *

Midas pulled into Sweeton at three in the morning. The welcome sign at the city limit marker read, "Sweeton is Sweet on You." The words were surrounded by red hearts directly above the words, A POPULATION OF 6,000 PEOPLE WELCOMES YOU!

"Well, thanks, that's going to make my stay here that much more pleasant," Midas announced aloud.

He had no intention of hanging out in the little town any longer than necessary. He was confident that this job might be the easiest hundred thousand he'd ever made. It crossed his mind that the offer of so much money for a job like this was perhaps a little too generous coming from the Slick Stick, but right now he had to focus on the job ahead.

Midas's choice of favorite work tools were a simple Sig Sauer nine millimeter pistol with a detachable silencer, and an ice pick. Both weapons sat in a specially designed, well-hidden quick access space built into the interior side of the driver's side door. Over the years, Midas had come dangerously close to using the weapons to end the lives of police officers whose intuitions had been uncomfortably on target during routine stops.

The other handy accoutrement was the false door area directly beneath the stainless steel truck bed. Its efficiency for storing newly dead bodies was ideal, but Midas also knew that in the murder business things sometimes went wrong.

According to Google Maps, he was ten short blocks away from Mr. and Mrs. Douglas's home. Most of the people the Stick sent him out to murder were not necessarily bad people, but the distinction between good or bad was something about which Midas was wholly indifferent. This was more than just a job. It was a vocation he enjoyed. The Douglas couple would simply be numbers fourteen and fifteen.

When he was three blocks away, Midas pulled the truck behind a store called Burt's Corner Groceries and began his trek on foot. Midas hated this part of the job because it was when he was most exposed. Fortunately, the obviously dirt-poor neighborhood had no streetlights, and the homes were close enough together that he could weave his way between front yards, backyards, and grass alleyways as he approached the target. At this point, any police officer, nosy neighbor, or barking dog stood little chance of taking another breath if they posed any hint of a threat to Midas.

The Douglas home was the type of dwelling Midas referred to as a shotgun shack. It was struggling to stay upright. Only touches of remaining white paint. The most attractive aspects of the home were the perfectly maintained flower beds that were no doubt an effort to draw attention away from the reality that the old home was on life support. Midas respected that the Douglases were people who were trying to make the best out of the hand they had been dealt in life. If he'd had the chance, he would have let them know that.

Midas made his way to a side window directly above one of the largest flower beds. The Douglas living room was on the other side.

"What have we here?" he thought to himself when he noticed a large propane tank to the left of the bed.

Always able to improvise, Midas began visualizing how this murder would unfold.

12

Gina and Cara landed at Boston International in London quality fog. They were already running late to start their twenty mile drive to the Massachusetts correctional facility that had housed Brian Meyers for three years. His crime? Guilty of trusting Congressman Bob Minds. Gina and Cara had flown to Boston to get a firsthand account of the story Cara had uncovered in her research of the congressman. Meyers had been convicted of offering bribes to an honest regulator who supervised the logistics arm of the ORR, the Office of Refugee Resettlement. The huge new influx of refugees into the United States was a gold bonanza for companies like Phoenix. Minds was focused on promoting children's housing facilities as a place child refugees could call home. Blessings from both the ORR and ACF would backup Minds's efforts.

They pulled into the parking lot with fifteen minutes to spare. Meyers was housed in a minimum security section of the prison, but the two lawyers found it to be a highly sophisticated gauntlet of safeguards.

Meyers sat in a small, allegedly private meeting room adorned with pea green paint that was flaking off in large patches from the ceiling to the floor. The dim florescent lighting flickered. The odor of sweat, urine, and old sneakers was overwhelming to the point that the palm of Cara's hand reflexively moved to her nose. She caught herself, though, hoping Gina hadn't noticed.

Gina was accustomed to sitting in such places after having spent a few years as a prosecutor both for the DOJ and the state of Florida. The smells and other putrid aspects of prison meeting rooms had a negligible impact on her. Most of the time her goal was to talk to prisoners who were angry enough to target people who had been accomplices, financiers, or strategic organizers of other peoples' criminal conduct. The ones still living the good life. Often the ones who were sent to prison were ready to talk. Gina had become a master of collecting leads to go after the prisoners' pals.

Meyers had been living that good life as a small-time lobbyist who had made a career move from CEO of a large Massachusetts insurance company. After building a reputation as a reasonably effective lobbyist, particularly in areas of finance and insurance, Meyers had been looking for a whale client to give him the big break he believed would inevitably come his way. He had made the wrong choice.

After Gina and Cara took their seats across from Meyers at the small rectangular table in the middle of the room, the guard made his exit and took a position behind a four-by-six window so that he had an unobscured view from the other side of the wall.

Gina spoke first. "Brian, first of all thank you for the quick response to our letter. I'm not sure we have ever had a four day turnaround like that, especially with a phone call. You asked us to come and so we are here. What now?"

Meyers said with a trembling voice, "I feel strongly that we should not start this meeting without us praying together. Can we join hands, stand together, and pray?" He held out his left hand to Cara and right to Gina.

Cara reached out but Gina quickly responded, "Brian, the hands part will bring that guard back into this room. How about we pray with you and hold off on the hands thing for now." Cara realized her naïve mistake and slowly pulled back her hand. She was the first to admit that she still had a lot to learn.

"Oh, of course," Meyers said. "But know there are angels in this room. Where I go these days, they go too." He sounded sincere without a hint of being a religious zealot. He then held his right hand high, bowed his head, and delivered his prayer as if he were a strong, focused CEO addressing a room full of executives. "Lord, protect us. Protect the ones we love. Keep us safe from harm. Show us your grace with your protection. Lead us away from the enemy. Bless us with your power and the love you show us every day. Be mighty in how you guard Ms. Gina and Ms. Cara as they set out on this important journey you have put before them. In the name of Jesus, our Lord. Amen." Meyers then smiled individually at both Cara and Gina and shook his head as if it was his sign of approval.

Gina recognized that it would have been ignorant and unsophisticated to not appreciate the sincerity that Brian Meyers exhibited in that short prayer. At the same time, it would have also been unobservant not to have picked up on the point that "personal safety" and "protection from harm" were the centerpieces of it.

"Thank you for that, Mr. Meyers," Cara said with genuine appreciation.

"Yes, thank you," Gina added. She instinctively suspected that Meyers exhibited "born-again" Christian vibes and that it was probable he was sincerely reaching out for redemption of some kind. Gina felt genuine respect for that. "Now, from what you said on the telephone it sounds like you have much more to say to us than we have for you, so would it be okay if you lead us through this conversation?"

"I am a living example of pride before the great fall, Ms. Gina. It was pride that allowed me to believe what I knew was wrong from the beginning, but the enemy works in effective ways. It started with a call of high praise for how effective and respected I was as a lobbyist. I was made to feel puffed up and proud, just like the great King Saul before he met his end. I was told by a man who was a very close friend to Congressman Minds, who I had never met, that I was ready to move into the stratosphere of lobbying if I could prove I was trustworthy enough. I was tasked to help fix a problem they had in Alabama. You must know about that."

Gina and Cara glanced at each other. *Alabama?*

Gina quickly rolled with it. "We do, Mr. Meyers, but why don't you tell us more about it?"

He sighed. "To this day, I pray for that young boy. At the time, I had no idea what he had gone through, but God does forgive." Meyers cleared his throat. "I believe his name was Jordan. I can't recall his last name. Thirteen years old. A boy who had been placed in the Alabama facility. He died at the hands of a security guard named Perkins. But you know that."

Actually, they didn't. Cara made some notes on her legal pad and allowed Gina to respond. "Yes, and we are indeed looking into that." She made eye contact with Cara, who understood that this was something big and that they *would* be adding this information to their list of leads. "Back to the connection to Congressman Minds . . . the facts we've collected so far, Mr. Meyers, point to the person making that call as being Ron Jacobi, who was initially investigated along with you for bribery. Is that correct?"

"Yes, he was the Jezebel who seduced me. Ron Jacobi. Supposedly, if I would show good faith by delivering a package to a certain government supervisor, I would be given a lobby contract by a multinational corporation called Phoenix Industries that I'm guessing you already know plenty about. They owned the facility in Alabama. That supervisor, according to Jacobi, was expecting delivery and would be fully cooperative in listening to details about what Jacobi expected of her. Her role as supervisor to a department that oversees the welfare of unattended children crossing the border was critically important to what Jacobi was trying to accomplish. Jacobi needed her help to secure government contracts."

"Fill in a few blanks for me about Ron Jacobi. The best we can find about him is that he is a political big shot wannabe who is enormously wealthy but has never run for or held any public office. Did I get that right?"

"Partially right, but Jacobi is much more complicated than that. You are correct that he is wealthy, but what you must also know is that old family money came from the seeds of Satan himself. His father helped build Boston's' organized crime syndicate that has resulted in that town becoming a modern Gomorrah. Today, Jacobi's family claims to be long out of any kind of crime business. Everyone believes they are now just builders and developers, but I know better. I stared into the face of the whole gang of devils who put me here."

"Can you be more specific?"

"Jacobi is the leader of the political arm of the family. He can't run for office, but he is the one who buys all the politicians. He's known as a political fixer who has a go-to contact in both parties when they need money or a political dirty trick or two. That is why he is not sitting in this fiery furnace with me. His family and a few political paybacks bought his way out."

Cara interjected, "Mr. Meyers, as we told you in our brief phone call, our firm represents the mother of a child who was beaten to death in one of the facilities owned by Phoenix. What our research has shown is that the expansion of the company's adult prison operations and the children's housing operations has been exceptionally fast over the last five years. As we dive deeper, one of our goals will be to show that the overall methods of operation in all the children's facilities are the same and substandard across the board. With what we've seen so far, the kids being housed in any one of the Phoenix operations are at serious risk. Is there anything you can help us with in that regard?"

"There are a few ways I might help you. I can tell you that part of the message I was asked to deliver to the supervisor I was supposed to bribe was that the hiring standards needed to be lowered to the point that no special training or education be required for anyone working in the facilities. I was also told to sell the idea that specific operational budget requirements by the state or federal government should not be included in any bid process. The heart of the pitch I was supposed to make was that too many cumbersome regulations would run companies like Phoenix away from even wanting to bid. My goal was to have her department put a list of points like that into a report that she could provide for any government office that asked. Also, I can help by telling you that Bob Minds's filthy fingerprints are all over this. He either owns the Jacobi clan or they own him."

Gina asked, "Brian, do you have a written list of what was included in the demands to that supervisor?"

Meyers paused for some time before he looked up at the ceiling and smiled as if someone was watching ten feet above his head. "Now, it's a fact that the prosecutors got all the files I had put together on this, but the Lord taketh away and the Lord giveth. I not only have a copy of everything I kept from Jacobi, but Sammy, my brother—not my real brother, but a brother in Christ—who is as good with a computer as anyone you will ever meet, hacked his way into the bowels of the Phoenix system. For three hours, Sammy collected piles of data before they were onto him. He intended to extort Phoenix, telling them he would publicly release the information if they failed to pay him one million dollars. I talked him out of it because I believed that Phoenix file he had might be my ticket out of here. He has shown me pictures of the material he downloaded. I'm thinking that might be more important to you than it is to me because I now realize I'm exactly where God wants me to be. Sammy will be able to get you my file and all the material he has stored on his computer, if you give me the details of how to send it."

"And your role in the Alabama case was . . . what?" Cara asked before Gina could.

"Oh, that happened after the bribery thing but before I was caught for it. I was tasked with paying off some officials there for records that Jacobi needed, and, in turn, Congressman Minds. The case went away. I don't know what they did to make that happen, though."

Gina and Cara spent another half hour with Meyers more out of kindness than necessity. They had the beginning of exactly what they came for . . . the beginning of a paper trail.

* * *

The only bit of light in the Douglas home came from a nightlight in the kitchen. Midas liked it. The illumination came from the two eyes of a fake owl that sat on a perch next to the sink.

He sat for a moment at the kitchen table appreciating the smell of fresh vegetables and fruit in the tiny space. After taking a moment to wash the blood off his hands and the icepick that had quietly and painlessly pierced the brains of Mr. and Mrs. Douglas, Midas felt serenity. He rarely felt kindness toward the people he murdered, but there was something particularly peaceful about the old man and woman. Mr. Douglas's head rested on his wife's shoulder, and the loud snoring directly in her ear must have been something she had accepted over the years. He found it curious that the couple did not have the wisdom of sleeping with the bedroom door locked. Midas had often thought that if he ever got the chance he would write an opinion piece for a newspaper and warn readers about what he knew about the stupidity of unlocked bedroom doors.

He was hungry, so he took a few minutes rummaging through the kitchen cabinet for peanut butter and bread. Didn't old people always have peanut butter? He had grown up eating it as a regular staple when his mom was out working the bars at night.

His watch indicated there was enough time for a quick sandwich, but then he had to feed the big flame, as he liked to say. The rickety place would go up in smoke faster than a scarecrow on a barbecue.

* * *

At seven the next morning, Carol and Jake drove past the smoldering embers that used to be the Douglas home. Carol had a difficult time controlling tears. She couldn't help considering that she might have been personally responsible for the tragedy.

"There are no coincidences," Jake said, as they gazed at the two city police cars parked on the street in front of the address.

"Dan Douglas described it as their 'happy home' for he and his wheelchair-bound wife," Carol muttered. She had to push away the sorrow and pity she felt for the couple as she drove past a third time. Concentrate on the barrage of troublesome facts Douglas had disclosed.

They had twenty pages of notes describing Trayvon's torment.

"Jake, let's move out of here before those two cops start looking at us as suspects."

"There are not going to be any suspects, Carol. 'House Burns Down Killing Two Longtime Sweeton Residents' will be the only headline today. There won't be any questions. There won't be any investigations. Those glowing embers we're looking at are the end of the story unless our team does its job."

13

Big mistakes in the practice of law can be damaging for the poor lawyer who called things wrong. Gina was therefore jubilant when Cocker-Bradshaw, a silk-stocking hundred-year-old corporate defense firm, made its big mistake.

The case against Phoenix had been filed in federal court for less than four weeks when their defense firm provided a big opportunity for Bergman-Deketomis. There had been no need from a time standpoint for them to file the motion they did. Gina wondered if it was an oversight by one of the younger lawyers in the two-thousand-lawyer firm with offices around the world.

The motion was asking for an expedited status hearing based on the complaint pleadings that Gina had filed. The mega defense firm was arguing that there were exigent circumstances that required immediate consideration for the judge. The motion went through twenty pages of arguments stating that the federal government was giving Phoenix contractual direction on how their businesses were permitted to be organized and function. The pleading stated that the lawsuit on its face had an immediate chilling effect on Phoenix's ability to operate within the mandates of the federal contract. In other words, a lawsuit like the one filed had the potential to interrupt the launching across the country of Phoenix's brand new facilities for thousands of unaccompanied minor children crossing the border. The pleading actually went as far as arguing that the Bergman-Deketomis lawsuit had the capacity to create a national security problem.

Gina had tried many jury trials, had graduated first in her class from Rutgers Law School, and she was editor of the *Rutgers Law Journal*. She always kept her research and writing skills sharp twenty years into her lawyering career. Many lawyers who specialized in jury trials often failed to do so because they had underlings who did that for them. Deke was often heard saying that some lawyers were gifted with remarkable trial skills, some were superb writers and researchers, but very few were both. Gina was that exception.

The defense motion had opened a door. It would have taken months for depositions and meaningful discovery to get underway. This motion had the capacity to change all of that.

Still, it was a mystery to Gina. Defense firms made millions of dollars usually delaying and protracting a lawsuit. It was typically a billable hour scam where minions of lawyers in a big firm like Cocker would bill every second they breathed with mostly meaningless motions and memos at as much as $2,000 per hour in some cases. The victimized corporate defendants were rarely sophisticated or focused enough to appreciate the massive amounts of money going out the door. Senior defense lawyers in most big projects had learned early on in their careers the fine art of delivering fear and assurances in the same sentence for anyone asking about the exorbitant fees that were being paid. By seeking an early end to the litigation, the Cocker firm was willing to short circuit their cash cow opportunity. This spoke volumes about how critical this unusual legal maneuver was to them.

The motion would take a simple response. It would be yes, there were time-sensitive issues surrounding the case. Yes, there would be some immediate prejudice and harm that could result from delaying the progress of the case. And, yes, the Deketomis firm would agree that a quick hearing was warranted. The only difference in the body of the motion response was that the Deketomis firm would be prejudiced by not having that immediate hearing the Cocker firm was asking for. Gina guessed that an immediate early hearing also raised the possibility of immediate discovery that would ordinarily be delayed for months.

Cara walked into Gina's California-casual decorated office and plopped down in the middle of the overstuffed white and silver eight-foot couch in what Gina referred to as the chitchat side of the room.

"I don't know what to think about Cocker's first move here, Gina. No traditional motion to dismiss based on the pleadings. No delay to run out the time they could have taken to file their first pleading. Just wham, bam, let's have a hearing. What're your thoughts?"

"My thought, young lawyer, is that this is an important opportunity for us to strike the first blows with attack depositions. Any direction they head with this motion in front of the judge is going to open up our chance for at least minimal discovery that would ordinarily be delayed way too long."

"So it's all about discovery."

"Correct. Whatever position they take on why this case should not proceed will give us reasons for quick depositions. There is virtually no way we wouldn't be afforded the opportunity to ask witnesses under oath to validate or deny the claims being raised in the motion. Even with their best and most extreme argument of national security risks posed by the lawsuit, we should be able to take a few depositions long before we ordinarily would. It's basic Due Process Class 101. Our task is to be ready to begin every deposition with the most inflammatory facts we can gather quickly and begin putting Phoenix on trial long before they ever walk into a courtroom. The lesson here is that being creative in lawyering has its pluses unless that creativity creates a trap along the way. These overly creative boneheads have already put one leg in a big, potentially fatal trap by giving us an early head start like this. Bad, bad strategy on their part."

As she listened, Cara felt fortunate to have Gina as a mentor. Cara had experienced the challenges of working as a female trial lawyer in a world with an overabundance of testosterone. She had been in courtrooms and depositions with that warrior of a woman who had routinely shredded the case of so many pompous corporate defense lawyers that she had lost count. When her father called on Gina to be in the courtroom with him, the bad guys were going to suffer. Cara had been a young teen when she'd first met Gina at family functions with the firm. Even then the attorney had struck her as a woman with class and charisma. In the four years of Cara's tenure at the firm, she had witnessed firsthand how Gina made her mark both in the office and in the courtroom. Cara thought of Gina as one of the key people besides her mother and father who helped her pilot through life as a twenty-nine-year-old unmarried woman.

"Judge Rogett is probably the right judge for this case," Cara surmised. "I've been in front of her before. I respect that she is such an innovator. She made me a believer in the way she handled the optic lens litigation. Seventy-thousand claims nationally, all in her court, and she creatively and forcefully cajoled both sides to get all those cases resolved. I'm impressed with her. Do you mind if I write the motion response?"

"I think that would be great, Cara. As you write this one, avoid complex arguments. Just keep it simple and keep your eye on the fact that we want to get in front of the court as soon as possible." Gina sat back in her chair and then smiled. "By the way, I hear that congratulations are in order."

"Pardon?"

"Claudia Clapper. You got her into rehab."

"Oh! Yes. Well, it took some doing."

"The place is in Colorado?"

"Right." Cara didn't tell her that it was Zach Morrison who had suggested the facility. That was still a pending issue for Cara, as he had nudged her about making the decision to leave Florida.

"That's fantastic, Cara. I'm sure your father is proud that you could do it."

"Let's hope Claudia sticks with the program. That's always a big *if.* And, as far as my father goes, he was very skeptical about Claudia. He was skeptical about me convincing her, too. He wasn't exactly cheerleading me in the process."

"Well, that brings me to something else I want to talk to you about, Cara."

"Yes?"

"It concerns your father."

"Okay."

"I'm having a little more of a difficult time keeping him grounded about this case. I totally understand his plan. He wants to use this case as the template for targeting, state by state, all these children's facilities.

The more I read the material that we got from Sammy, Brian Meyers's 'brother in Christ,' the more I'm convinced that we can absolutely accomplish a national strategy, at least for Phoenix. I'm optimistic about other national organizations as well, but we have to tamper down Deke's rage. I spent an hour reviewing the Meyers material with him two days ago. He moves from absolute, unfettered rage to moroseness in sixty seconds. He appears to me to be more of a ticking time bomb than a Hall of Fame trial lawyer. I've just never observed this with him. There has got to be more to his story than anyone really knows. What is your take?"

Cara crossed her arms. "Hmm. Well, I can tell you this. You know we have a monthly family dinner at Jaco's. Well, last week I saw first-hand what you're saying about Dad. It was the same kind of peculiar, bewildering reaction I saw a month and a half ago when he talked to us about this case. I didn't see the fury you're talking about then, but last Thursday, I did. So, I get what you're saying."

"I'm not sure anyone has completely unpeeled that onion, Cara, but knowing your dad, my guess would be that to this day he has not shared everything with anyone, including your mother."

14

Michael Carey had traveled to Pennsylvania, Colorado, and Massachusetts interviewing witnesses and piecing together a vast collection of terror tales surrounding the operations of the Phoenix institutional children's housing facilities. He had conducted interviews with former employees, former victimized occupants, state regulators, and even small support groups that were emerging in places like Boston and Philadelphia. Michael's success as a lawyer was in part due to his ability to systematically assemble data and factual findings that created hints of a pattern. This pointed to Boston as being the hub of all the spokes that turned the wheels of dysfunction in all of the facilities, including the Florida camp where Trayvon Clapper was murdered.

He had collected a box of documents, including mandatory directives from Phoenix, emails, pages from what appeared to be operational manuals, sympathy letters sent to parents acknowledging the deaths and disappearances of their children, and two dozen boiler plate letters that appeared to be personalized by facility staff. The latter were digitally produced, handwritten missives from a particular staff member who professed to be very close to the camp occupant and was giving a personal rundown on how well the child was prospering. Some were addressed to the parents of a child, others were to court-appointed guardians, and a few were sent to the folks who had started GoFundMe sites generously sending money to a few of the kids. The commonality of almost eighty percent of the documents was that they all likely originated from Phoenix's Boston headquarters.

Thanks to a lead from one of the children's housing "survivors," Michael learned that the First Trinity South Church in Boston was the location for a monthly meeting of a support group that discussed the suffering the members had experienced during their time at various facilities around the country. He parked his rented Honda CR-V in an isolated corner of the lot away from the entrance, setting up a position so that he could observe other cars pulling in and people entering the side entrance of the old church. It was almost time for the gathering.

He was exhausted and road-weary. Thankfully, he had at least forty minutes to sit and relax before he had to play lawyer again. Normally he would use the down time to make a call home to his wife. Mona had grown accustomed to Michael's long weeks away. She understood the complexities of what he did for a living. Most days she said a prayer of thanks, asking for God's grace in protecting the man who had risked his life to save hers in war-torn Afghanistan. In rare moments when Michael displayed signs of defeat and being hopelessly overwhelmed, she would remind him of his courage and commitment to do the right thing. Her story always began with the sight of Michael racing for her just minutes before her life would have ended from a bullet or a bomb. Her four family members already lay around her. Smoke, the deafening sound of explosions, screams, pervasive hopelessness . . . but she would tell Michael how he had charged through it all with his eyes fixed on her like an archangel. He had spoken words she barely understood: "I'm Michael, we go." That victory changed both of their lives.

But there would be no call home at that moment. A white Lincoln SUV pulled into the parking lot and took a position practically blocking the entrance to the church. Whenever any other folks who arrived parked their cars and attempted to enter the church, two men emerged from the Lincoln and confronted them. The first time Michael observed the exchange it was uneventful, except that one of the men made his way to that newcomer's car and appeared to write the license plate number in a small notebook.

This routine occurred two more times. The men returned to the Lincoln and waited until another car pulled in and the driver attempted to enter the church, but he was prevented from doing so. The next time, it was a young male with a noticeably small build who wanted access to the church. Again, the men stopped the young man. This time Michael lowered his window and heard one of the men raise his voice at the newcomer. The visitor began to back up, almost cowering. Both men from the SUV laughed at him. The license plate number was noted and the young man got into his car and left. One of the men flipped a bird at the exiting vehicle. The two men laughed as if something exceptionally hilarious had just occurred.

Michael could not piece together what he had witnessed. Who were these men, what was so funny, and why were the support group people being turned away?

Another vehicle that looked completely out of place pulled into the lot. It was a new silver and black Corvette Z06, something that sold in the neighborhood of $200,000. The impeccably dressed Hispanic woman that climbed out of it was a contrast to her surroundings. She knew she looked great and, in character, sashayed toward the same door.

One of the men seemed to know her. He grabbed her by the arm and blocked the heavy black purse she swung at his head. It was game-on. Michael heard the woman scream for help in between a mixture of swear words. The man wrapped his arm around her torso . . . and then Michael was out of his car.

He ran at full sprint toward the melee, and within seconds the man assaulting the woman hit the ground as if an anvil had fallen directly on his head. Michael prepared to deliver another blow to the downed thug while keeping an eye on the other one, but the woman pulled a gun from her purse. She pointed it at the sprawled man, who was no longer conscious. Michael swung around, clasped her gun-arm, and diverted the pistol just as she squeezed the trigger. The round barely missed the man who was still standing.

While Michael struggled with the woman to prevent her from shooting again, the remaining guy ran for the Lincoln SUV and made his exit, its wheels screeching across the pavement. He had left his partner on the ground, enforcing the truth that there was no honor amongst criminals and thieves.

The woman's demeanor was somewhere between shock and seething rage, but she had given up the weapon into Michael's hands. She stood motionless, staring at him.

"Are you all right?" he gently asked. When she didn't answer, he continued. "You're fine. Take a deep breath. But . . . listen, we have to leave now." He carefully placed a hand on her shoulder, and then he offered the pistol back to her. He knew this act would give her the confidence that he was there to help. "Let's talk. I have a strong suspicion that we're after the same people. I'm here to make sure they're punished, too. Please, please trust me."

Her eyes darted all around to make sure no one else had seen them. The gunshot had not attracted any attention. No one emerged from the church. Eventually, she tentatively nodded.

"We can go in your car or mine," he said. "I think you're a little shaken up. Why don't I drive us somewhere so we can talk?" He held up his hands in a surrender motion. "I'm an attorney. I may look like I'm one of them, but I'm not. Really."

Most women would not have done so, but there was something about Michael that reached her. He may have been something of a giant, but she sensed he was indeed a gentle one.

"Okay," she whispered.

They walked toward Michael's rental, but then he noticed a small red book on the ground. He snatched it up and put it in his leather jacket pocket.

He opened the passenger door for her and she got in. Once Michael was in the driver's seat, he drove them both out of the lot.

15

Jeff Grandy was sitting in Deke's office making notes on a legal pad when Deke walked in. He handed Deke a copy of Judge Ashworth's order, wasting no time with "hello" or "how-are-you."

"No surprises here, Deke. She did exactly what we thought she might do. As of today, you have officially been removed as an attorney of record in the Kaplan case. She wrote the order as if she was doing the firm a favor by not removing all of us. In her regressive mind, I'm sure she thought that would be possible. The most important aspect of the order is that almost every poorly written paragraph and conclusion provides a dozen ways to approach having her decision reversed. It's what we anticipated, so the important parts of our document are already written. We'll have an emergency appeal filed late this afternoon."

"Haters are always gonna hate, aren't they, Jeff?" Deke answered with indifference. "The only good thing about this order is the timing. It will open the door for me to spend more time on the Trayvon Clapper case."

Deke gave the order a quick review.

"What do you think?" Jeff asked.

"Let's try to show the good judge that carrying around all that hate has the capacity to cloud her judgment. Tell Peter I appreciate the two of you spending so much time pushing that mop behind me. Just like the judge, there is a lesson here for me, too. My big mouth has a good chance of obliterating my common sense."

After Jeff left his office, Deke didn't spend another minute thinking or worrying about Ashworth's order. If the ball could be moved, he was confident they'd find a way to move it.

Diana buzzed him from her desk. "Deke, I have Michael on the phone. I'll put him through. He sounds pretty jazzed up."

Deke put his colleague on speaker. "Michael, I thought maybe you were lost out there in the heart of darkness. I haven't heard from you in days. All good?"

Michael's voice was always comforting to Deke. No matter where he was in the world, the man's timbre projected confidence and strength. "All good here, Deke. I've tried not to bother you until I could honestly say I was getting some good results out here. If I ever talk bad about AI again, cover your ears because the leads that Cara's been getting from that AI vendor she hired are damn well on target. Do you remember in our first meeting she brought up Congressman Minds from Boston?"

"The politician and that Skyler woman he is tied to. Yes, I remember."

"As I talk to you, I'm not sure who is playing who between the congressman and Skyler, but one thing is absolutely certain. They are up to their eyeballs with money they're stealing from Phoenix and a half dozen other corporations trying to do business in Massachusetts. I was involved in a little dust up last night and met a new friend."

Deke interrupted. "Whoa, hold on. Dust up? After what happened to Mr. Douglas and his wife, physical conflict needs to be avoided at all costs. Michael, put that on a scale for me from one to ten."

"Barely a five, Deke, nothing to worry about. I had some help from my new, very important friend, Maria Valdez. I'm not sure whether I saved Maria from a couple of thugs or if I saved two thugs from Maria. This woman has more mettle than a bullfighter, and she's a virtual encyclopedia when it comes to Bob Minds and his working girl, Skyler. I'll tell you Deke, I know we are in a business where we see sleaze almost every day, but the congressman and Skyler Bannock's story is a sordid road show. What I'm about to tell you indirectly has some impact on the Trayvon case, but it has a much bigger play in the national case you want to build against Phoenix. Skyler and the congressman have as much to lose as the entire Phoenix international organization, and right now we have the potential to be their biggest threat."

"First of all, before you go further, are you safe, and when will you be home? Mona gave Cara a call and said you had not called home in two days."

"I'm fine, Deke. I've just been caught up in one of those momentum pushes where you forget what time it is. I'll call home when we hang up. We can go over more specifics when I get the team together but here are the highlights."

Deke went around the desk and sat. He grabbed a pen and jotted notes on a pad as Michael spoke.

"Maria was part of a very exclusive working girl team that was organized and run by Skyler. Deke, the team of girls is so exclusive to Skyler and to the congressman that if there's any hint whatsoever that they might have a sexual relationship with anyone else other than their assigned johns, then they not only lose tons of income but they also run the risk of losing their good looks. Maybe even their lives. I'll share a few of the stories about girls who went astray when I see you. What Bob Minds has going with Skyler Bannock is nothing less than a highly disciplined harem of about ten incredibly effective women. They are engaged in a system similar to what foreign governments have in place to entice and ultimately blackmail American politicians and people they need something from. However, here they focus on corporate wish lists."

"Yikes. Sounds like what you are describing is the whole Epstein show only with adult professionals."

"Well, I can't conclude that they are all adults, but they are certainly well-trained and highly paid professionals, specifically assigned to anyone who might pave the way for Phoenix and other corporate players. According to Maria, who has worked for Skyler for three years now, the harem covers Wall Street finance targets, regulators, politicians, and law enforcement officials from the ground up. Skyler is the madam, so to speak, and sometimes does the work, too. Congressman Minds is the silent partner in her operation and has a lot of say in how Skyler operates. She does his bidding."

"How in the world does a United States congressman get away with consorting with a woman like that? They can't have kept their relationship a secret. And there are things called ethics!"

Michael laughed. "In our US Congress? Are you kidding? I've looked into Skyler Bannock a little more. Over the years, Boston local media has subtly suggested that there is some kind of relationship between Minds and Bannock. She's a former pole dancer. Now she's apparently in the, ahem, 'concierge' business. If she and the congressman are romantic, it's speculation. Once, after a reporter had snapped their picture in the lobby of the Raffles Hotel and asked about the two of them, she replied that they were 'just friends.'"

"Right. I believe that," Deke said with sarcasm.

"Apparently she's kind of a minor celebrity in Boston. Her appearances in the press and society pages reveal her as a strikingly attractive woman with a tasteful sense of high fashion. Her mystique has the media embracing her like goofy teenage celebrity hounds. One shallow gossip writer declared her 'Boston's very own princess.' Photos occasionally appear of Skyler at the Cape's many clubs and five-star restaurants, often seated with wealthy and powerful men. The beachside shots of her thong bikini-clad perfect physique are, uhm, most popular. The media has grown to accept Skyler Bannock for being a classy lady who no doubt will end up with her own talk show someday. Don't you just love what journalism has evolved into?"

"What a world." Deke drummed his fingers on his desk for a couple of seconds. "I'm still not clear about the 'brush up' as you call it, your new friend, Maria, and how in the world you know all this."

"Maria lost a daughter in one of the facilities here in town. When I say lost, I mean it. She's been missing for nearly four years now. It happened before Maria was involved with Skyler, back when Maria was down-and-out, living on the fringes in poverty. My guess from what we've seen in the past is that she is now a sixteen-year-old being trafficked by someone, somewhere. I have no proof of that, but that's my guess after hearing the facts from Maria. Anyway, Maria eventually got a job as a stripper and Skyler discovered her, recruited her, and made her rich doing dirty work that benefitted Phoenix."

"She will testify to this?"

"Yes!"

"And tell me again how you met this Maria woman?"

Michael explained how he was in Boston to attend a support group of people who had been impacted by tragedies connected to children's facilities in general, not just Phoenix programs. "She was there to attend a monthly meeting of the group. Here's the clinker. Maria was with a client that Skyler had sent her to, and it turned out this client worked for Phoenix. He was one of those guys who liked to talk about himself when he was with a beautiful woman, and somehow, the names of children's housing facilities and his job with them came up. He mentioned the very facility where Maria's daughter had been placed—and then lost. Maria did some digging and realized that the very people she was working for were responsible for the negligence in the school where her daughter went missing. Maria was shocked and angry, and she felt betrayed. She started attending this support group at this church in Boston, hoping to deal with her grief and remorse. She stopped answering Skyler's messages and calls."

"In other words, she left Skyler's employment."

"Right. The thugs I told you about were in the church parking lot, stopping and discouraging members from attending, and monitoring the people who did attend. But I think they were also specifically looking for Maria. Maria did say she thought she might have recognized one of them. She believes they were sent to 'rectify' the problem of Maria being a wild card. Maybe Skyler realized that she hadn't properly reviewed Maria's background and learned that the woman had lost a child in the very system that Skyler and her congressman partner protect."

"Where did things go after the parking lot?"

"I drove her to her condo that, oh, by the way, is one of the most exclusive, high rent condos in Boston. A place called One Dalton. Google it. It's big money to live there. She told me it's where she works, so I left it at that. Deke, for two hours, Maria sketched out the Minds and Bannock team's entire operation, and it is damn impressive. She had what appeared to be an epiphany as I explained what our case was about. She's trying to accept the ugly irony about her work for Skyler and the possible connection to her missing daughter."

"Michael. Several things. First, get out of town today. In fact, I will send the jet to pick you up. Create the most detailed report you can for the team and call your wife. This is way too much to cover on the phone."

"Okay, but I need to tell you one more time sensitive fact. Maria told me about a person she described as the creepiest human being she's ever met. Some dude named Midas. She said we need to be aware that there's no limit to what he's capable of doing for Skyler. And guess what—he calls her 'Sis.'"

"His name is Midas Bannock?"

"No, I don't think so. Maria wasn't sure, but it's not the same. Different last names. But Maria is almost positive that Midas is Skyler's brother. Or stepbrother."

Deke considered what he'd just heard for a beat.

"Are you there, Deke?"

"Yes, I'm here. It's possible we might already have that guy Midas in our backyard. I need to tell Carol and Jake to come home immediately, too. I'll see you tonight."

After ending the call, Deke stood at the picture window and noted the dark clouds in the sky. A storm was coming, and he knew it wasn't just rain and heavy winds.

His team had experienced danger many times over the years, and his gut told him it was happening again.

But this felt different.

16

For years, Deke had referred to Gina Romano as the firm's Shield Maiden. She showed a level of fierceness he believed to be similar to a Viking maiden warrior. On her fortieth birthday, Deke had organized an expensive party for her at which all attendees were asked to show up in Nordic dress. To no one's surprise, Gina's elaborate costume was that of Brynhildr, one of the Vikings' most well-known Valkyries.

However, Gina knew when a strong Shield Maiden persona was better left outside the courtroom.

She led the lawyer and paralegal procession into Judge Kate Rogett's courtroom, prepared to let the Cocker-Bradshaw lawyers leave themselves wide open for the list of requests she was prepared to make to the judge. The eight Cocker-Bradshaw lawyers sitting at their counsel table had already begun telegraphing their smug, superior sense of importance as Deke, Gina, and the team organized their own table.

The bailiff announced, "All rise. The United States District Court is now in session, the Honorable Judge Kate Rogett is presiding. Please be seated."

The judge entered and took her place. She was a rarity in the federal judicial system. Respected by both sides to a large degree because of her firm and fair consistency, a lawyer was expected to be prepared, be honest, and not burden the court with meaningless, fee-generating motions.

Cocker lawyer number one was lining up to violate every one of those expectations.

Judge Rogett stated what issues were before the court and called for the Cocker man to approach the podium in front of his table and argue his motion.

One of the failures in most large law firms like Cocker was an archaic pecking order of who does what in everything from writing motions, taking depositions, trying cases, to arguing motions in front of judges. Typically, the lawyers who did all the work preparing the research and actually writing the motions were asked to quietly stand down so that more senior partners could look exemplary on the backs of those folks who did real the work.

Rogett was used to seeing the downside of that play out on a regular basis in her courtroom.

The Cocker attorney began his argument. "Your Honor, our motion is straightforward. If you will look at page fifteen in our motion before you—"

The judge interrupted. "Counselor, I have no page fifteen."

One of the worker bees sitting behind lawyer number one stood up and whispered something in the man's ear, handing him a document.

"My apologies, Judge. What I was reading from were notes, not the actual motion. If you could go to page five, you will see our grounds stated clearly. The lawsuit filed by the Deketomis firm has the potential to create a national security risk because of the contract Phoenix has signed with the federal government. That contract grants my client the authority to provide housing for the thousands of unattended children coming across the border. At this juncture, as you can see by the attached Phoenix affidavit—"

Again, Judge Rogett interrupted, and whispers in his ear took place a second time. Nothing was handed to him.

"I'm sorry, Your Honor, the Phoenix affidavit was withdrawn and replaced with another affidavit from the office of Homeland Security, which you should find—"

"Yes, Counselor, I actually did find that affidavit and had the opportunity to read it before I began this hearing," Rogett growled. "I came prepared, which is something you might focus on in the future. I hesitated to set this hearing because the affidavit was so equivocal and uncertain on exactly how the inner workings of Phoenix might have any relevancy in arranging housing for immigrant children and national security. Provide me something more complete and I will reserve ruling on your interesting motion. Mr. Deketomis, let me hear from you."

Lawyer number one took a seat and stared daggers at his colleagues as if they had somehow been responsible for his poor effort. Most everyone at the table understood there was a clear argument to be made without any affidavits. The simple assertion of the existence of the contract, which was attached to the pleading, should have given the lawyer plenty to argue before the judge had toasted him. More importantly, it would have kept open the opportunity for the attorney to make at least four critical points that might later be factors in the case. Now the effort was delayed, and the Deketomis team's next play was predictable.

Deke stood at the counsel table to address the court.

"Your Honor, my partner, Gina Romano, prepared the thirty page brief that I hope is in front of you. She will argue on behalf of Trayvon Clapper."

"Fine. Ms. Romano, let me hear from you."

Gina approached the podium and began. "Judge Rogett. The defendants have clearly already shown their hand about the unusual partial defense they have put on the table. The very fact that we are already in front of the court with this unusual motion hearing barely three weeks after the complaint was filed is uncommon in and of itself. Those developments, however, may provide an opportunity for the court to continue moving this case quickly if only we can be provided the right to begin taking a few depositions, particularly as to this government contract defense that will at some point in the future be subject to this court's ruling."

Lawyer number one was up on his feet as quickly as a malfunctioning jack-in-the-box. "Judge, there will be plenty of time for Ms. Romano to begin her depositions. It would be extremely prejudicial to the defense to allow early depositions before the federal rules would ordinarily make them permissible."

"Counselor, you opened this door of early opportunity with the motion you filed. Ms. Romano is correct. At some point I am going to have to rule on your motion, and I would have to give the plaintiffs the right to take depositions before that ruling. No better time than the present. I will make my ruling as to expedited depositions by tomorrow. Just to be clear, I'm inclined to grant Ms. Romano's request. Thank you all. This entire exchange has been interesting."

Judge Rogett stood and gracefully exited the courtroom.

Lawyer number one could be heard raising his voice at a young female lawyer as their group headed for the elevator.

17

The sixty-something-year-old Sweeton security employee sat in a chair much too small for his massive build. The menacing glare he projected at the two other men in the room was a permanent feature. Three-day-old whiskers and his overall disheveled appearance indicated that he cared little about impressing the lawyers who had been grilling him for an hour. The high-pitched, whiney, and childlike voice did not fit his body.

Fred Perkins had created another shit show for Phoenix. Just like the other event that occurred two hundred miles away in Alabama, the problem needed to be cleaned up. Local law enforcement and the county coroner's office had to create reports that made Perkins's manslaughter of Trayvon Clapper look like an accident. In the Alabama event, witnesses were both threatened and coached, physical evidence was removed and destroyed, and life carried on. Until the next tragic event, which had now materialized. And Perkins had been involved in both incidents.

Perkins knew how the Phoenix perks program worked. The large amounts of money Phoenix spread around in all the right places was appreciated, relied on, and even demanded in some instances. Every attitude-drenched word that came from his mouth was a reminder to the people in the room that he knew details.

Tim Matoric was one of the "money grinders" for the Cocker firm. Every second Matoric was awake and thinking about the Phoenix case was billed at $1,500 an hour. He had never tried a case in his life, but he was the go-to guy in place to negotiate the case. Or make it go away.

Matoric had dealt with Perkins in the past and had negotiated the paltry settlement for the single, alcoholic mom who had given up custody of her thirteen-year-old to the state childcare system in Alabama two years earlier. Her child was the victim of the prior "accident," as folks around Phoenix called it. Part of Matoric's plan involved an invitation to Perkins to permanently retire and thus hopefully never see the freakish man again.

The lawyer cleared his throat and asked, "Mr. Perkins, from what we have gathered from witnesses, you apparently slipped and fell on top of the Clapper child. Is that correct?"

"Yeah," was Perkins's only response.

"And you yourself were dazed and possibly unconscious for a moment or two. Could that be what happened?"

"Uh, yeah. It was fuzzy. I can't remember. Help me with that."

The whiny voice was the creepiest and most unsettling aspect of the giant. But Matoric took his problems as he found them. Any effort to meaningfully rehabilitate them was usually pointless. Perkins was a special problem for Phoenix, and Matoric knew he had to proceed cautiously. *Knowing where all the bones were buried* was more than an idiom when it came to a guy like Perkins. He was one of the very few employees who had needed to be considered a long-time necessary fixture in the organization. Up until now. After all, the man had stories dating back to the old Florida Dozier facility, where he had been a teen resident. Forty years earlier, the bodies of young boys were buried there in unmarked graves.

Stories about Dozier, located less than an hour from Sweeton, had been told in books and a documentary. Whatever tales were in Perkins's head needed to be kept there. Today the discussion was not about Dozier. It wasn't about Alabama, either. It was about the manslaughter committed at Sweeton, Perkins's latest stomping grounds. The man had crushed a fifteen-year-old's windpipe, ribs, and spleen. Perkins had intentionally thrown his full three-hundred-pound body onto the child, suffocating him.

Matoric continued, attempting to lower the tension in the room. "Fred, we're going to come up with a way for you to retire so you can hunt and fish and spend a little more time with your family. How does that sound?"

Perkins broke into a laugh that resembled that of a preteen girl. "I ain't going nowhere. I ain't huntin'. I ain't fishin', and I don't have no damn family I want to hang out with. This is my job, and it makes me happy. Do you want me happy, Mr. Lawyer?"

Matoric had expected this. Being the chief guard where Perkins and his staff could ride dominion every day over fifty boys who had to call him "Sir" was more than a job for the monster. The guy considered it "fun." Perkins enjoyed the games of pitting the weak ones against the predators. Matoric figured that the thrill was in the total submission Perkins saw every day from the institutionalized boys. It was payback for Perkins. When *he* was that age, he would have been on the receiving end of getting his ass kicked by the same crowd of boys for being stupid, overweight, and talking like a girl.

And Perkins was predatory enough to understand that he stood a good chance of getting what he wanted from Sweeton and the folks at Phoenix.

"What can we do for you, Fred, to help us through this difficult time we might be faced with because of this new accident?"

Matoric was a pro and knew the importance of keeping an understated, even tone. He was well aware of what the bad publicity would do to the relatively new Phoenix operation. Perkins had the capacity to shut down Sweeton. Protracted reinvestigation would, by law, have to be undertaken. It might even give rise to forensic archeologists doing searches at Sweeton for remains buried in unmarked graves only because of the long, tragic history of the Dozier facility years before. Phoenix would experience losses in the millions, and it was a possibility that even their licenses to operate might be suspended for months. Worse yet, Matoric could never be certain that there weren't unidentified bodies buried at a facility where Perkins had been in charge.

"I'll tell you about a few things you can do for me," Perkins said. "After you kiss my ass, you can put me in a new truck and one of them new places there in that fancy new neighborhood down the road from here. How 'bout we start there?"

The Perkins in front of Matoric was not the same person he had negotiated with just two years prior. Perkins had been thrilled with not being prosecuted for murder. Now Perkins was a full-blown predator who played the role of an enforcer around the camp.

"Fred, there are a few things we can do for you after all this ugly incident blows over, but a new truck and a new home can't figure into that because of the attention and red flags it would raise. There are lawyers who are preparing to take your deposition. But perhaps we can do something like that after a year or two."

"Sure, I heard all that bullshit the last time. When y'all were going to buy me a condo in Boston and let me be one of the head honchos up there. But here we are with that pissant raise you gave me and you trying to load my mouth with good things to say when that lawyer talks to me. I call that bullshit. You have to make sure nothing slips out of my mouth by mistake, don't you? Hell, I already got a free pass from the cops about what happened to that little worm who couldn't play by the rules. You're damn lucky we found that little notebook with his stupid drawings and notes he was gonna use against this place. Best you and that dickhead there taking notes give me exactly what I want. Write that down, Mr. Dickhead."

Matoric gazed at the folded hands in his lap for a moment before he spoke. "Fred, there is only so much I can do to make everyone happy here. I'm going to set up another meeting so we can spend more time together discussing all this. In the meantime, why don't you consider some other kinds of demands that maybe we can deliver after some time passes? I simply don't see a new truck and new home anytime soon. That's not to say it can't happen two years from now, but you are going to have to help me a little here with what you're asking for."

"Sure, no problem. I'll help you and those damn lizards in Boston after I call those lawyers who've been sneaking around town asking all them damn questions. Sure, I'll help you."

"I think we're done here for now, Fred." Matoric stood and motioned to the young lawyer with him that it was time to leave.

"Y'all stay in touch with me now."

As he left the room, Matoric shook his head. Perkins had no understanding how the Phoenix group would stay in touch. It was too bad. He had done all he could do for Perkins.

* * *

Maria Valdez had made all the arrangements.

Puerto Rico was the only possible destination, for it was there that she could find plenty of muscle among her brothers and family to keep her safe. She had hurriedly sublet her condo, left no traces of where she was headed, and withdrew enough cash from a rock solid bank account to last for several months. All she needed to do was drive to the airport, park the Corvette in the long term lot, and get the hell out of Dodge.

As she made what she thought was the final strut from the condo to her car, she saw him.

The guy she knew as "Midas."

"Maria, I've just met a girl named Maria!" he said with a singsong voice, a smile wide across his creepy white face as he approached.

She halted in her tracks. Her stomach lurched, and she felt ice up her spine.

"Going somewhere?"

Maria did her best to put on a happy face. "Why, hello there! I haven't seen you in a while. You doing okay?"

"I'm just fine, Maria." He was close enough that she could smell his cologne, some kind of fancy French stuff.

She tried to move past him. "Well, I'd love to chitchat, darling, but I'm terribly late for an appointment."

"Nuh uh," Midas said, blocking her way. "We need to talk. Let's go back to your condo, honey. Like, right now."

"Midas, dear, I'm *late*. I really have to go."

"You have to go back to your condo so we can have a *chat*. Do we understand each other, *dear*?"

Maria's survival instinct kicked in and she did the only thing possible. Since he was standing right in front of her, she abruptly used the

Rockettes-style dancing move she had learned as a teenager, jerked her leg straight out, and slammed the toe of her heel into his groin.

"*Agh!*" he cried, stumbling to the side and falling over.

Maria bolted to her car, ten feet away. As Midas rolled on the pavement, clutching himself, she got in the car and locked the door. But, miraculously, he was up and on his feet before she could turn the ignition.

He attempted to smash the driver's side window with an elbow. Once, twice . . . the force he used didn't seem to hurt the bones in his muscular arms.

"Open up! Maria! Get out of the car! Now!"

The Corvette's engine revved and she stepped on the gas to make a desperate exit.

Midas leaped upon the hood and held on for dear life.

The car screeched out of the drive and into the street. The man continued clinging onto the vehicle.

She leaned on the horn. The loud blaring did nothing to budge him. The man she knew to be a killer remained on the hood like a magnet.

Maria roughly turned the steering wheel, making a sharp turn onto a cross street, and then she slammed on the brakes. That did the trick. Midas went flying.

The last thing she saw in the rearview mirror was him lying in the street, unconscious.

As far as she could tell.

18

The pictures Deke projected on the screen were close-ups of Fred Perkins sitting in what had to be the sketchiest bar in Sweeton. The man was alone, leaning on his elbows on the bar with his face hovering just above the beer mug in front of him. It appeared that Perkins's well-worn white shirt was unbuttoned halfway down his chest and the blue jeans he wore were struggling to hang on just below his protruding, hairy stomach. In another shot, his butt crack was in focus. Deke displayed pictures ranging from the big man eating alone at restaurants to sitting in the small nature park situated next to Sweeton High School. The common aspect in each of the twenty shots was that Perkins was always by himself and sporting an expression of anger.

"One of the biggest ironies about this man is that he was a product of the very system that contributed to the death of Trayvon Clapper," Deke said to the team gathered in the conference room. "As a teenager, he spent four years at one of the deadliest child institutions in America, the old Dozier facility. It wasn't because he had dysfunctional parents. He was there because he was a violent little shit who didn't function well on the outside. This is the man who killed Trayvon and was then the benefactor of a complete whitewash job by every government official in Sweeton who was beholden to Phoenix. And, thanks to what Gina and Cara uncovered through that Brian Meyers fellow, we now know about Phoenix's Alabama facility. This same man, Fred Perkins, was also involved in the death of a child *there* two years ago. He thrives on violence and the kids in these facilities are convenient targets. We will probably find out that he was the kind of child who tortured cats and dogs growing up."

Michael Carey emitted a low grunt of disgust.

Cara's jaw dropped. Her father was usually more nuanced than that. His words were uncharacteristically emotional, to put it bluntly.

"Excuse me, Dad," she said, raising a hand to be recognized.

"Yes, Cara?"

"Do we really know Perkins was a violent teenager? Do we have his records?"

"The fact that he's killed two children who he was supposed to be protecting, and the fact that he was at that hellhole Dozier as a child himself, tells me what I need to know."

"So that's really speculation," Cara continued. "I'm not defending this monster, but I'm wondering if Perkins had violent tendencies from the get-go, or did he develop them because of the abuses he likely received at Dozier? Instead of getting the help he needed, Perkins was made into an even more dangerous animal. That's the fault of the reform school system."

Deke just stared at her for a moment. Cara didn't flinch. She knew he was still upset with her regarding the possibility of her joining the firm in Colorado.

After a few awkward seconds, Deke moved on without addressing his daughter's comment. "The good news, though, is that the free pass Perkins got makes our case that much stronger. And if we do our jobs properly, we can ignite the interest of the FBI and take decision-making away from all the fanboys who are protecting Phoenix in that useless, nothing little community and in several other communities around the country. Let's begin our discussion with Michael telling what we need to be aware of from a pure safety concern."

Useless, nothing little community. With this atypical and judgmental remark, Cara was certain that her father was too close to this case.

Michael took the remote and threw another picture on the screen of an attractive blonde in a tight cocktail dress that revealed more than enough leg. "I've prepared a detailed report about this woman, Skyler Bannock, and her 'friend,' Congressman Bob Minds. Until I was briefed by Carol and Jake, I would have never said that the specialized harem of high price escorts that I described in my report would have had any specific direct impact on the Trayvon Clapper case. Remember, I began my investigation with an eye toward the bigger national case that Deke wants to proceed with against all the Phoenix facilities as well as a few other national groups. As everybody in this room has learned in our experience, coincidences are rare. You've all read Carol and Jake's report. The death of Mr. and Mrs. Douglas was not random bad luck. Rest assured the bullshit conclusion from the sheriff and coroner who investigated those deaths is a fantasy."

Another photo appeared on the screen. On first glance, one might have thought the man in the picture was a glam-genre rock star. The complexion was eggshell-white. Eyeliner was meticulously applied on one eye, as if he were the main character from *A Clockwork Orange*. Jet black hair was tightly pulled back into a small man bun. A slight smile revealed perfect teeth.

"Let me introduce Midas McDonald," Michael continued. "That is his name as of today, anyway. Our investigators have confirmed that Midas is the stepbrother of Skyler Bannock, which is why the surnames are different. If I can believe even half the stories I was told about this man, he is a nuclear thermal threat to everyone in this room. It would be shortsighted of me to suggest that there is anything any one of us can do to keep a safe distance from him if we're truly going to do what needs to be done in the Trayvon case. Many of us have been exposed and even been the victim of violence in past cases. The caliber of danger here is identical. No one in this room decided to be a plaintiff's lawyer to expose yourself to the kind of risk I am talking about here."

Michael stopped talking and moved through a half dozen more Midas pictures for a solid three minutes. He wanted his words to sink in. In his years as military special ops, Michael had seen how a false sense of courage, bravado, and noble intent could end badly.

"When you review the white paper I prepared for all of you, one main takeaway should be that the list of the ten escorts I named are women who, according to my source, have for the last year been designated to targets that would benefit Phoenix. I know we've seen similar kinds of operations like this before, just like the old 'honey traps' during the Cold War, but nothing as exclusive as this. What that tells me is that Skyler and Bob Minds are being paid big money by Phoenix right now, and my bet is that Phoenix has no real appreciation for just how far Minds and Bannock will go to continue collecting it. Including the unleashing of Skyler's brother. I truly believe he is their secret weapon. That's all I have for now."

Michael handed the remote to Cara. She stood and took over the presentation, having professionally brushed aside the momentary awkwardness with her father in front of the group.

A list of text appeared on the screen. "The bullet points you see are a composite from several different sources we've developed in this case that should shine some light on how the Sweeton facility operates. You have in front of you a report going into key details about each one of the entries on the list. When we meet tomorrow, we can discuss each item in detail if you'd like."

The list on the screen read:

- Phoenix right now under threat of license revocation / Sweeton
- Sweeton Little Red House / House of Horrors / Trayvon 4 times
- Sweeton Fight Club / Gambling by Guard Staff / Strong v. Weak
- Beatings / Sexual abuse as punishment
- 10 hospital visits allegedly related to organized fights
- Sweeton facility cited 50 times for understaffing, all positions
- Witness testimony / Possible but not verified unmarked graves like Dozier
- 2 Books about Dozier / Dozier graves, boys' bones
- Employees common to both Sweeton and Pemberton, and Dozier
- Sweeton and Pemberton facilities cited for employing felons on 10 occasions
- Virtually no background checks
- Zero education requirements in order to be employed at Sweeton
- Mostly minimum wage
- Equine therapy, nature hiking, field trips, feel-good sales pitch is rank fraud

- The 1 nurse at Sweeton has no nursing degree
- The 2 counselors at Sweeton have no counseling degree
- Sweeton doctor previously had suspended license / Opioid pill mill
- Doctor at Sweeton never examines patients, only reviews reports by the staff
- Sweeton kids are made available for farm work / 5 dollars an hour / Half to Sweeton
- School is 3 hours a Day / Work to maintain campus considered class
- Woefully undereducated Sweeton staff must sign a 200-page Standards of Practice list
- Sweeton employs 30 percent of community / Pemberton 5
- Administration for Children & Families (ACF) 28 filed complaints for abuse
- Lists of Enforcement Actions by ACF for Endangerment = 5
- Sweeton staff must sign Non-Disclosure Agreements
- There are 5 surveillance cameras at Sweeton, only 1 works, no sound
- There are no nutritional standards that must be met / Corndogs, French fries, peanut butter
- Kids at Sweeton are not allowed to wear shoes / Runaway risks

Michael's phone rang as Cara put up a second slide that was a composite of all the details for each of the sanctions, warnings, and complaints that had been filed against Sweeton by state and federal agencies. He interrupted her, saying, "Excuse me, Cara. Can we pick all this up tomorrow? I'm just now getting some new information about Midas McDonald that we all need to follow up on immediately."

He stood, whispered something into Deke's ear, and hurried out of the room.

"That's all for now, people," Deke announced. The team left, curious about Michael's call, but no doubt more conscious of their personal safety.

Michael met Deke in his office.

"Talk to me, Michael," Deke said.

"Midas McDonald confronted Maria Valdez. She's beyond terrified." He relayed what the woman had told him about her encounter with Midas McDonald in front of her condo. "We ain't in Kansas anymore, Deke. This whole ugly scene is starting to remind me of the banking terrorism case that took me and three of our people miles into harm's way. I'm okay with that, and I'm sure you're okay with that. No doubt Jake will be good. What I'm having trouble with is the idea of placing Cara, Gina, and Carol up on the front lines. Carol is certainly used to this type of threat as the head of security, but still . . ."

Deke dropped into his seat, markedly concerned. "No argument from me, Michael. Like I told you, we can bring in the same team we used in the oil spill case. Great contract lawyers and investigators accustomed to big risks are what we need right now. I don't want to delay this talk with the ladies. We know what to expect from all three of them. I can control the Cara part of this, but we're going to hear an entire litany about all the dangers the other two have faced in the past and how in their minds it was just part of the job and—"

"Deke, everyone building a case against Phoenix has become a potential target. Look, it's clear to me that the real threat is not coming from Phoenix. It's coming from Skyler Bannock and Bob Minds as they try to keep the big money flowing. The more damage that's done to Phoenix in any capacity raises the possibility that their services will no longer be needed. All the millions they're banking from the Phoenix gig alone could suddenly be in their rearview mirror if they're unable to stop the war that's being waged against their corporate sugar daddy. Let's get it over with. I'll call the three of them now and ask them to come to your office. Are you good with that?"

"Just buckle up, my friend. This will not go well."

Fifteen minutes passed before Cara, Gina, and Carol walked in together. "So, what's up, Deke?" Gina asked before they took any chairs. There was attitude in her voice, as if she knew exactly what was coming. They all did.

"First of all, how about we all take a seat? Michael, tell them what you told me about Maria Valdez."

The three women sat and then listened in shock as Michael relayed how his new witness barely evaded what could have been another violent, likely fatal attack on a whistleblower.

Deke then continued with the command of a leader. "Everyone in this room is aware of the many times this law firm has beaten the law of averages when it comes to our personal safety issues. Gina, you've been hospitalized as a result of one of our cases. Carol, you and Jake almost became statistics in the banking case we did, and don't tell me you weren't shaken by it. Last year I almost lost my own life in Chicago. Sometimes we forget that we're a law firm and not a strange collection of Marvel action heroes. Reality, as all of you know, is often catastrophic when we kid ourselves into believing that fate always favors us. The truth is that for years now I've been afraid we too often tempt fate. I have lost count of all the hours I've spent lying in bed, terrified that you, Carol, or you, Gina, are so exposed to the intrinsic dangers of what this law firm does. And forgive me, Cara, but how much more magnified do you think those hours of terror will be for me when I know it's you on the trail of one of the psychotic types that always hangs just below the surface of the cases we handle? So, let's start this discussion with that on the table."

Gina started to speak, but Cara was a second ahead. "Dad, first of all, yes, we get it, that was a lovely speech. But we've seen this developing around here since the Douglas murders. Now this with Maria Valdez. Yes, it's scary. Don't think for a minute that I don't appreciate your concerns for our safety. I'm pretty certain we all do. But I want you to think about something. All three of us have had the choice of working in silk stocking law firms where the biggest risk they ever know is whether or not their cappuccino might spill down their pressed white shirts. Or maybe we could have decided to chase ambulances in car wreck cases where our biggest threat might be running into the back of the damn ambulance. The truth is, Dad, through my whole childhood I've watched everyone in this room accomplish the impossible on behalf of people who had zero possibility of ever getting a fair break. 'The Golden Rule will prevail and the few people with all the gold make all the rules.' Sound familiar, Dad? It's a saying that Andy and I heard around the dinner table most of our lives."

"Well said, Cara," Gina muttered.

Deke's expression was troubled and concerned. His thoughts went to *Maybe she* should *leave this firm and take that job in Colorado where she'd be out of danger?* Whatever . . . he knew that Cara was likely not going to be swayed from her commitment on this case. More importantly, he knew that a wrong decision from him would affect the respect she had for him as a lawyer and as a father.

Michael, on the other hand, was obviously far less impacted by Cara's heartfelt statement. "Cara, this is not one of our typical cases. Most of the time we're unaware of life-threatening possibilities until they surface unexpectedly. Here we know we're putting the three of you in the path of a high-functioning psychopath who has probably been responsible for two deaths already and just yesterday tried for a third. With all due respect, nobody in this room besides me and maybe your dad, and, yeah, very likely Carol, are equipped to deal with a development like this."

"I was gonna *say*, Michael . . ." Carol grumbled.

Gina replied, "It's not really accurate to say the three of us are not equipped to deal with a threat like this Midas nutcase. Do we have your physical size and your physical training? Of course not. The challenge for us will be to use our brains and our instincts to avoid the possibility of this guy ever getting close enough to become a threat. Frankly, I would be amazed and actually downright pissed off if you tried to convince me that we can't do that. Something you two take for granted, like walking to your car alone at night, we're constantly using life-learned skills that neither one of you ever needed to develop. Try being a female and doing something as simple as going for a two-mile run at night. Let us be us, Deke. We will proceed with total respect for everything you and Michael have said here today."

Cara and Carol nodded and verbally concurred.

Deke looked at the ceiling in exasperation, stood, and strode around the office. The others watched him, wondering if he was going to explode or smash the picture window beside which he eventually halted. Then Deke abruptly turned to them.

"No."

"Excuse me?" Carol asked.

"*No.* I can't let you put yourselves in harm's way. Not this time. Not on *this* case."

"How is it different from any other perilous situation we've been in? Deke, with all due respect, you're not yourself. What the hell is going on?"

"He's too close to this case," Cara answered. There. She got it out in the open.

Silence.

Deke glared at his daughter, then turned back to the window. Two sailboats were making their way out into the Gulf of Mexico.

She's right, he thought.

Bucky Carlton.

The water. The boats. The sunny day.

Breathe.

The peaceful scene outdoors eventually advised him of what to do. His decision would be a compromise, but nothing would ever quell his fear for the three women he loved and respected so much.

"Michael," he began, turning back to the room. "If they remain in the field on this case outside of only office roles, what ideas do you have about keeping them safe?"

"Nobody in this room is going to like my answer to that question because it's going to range from a nine millimeter to a switchblade, to stun guns and Tasers." As he spoke, Michael revealed the nine millimeter holstered at the base of his back, underneath his jacket, and the four-inch black tactical switchblade he pulled out of his jacket pocket.

Deke, Carol, and Jake were the few people in the firm who knew that Michael was always armed. He rarely pulled a weapon because he was more than capable with his elbows, knees, and fists. Still, Gina and Cara were surprised.

"For now, Michael, let's focus on your mention of a Taser. Is that a practical solution?" Deke asked.

"It's not a solution, but it's a start. Carol has been carrying a fifty-thousand-volt Taser for years along with a small thirty-eight. Is that a solution? Not always, but it's gotten her out of more than a few jams over the years, hasn't it, Carol?"

Carol had years of training in self-defense involving weapons, but she was walking a razor-thin line when it came to the safety question for Cara and Gina. Not for herself. She would never want them to know that, though.

"Fellas, I'm wondering about your own ability to adequately protect yourselves if a psycho freak like Midas ever actually targeted you specifically. At the same time, I want to honor my colleagues' commitment and confidence. In my law enforcement years, I spent far too much time being underestimated by men. Here's how I see it. It would be a mistake to take any one of us out of the field. That's where cases are built, not behind a desk. There are so many newly developed self-defense weapons available. Specifically designed for women who don't want to carry a gun. As Michael said, I carry a Taser that will deliver more volts that you can imagine into the face, neck, upper shoulders, or hips of anyone within forty feet of me. And you know what? If they do get up close and personal, it even has a one-touch stun gun capacity that will turn them into a heap of Jell-O right at my feet. The longer you hold it on 'em the more damage you can do. I can have more Tasers and stun guns here tomorrow, and we can practice using them for hours if that's what it takes. Deke, trust me that I am all in when it comes to the concerns you and Michael have. But in the words of Gina, 'let us do us.' Until you have more reason not to."

19

Judge Kate Rogett made the decision Gina was hoping for, and she was preparing for the firm's first move.

The start time for depositions and discovery would be expedited. The treasure trove of documents that had been compiled was almost too good to be true. More importantly, the task of determining which fifty documents would exact the most damage to Paul Baker in the upcoming deposition was daunting. Deke and Gina joked that they could have randomly grabbed any handful of them and carried on a bloodbath depo of the Phoenix senior executive.

She and Cara had been working on the stacks of paper for hours in the conference room, which Gina liked to call the 'war room.' It had been a busy week.

Cara waved three documents above her head. "How about these? I couldn't have made these up. Let me read you the quote of the hour from none other than Baker himself." She cleared her throat. "'It appears to me that unless we get the cooperation of someone at the highest level of the ACF, we are dead meat. You all know what that means when the dominos start falling. Not only no penetration into the child immigration space, but probably the suspension or revocation of our licenses at some existing operations. I feel like the proverbial boy with his finger in the dyke.' Now, there is no mention specifically about which dyke he has his finger in, but it was sent to two midlevel managers who emailed him on the same day describing an 'accident' at the Sweeton facility."

Gina said, "These are the folks who told the judge that allowing our case to go forward would be a threat to national security and that an immediate dismissal is appropriate. Deke will make a few defense lawyers' heads explode when he walks that one out. I haven't found anything as sexy as that in the last hour, but I've uncovered a pattern that's maybe important." She stood and placed twelve financial statements across the table. Together, she and Cara bent over them. Cara noticed that a dozen or more of the entries had been highlighted. Some bright yellow and others bright orange.

"What are we looking at?" Cara asked.

"Either a weird anomaly or a pattern. On day one, Phoenix wires money to a Kentucky bank, and always on day three after that, a huge bill for what must be a truly exceptional room at the Raffles Hotel in Boston appears. The only way it even caught my eye is because that hotel is where a true onetime love of my life used to take me when he was performing now and then with the Boston Philharmonic as a trumpet stand-in. But that's another story for another day." She gave Cara an exaggerated smile. Then, back to business, "Cara, how about cranking up the AI magic and see if any of the names or events you've searched have any connection to Peoples Bank of Louisville or Raffles Hotel. I'm always amazed at how seemingly random events like this turn out to be solid connections to the heart of a case."

"I'm on it now." Cara waved and left the room.

Gina poured a fresh cup of coffee, dimmed the lights in the room, and took a seat in one of the comfortable recliners. Lawyers spent many hours in the war room at all times of day and night preparing, researching, reviewing documents, strategizing, eating, and sleeping. A stylish full shower and sauna next door to the room at least gave the hardworking attorneys some semblance of R and R when they could—and were willing to—take a break.

She had been raised in a six-million-dollar mansion surrounded by a ten-foot stone and mortar fence. The place had decorative gardens, marble fountains, and resident peacocks roaming the grounds. The fence had hidden what Gina had experienced growing up with her brother. It could never have been characterized as an actual home in her mind.

One victory was that, being born to a Sicilian father and Jewish mother left her with elegant beauty. It was a quality she had possessed as young as thirteen. Her alcoholic, drug-addicted mother had attempted to convince her that the reason her father had behaved the way he had was because he loved her so much.

Sick.

The Romano Mansion days had left Gina as damaged goods. She had even been the caregiver for her younger brother, a regular target for her father's rage. She had written a short story titled "Big Stone Fences" as an assignment in her college creative writing class. It was about concocting a plan to hang her father from the top of the twenty-foot marble staircase. In the story, the plan fails because of her brother's lack of physical strength to hold the rope after securing it around her drunk father's neck and shoving him from the first landing. Her instructor had given her an A and marked it with the words "Angry but Creative." She never disclosed to the teacher that the story was true.

She didn't miss her father, who had died of a stroke not long after Gina had entered law school. Her mother? They spoke, but that was the extent. Gina didn't see her brother often enough, but they were still close.

It was a fact, Gina reflected, that her path to recovery from the traumas of her past lay in the power of being a law partner to Deke. He had truly helped her.

She had been given the opportunity to make certain there were less awful people in the world. Now, as she observed her boss go through his own emotional crisis, obviously tied to his past, Gina could sympathize. She wondered how she could help him overcome those demons while they were fighting for justice together.

* * *

Midas had spent the better part of an hour straightening up the disaster in the shack of a home. He had even made the queen-sized bed that smelled of body odor. The mattress dipped on one side, leading him to conclude that the big man slept there. The bathroom was particularly smelly. The tub was more black than white from filth and inattention. The toilet seat was cracked in half, hovering above a toilet bowl that might have been a small open sewage deposit. Finally giving up his desire to make the space respectable, Midas moved on to the kitchen.

Open half-eaten cans of tuna fish and green beans sat on a three-legged rusted metal table. Green linoleum covered parts of the kitchen floor, but large sections of dirty concrete were exposed. Stacks of dishes sat in a small sink with not much porcelain left.

Bringing order to that part of the shack was also beyond the cleaning skills of Midas McDonald.

Most of the time he liked walking around someone else's home and snooping through drawers and closets. He usually achieved a sense of accomplishment when he left a home cleaner and better organized after a killing. In his mind, it was his apology to the victim. But there was nothing about Fred Perkins's disgusting little shack that Midas could make orderly except for making the dreary bed.

Midas took a seat in the so-called living room. There were four pieces of furniture. Two wooden lawn chairs with red cushions were positioned on either side of a cracked glass lawn table, alongside one wooden crate with the words "Sweeton Pies" in large green letters on two sides. An early model midsize smart TV hung on the wall. Empty and partially full beer cans sat on the floor in triple rows next to the lawn chair where Perkins must have spent most of his time. Porn magazines were stacked somewhat orderly in the second chair. Those appeared to be Perkins's prize possessions. Midas was surprised that such stuff was still available in print. He'd thought it was now only online, but he wouldn't know. That wasn't his thing.

Midas took the top magazine and began turning through the pages. He focused on the faces. The variations of makeup interested him, not the flesh. A lot of the makeup was what he thought of as "honky-tonk trashy." He wasn't above slapping that kind of makeup on his own face when the occasion called for it. After all, he had experience as a theatrical makeup artist. He enjoyed being "other people" at times. His mother had adopted that kind of comfort makeup in her years as a working girl on the honky-tonk circuit. His beloved sister, Skyler, had applied it when she was working the poles around Louisville, Kentucky. He had been thrilled when he finally convinced Skyler that less was more.

Midas often wondered if the feelings he had for his sister were "love." Was it that, what other people thought love was? Or rather a strong admiration for the girl he had taken such an integral part in raising? He had been, and still was, more intuitive and calculating than his sister. And yet now he was the one working for her rather than the other way around. That was all right. He respected Skyler for that.

The Slick Stick, though, would never see it coming. One day all of his money would end up in the hands of the two people who really deserved it.

Midas pulled himself away from the daydreaming. It was time to pay attention to what he was being paid to do. Another big paycheck from Congressman Minds that would be evenly split between Midas and his sister, once this slice of history was behind them.

Making another pass through the shack to find something that would help him stage the murder scene the way Minds had desired, he found a metal baseball bat under the bed. It had no doubt been placed there as "protection."

Midas broke out in a guttural laugh. The irony!

He then replaced his thin surgical gloves with a new pair and began the quiet wait at the door.

20

Deke read the appeal that Jeff and Pete had filed with an expedited request for review. Besides the fact that its purpose was to save him from a spiteful judge, he was also thrilled to see the simple level-headedness the two lawyers had used to hopefully change the direction the judicial system had been moving in the last several years. It was just common sense that a judge should not be allowed to cooperate with corrupt corporations in hiding secrets from the public when it could result in needless death and injury.

It was happening a lot in courtrooms all over the country. The Kaplan case was typical of the Hide and Die policy that second-rate judges like Ashworth were buying into on behalf of corporations. The judge had overwhelming evidence that the product the Kaplans were selling was contributing to the fatalities of men and women, young and old, every year. Ashworth had become a mere extension of the Kaplans' lies. They had spent hundreds of millions of dollars every year convincing doctors, regulators, legislators, and the general public that their special narcotic was safe and nonaddictive. They then focused on spreading political money. Few politicians were willing to hold hearings. The biggest victory for the Kaplans, however, was their ability to fund advertising. No corporate news organization was willing to do an exposé to report the facts. The advertising income flowing into the media far exceeded the importance of human life.

Deke wasn't convinced that this appeal, or even a hundred like it, would overcome the power of greed or how the judiciary viewed the issue, but he was proud to have his firm's name on the document.

Michael Carey walked in carrying a body language that indicated bad news. "The murders just keep coming," he said as he read from a document in his hand.

Deke straightened in his chair and pushed aside the papers he was reading. Part of the job of a competent lawyer was to be able to switch focus from one case to another in the blink of an eye. "Please tell me it's not Claudia Clapper."

"No. This time it's Mr. Fred Perkins. Just ten blocks away from the Douglas murder in Sweeton. There have probably never been two murders back to back like this in that town until we showed up."

"What details do we have?"

"From what I've been able to piece together, Perkins's legs were broken at his knees the same way Trayvon's were. They found the baseball bat that accomplished the deed right beside his dead body. That bat hit a triple if I'm to believe what my source told me. A single with perfectly placed contact to his left temple, immediately followed by a well-placed swing right behind his knees. And you're really going to love this." Michael waved the paper in his hand. "Perkins suffocated just like Trayvon. They apparently found a dish rag stuffed down his throat."

Deke covered his face with his palms as he shook his head. With a big sigh, he slapped his hands on the top of the desk and said, "And they no doubt found a note saying, 'I did it,' signed by Claudia Clapper. Which, we know, would be ridiculously false."

Michael looked at his notes. "No written confessions at the scene, but a witness did come forward. He thought he saw a woman with green hair and a large Black man make several passes in a truck by the Perkins house in the morning hours before the murder."

"Of course he did. Let me guess, the witness just happens to work at the Sweeton facility." Deke's sarcasm was tangible.

"No. Better than that. The witness was a city councilman and, oh, by the way, an upstanding lifelong resident of Sweeton. That's the way my source put it. What do you think, Boss?"

"First of all, who's your source?"

"He's a SWAT team commander in Tallahassee that I used to jump out of planes with in really scary places. Solid as a rock. He got all this info secondhand as it's been developing in the last eight hours. He followed the story about me and this firm representing Claudia, and he wanted to give me a heads-up."

"Well, somebody on their side is grossly incompetent. Claudia is fifteen hundred miles away from here in rehab in Colorado. And how could they not know that Bruno was extradited to California quite some time ago? Sounds like piss-poor planning by the idiot congressman. You see, this is just another example of my theory that an operation as big as Phoenix is not calling the shots. It's certainly not their legal team doing it. At best they're sitting back and letting the crazy train go where it wants to. They're separating themselves from these murders with no input and no involvement. Total deniability. But they know full well what Skyler and company are capable of."

Deke rose from his chair and began what his paralegals labeled the "Deke Shuffle Circuit." It was when time stood still for him as he walked around his office, silently processing new information before responding. Michael took a seat, knowing it might be a minute. Eventually, Deke took the seat next to Michael.

"I'll tell you what I think," Deke said. "What's important is that this allows us a clear look into what the congressman's team is thinking. Even as off base as it is. That has real value to us. Buffoons are in charge. The people running a multibillion, multinational corporation such as Phoenix are not buffoons. You might disagree, but I don't think in a million years that any of this is being engineered by Phoenix."

"Well," Michael said, "to be fair, they *are* using Minds to do their dirty work, even if they turn away and pretend it's not happening. Sounds pretty buffoonish to me. And culpable."

"Michael, in the congressman's head, he could murder the Douglases and make a clean getaway. He could stage a setup murder of Perkins and maybe get away with it. But there is no way he could murder Claudia, trying to end her lawsuit, without someone calling bullshit. So, the compromise low-risk play is to destroy her case with a prison sentence. This is an attempt to frame Claudia. In fact, I'd go as far as saying the Phoenix folks have never met or likely have never heard of that wacko Midas. It's his signature that's all over the Perkins murder."

"I agree, it makes sense. And the Skyler and Minds operation goes way beyond their work with Phoenix. According to Maria, that specialized hooker business Skyler's running touches everything from the pharma industry to the oil and gas industry. Phoenix is just another client, but it's the one that pays the most money. Deke, I think Minds is so focused on the Trayvon incident because, unlike Phoenix, he isn't sophisticated enough to understand the big picture. In his and Skyler's brains, if the Trayvon case goes away then the Phoenix problem goes away. And then they don't lose their cash."

"Michael, with all the noise you've been making around the country at most all of their facilities, Phoenix surely must understand that our focus moves beyond the Sweeton facility. I have no doubt that Phoenix sees that we're trying to shut down Pemberton, too, and every one of their other hellholes across the country."

"Phoenix might see that, but I bet Skyler and her sick brother haven't connected the dots yet. They truly believe 'no Sweeton case, no problems.' Kill a few people, put Claudia in prison, and it's payday. That's what they are counting on. Maria made it clear that we aren't dealing with rocket scientists. The class action we have in mind is nowhere on Minds's radar. We're not dealing with analytical long-range thinkers. It's a pole dancer who runs high-end hookers, a crooked congressman, and a certifiable psychopath."

"But don't underestimate the dangers here, Michael. After that first deposition we take, it's going to be crystal clear to even the slow learners what we're up to. That's when we put ourselves at a huge risk. It could be a two-edged sword for everyone in this firm. Skyler and her group will turn their attention to us once they understand that their threat is not limited only to the Trayvon case. Frankly, with what I've seen so far, it doesn't give me a warm, fuzzy feeling. And they're not going to send in the high-priced escorts to try and solve the problem."

"Nor the clowns," Michael quipped. "Actually, Deke, I disagree with you about the escorts. I wouldn't be at *all* surprised if you or I get targeted by some gorgeous dame offering a roll in the hay in a hotel suite. It's the kind of play they would make, to exploit human weakness, especially heterosexual male weakness."

"Michael, you may be right, but after thirty-eight years of a marriage I don't deserve, I have no doubts about how I would react. I'm pretty certain you're safe, too. For now, you and Carol help get Claudia lawyered up for what will amount to a nothing criminal case against her, unless she's learned how to teleport. A good lawyer will have this case stopped in its tracks within twenty-four hours. Even the Sweeton Keystone Cops aren't stupid enough to try to sell this one, no matter how much cash is spread around. It'd be too risky even for them. Let's keep our eyes on the ball and not be distracted by all the noise. This first depo matters."

Michael turned to leave but did a quick reverse. "Oh! We got the new Tasers and stun guns for the ladies. I'll hand them out today and offer intro lessons at their convenience."

"Fabulous. See that they're deadly proficient with them quickly."

"Sir, yes, sir!" Michael saluted and left.

Deke afforded himself a smile.

* * *

Paul Baker thought he was in hell.

He'd had his deposition taken in five other cases filed against Phoenix over the years. Those were nothing like what was being unleashed on him. His in-house general counsel had warned him that the lawyers at Bergman-Deketomis had a radically different style from most all other plaintiffs' firms. He had not, however, been presaged about the shock and awe that had him sweating and praying to heaven that his damn, dull-witted defense lawyer would ask for a break.

Phoenix blood was spilling all over the floor every time that Deketomis prick surprised him with another document that was more about the national dysfunction of the company than it was specifically about the Sweeton facility. His young defense lawyer should have stopped the depo and asked Deketomis where in the hell those documents came from. "Deke," as people in the room called him, was displaying on a massive six-by-five screen material that never should have seen the light of day. *Surely* how he'd obtained the documents should have been relevant, but the best his defense lawyer could do was whisper in his ear, "Stay calm. We're all right."

Paul jotted notes on his own legal pad as he desperately fought to explain documents that revealed that the national company, as a whole, knowingly understaffed their facilities. That they cut costs by hiring ridiculously unqualified workers and supervisors in areas ranging from in-house healthcare to critical counseling of the child residents.

In just two hours, Paul had been overwhelmed with attack questions about government money sources that financed their US operations, as well as the number of times the corporation had been sanctioned on a national level, or had licenses revoked. Not to mention all the details behind each event. He had been beaten over Phoenix political contributions, per diem payments for travel expenses, and even his personal preferences regarding Boston hotels. He had rarely been talked down to and humiliated to this degree. He wasn't used to it. He was the third in command at a Fortune 500 company! He had graduated first in his class at Wharton Business School with both an MBA and a master's degree in economics! He resented the country bumpkin ambulance chaser sitting across the table. The man had a damn smirk on his face as he dismantled the entire structure of Phoenix's US operations.

Paul was angry. Bob Minds had been correct when he'd told him that the seemingly "insignificant" lawyers in Florida were the "real deal." Bob had predicted that it wasn't only the Sweeton operation that was in trouble, but the entire Phoenix organization. Sure enough, the slimy attorney in front of him was focusing on issues much broader than a one and done kind of lawsuit, using documents they shouldn't have, in front of a defense lawyer who was pathetically outclassed and outmaneuvered.

There was little Paul could do as the blitzkrieg continued. He was already planning to fire his law firm. Assuring him that everything was okay, that they had this, that this would soon be over. What a joke!

Paul was also imagining how the slick, slimy congressman who had also humiliated him in front of his peers would pay for all this. The political thug and his whore business colleague had been silent on everything since their last hotel rendezvous, when they had promised that the five hundred thousand Phoenix had given them would silence all the regulators. "Nothing to worry about," they'd said!

Deke continued. "Mr. Baker, it's your duty to understand whether or not you are putting children at risk when they become residents at your Phoenix facilities, isn't it?"

Paul answered, "Well, I live in Boston and these facilities are all over the country, so I clearly can't know every detail."

"You certainly knew the details about the children who had lost their lives in accidents ranging from falling out of top bunks to being killed in knife fights in front of what you call trained supervisors, isn't that true?"

"Well, I'm not certain I know exactly what details you are referring to."

"What I'm referring to is this document sent to you by a 'Mr. Steve Caldwell.' How about you tell us who Steve Caldwell is?"

The twentieth document in the cross-examination appeared on the screen.

"Uh, Mr. Caldwell is head of safety assurance with our US operations, Mr. Deketomis."

"And whose name is at the top of that document? Isn't that your name right beside where it says 'To'?"

"Uh, yes, that appears to be my name. And I'm wondering where you got this document and so many of the ones like it?"

Deke gave the man a slight smile. "This is not the time for you to wonder, Mr. Baker. This is the time for me to ask questions and you to answer. That's how this works. So, I take it you did receive this document that shows the details of how each of these children died, and you also see that your so-called safety assurance specialist wrote in that handwritten note at the end of the document. What does he say? Could you please read that aloud for me?"

"Uh, it looks like it says, 'We have got to stop the bleeding.' Look, Mr. Deketomis, I can't be certain about what Mr. Caldwell meant by that statement."

"Seems pretty clear to me. You think he might have meant that too many kids were dying and being injured because your company chose to cut costs and save money? That you have a national operating structure that is so dysfunctional that kids like Trayvon are murdered right there in your facilities? You think he might have meant that, sir? What do you think?"

The defense lawyer stood. "Objection. First of all, you're harassing this witness and there is no way my client could possibly have known what Mr. Caldwell was thinking and—"

"Oh, we get it. You should object. You should also object to this whole disgusting story we've seen unfold in just two hours and twenty documents. Maybe it would be a good idea for you to tell the more experienced lawyers around your firm who probably should have been here that there is much more to come. Frankly, I have never seen a witness so underprepared and unprotected by counsel like I have seen here with Mr. Baker." First divide, then conquer. It was what Deke had taught all his young lawyers. "So I suppose we are done here unless you have any questions for your witness. We'd really like to hear those questions if you have a few."

The entire defense team stood in perfect unison, grabbed their briefcases, and quickly made their way to the exit.

Deke winked at Paul Baker and said, "See you in trial, pal."

* * *

By the time Paul exited the building, he had Skyler Bannock on the phone.

"Paul, darling, how nice to hear from you!" she purred enthusiastically.

"Cut the charm, Skyler. So, you damn hustlers extract virtually millions from my company and me personally and tell me that you will deal with the regulators. You told me two months ago at that meeting that, oh, by the way, was supposed to be just between us . . . you said not to worry, you had this. You knew what to do with all the cash or some BS like that. But less than thirty minutes ago, I had a room full of sharks showing me documents that had to come from some chicken shit government bumbler in regulatory, and God only knows where else. It has the potential to gut my company, Skyler. Tell your maladroit congressman cohort that I should have beaten his ass when he talked to me the way he did last time. And add the fact that he will never see Washington, DC again unless it's on a family vacation."

"Are you through, sweetheart?" Skyler asked with no change in her seductive tone. "Because I'm pretty sure you don't want me delivering that message to Bob. It would not be a great idea. And I shouldn't tell you what we have already done to help your company in the Sweeton misfortune that your moronic employees allowed to take place. But we have already delivered. All that is better left unsaid."

"Listen to me, Skyler. The last time I was left in the dark on the Alabama case you damn near had the entire company implicated in a bribery case, so your stock is not real high with me right now. And I don't want to hear anything about 'bedroom apologies' or whatever that term is you like to use. In case you haven't figured things out, this case is now about a lot more than Sweeton. Sweeton means nothing compared to the broad threat we are now faced with by this Deketomis prick."

He heard Skyler take a deep breath before she spoke. "Paul, let me be real clear here. First, don't even dream of calling Bob and speaking to him the way you just spoke to me. Second, don't interrupt the money coming our way. Most importantly, relax, everyone has their price. Let's see what that price is for your mean ol' lawyer friends to go away." She giggled.

"Skyler—"

"You know what is bothering me the most about this conversation is that Bob and I are always getting a good laugh out of that old saying 'lay down with dogs and you might get fleas.' How did you like those shots with me naked, you naked, and that whole bad dog scene at the hotel last year? Listen, Paul. Don't give us fleas. Both of us hate fleas, sweetheart."

Paul ended the call and cursed.

21

Ron Jacobi desperately tried to mask the fact that he was a vulgar thug. A handsome one, to be sure. Albeit small in stature, only five-foot-four. But he liked to think of himself as Al Pacino's twin brother, only with glasses. Not Al Pacino now, but the actor back in the 1970s, when the guy was a dreamboat to every woman on the planet.

But he also had the heart of a savage, just like the other fierce mobsters that he had been raised around his entire life. He knew that to be true. He was aware that all the stashes of millions of dollars he had secreted around the world would never change that. Most of the time he was pleased with his partial sense of self-awareness.

He and his mobbed-up family had spent millions on Bob Minds, more as a commodity than a political candidate. Ron considered Minds one of his least important purchases for political reasons, but he placed great value on the congressman because of the benefits his secret colleague brought to the table. Ron spent a lot of money on Skyler's underachieving friend and exposed himself to wildly unnecessary risks, such as the time he was the bag man delivery boy in the Alabama bribery job, for example. But in Ron's mind, it was worth it for a month of indescribable excitement with a woman who endlessly seduced him with Mata Hari electricity.

He was well aware that the claims that she was severing her relationship with Bob Minds and that she had never been with a more virile, thrilling lover were little more than enticing lies. Skyler was just being Skyler.

Money really could buy anything, including Skyler. Ron had once told Skyler that she was the valuable part of his political purchase and that her plebian colleague was simply *omaggio*, something his family called what others would simply consider a gift or gesture of appreciation. She predictably responded by parading nude in front of him, declaring that "this part of the purchase just keeps on giving." Ron could barely control himself when she spoke like that.

Unfortunately, it was that kind of play that brought him to be sitting in the waiting room of the Bergman-Deketomis law firm. He was already angry. It was supposed to be a meaningful negotiation, but they had him waiting for thirty minutes and thumbing through scuba diving, windsurfing, and *Cosmo* magazines.

A tall, broad man appeared to greet Ron and invited him to join the group in the conference room. Ron closed a magazine with a snap as if he had been caught reading America's nuclear codes. He peered at the huge smiling man in front of him through Coke bottle thick glasses. He extended a hand from where he sat. It was the gesture of a queen expecting her subject to kiss a ring.

The lawyer simply shook the hand.

"You don't look like the Nicholas Deketomis I've read so much about," Ron said as he stood. "Who are you?"

"My name is Michael Carey, and I'll be one of the team you will be meeting with today."

"Team? I was hoping to spend some private time with Mr. Deketomis to discuss some delicate matters."

Michael began escorting him down the hallway. "Yes, sir, that might develop today, depending on what you want to talk about in regard to the Sweeton case. At this point, all we've been told is that you were described as an ambassador here on behalf of Phoenix. We are typically not accustomed to dealing with 'ambassadors' in cases. Most of the time we deal with either insurance company representatives or in-house corporate counsel. We sure are interested in what you have to say about this case, though, seeing that you're an 'ambassador.'" Michael stopped and squinted at the man. "Has anyone ever told you that you look like—"

"A young Al Pacino? All the time. All the time. The ladies love me. Let's keep moving, big guy."

Is this overconfident young bastard making fun of me? Ron thought. He had not anticipated making a negotiation pitch to anyone but Deketomis. There was nothing illegal about the meeting that he had in mind, but he did understand that it would cause tons of ethical problems for Nicholas Deketomis if he chose to bite.

Michael opened the large double doors for Ron. The little man pranced in as if he were looking to buy the space. The eyes behind the thick glasses moved from the ceiling to the floor and over every inch of the large room as if he were taking inventory of its contents.

Everyone politely rose to greet the man dressed in black, custom-designed clothing obviously purchased at an extremely high-end men's clothing store.

"Mr. Jacobi, I'm Nick Deketomis," Deke said as he approached to shake the man's hand. "And this is Gina, Carol, and Cara. You've already met Michael."

Ron grabbed Deke's hand with both of his small hands to acknowledge the welcome. He held and tugged at it, causing Deke to wonder if he was trying to pull himself up to eye level.

"So, you're the man I've read so much about. The bigger than life lawyer. Would it be rude if I took a minute to take a closer look at the Chagall you have there on the wall? I'm assuming these are prints, Mr. Deke."

Indeed, the office walls were adorned with eye-catching framed artwork.

"Please just call me Deke, and yes, I wish they were originals. You would have thought they were with what our decorator charged us." Deke shot a glance at Gina, who rolled her eyes. What was with the phony flattery?

"Have you ever heard that Chagall also created stained glass windows and murals, Deke?" Ron asked. "In fact, two pieces of his stained glass have been with my family for forty years now. They are truly magnificent."

"I can only imagine, Mr. Jacobi, and please forgive us, we don't mean to be rude, but we are all bearing down on preparation for the next deposition scheduled in the Sweeton case. I wish we had more time today but, unfortunately, we don't."

Deke hammered home the message by sitting at the head of the table, ready to begin. He had been immediately turned off by the oozing officiousness.

"Of course. And I don't mean to be rude, but I have very specific directions to speak only to you personally about a Phoenix proposal to end this dispute between you and the company. Do you have any objections to that or are the Phoenix efforts already in vain?"

"I don't have any immediate problems with that kind of mysterious messaging, but the truth is that ultimately this team of people has serious input into how this litigation is resolved. If the need for a preliminary conversation between the two of us is essential, we can start there."

"I'm afraid it is essential, Mr. Deketomis."

"Very well." Deke addressed the others. "Sorry, team, but how about giving Mr. Jacobi and me a few minutes to ourselves."

The team shared glances with each other, stood, and left the room. Ron continued pacing. Deke was now somewhat amused by the Al Pacino look-alike.

The man spoke. "Sir, I can assure you we have done our homework on you and this firm. You have much to be proud of, but even with the many, many millions of dollars that flow through your doors every year, that naturally pales in comparison to the financial power and political influence of Phoenix. You have a wonderful thing going on for yourself, and I find it even more remarkable seeing it grounded in this small community out in the middle of nowhere."

Deke thought that sounded an awful lot like the clichéd mobster line, "Nice place you have here. It would be a shame if something happened to it." Nevertheless, Deke sat silently. Anyone who knew Deke would see a sleek cheetah watching his next meal that was unaware it was already dead.

"I have a one-time offer for you, Mr. Deketomis. Our people are considering paying you ten million dollars cash. Personally, with everything off the books. But in order for you to pocket that money, it will be necessary for you to immediately dismiss the lawsuit you now have pending and any other lawsuit you might already anticipate initiating against Phoenix or any of its subsidiaries as long as you live or this law firm is in existence. In other words, we make a quiet payment to you and you simply file quiet dismissals."

Deke wanted to throw the cretin through the large window overlooking the bay.

The man continued. "It would not be in the best interest of Phoenix for you to share any of this money with that unfortunate drug addict, Ms. Clapper, or anyone outside this room right now because of the optics involved with that and the obvious potential tax ramifications. That would make it appear that Phoenix had done something wrong, and it would further possibly attract even more disruption with regulators than what you've already caused. Is this picture becoming clear to you, Mr. Deketomis?"

"Crystal clear, Mr. Jacobi." Deke lay his hands flat on the table. "Let me answer you this way. Since you are such a fan of Chagall. Take a close look at that print on the wall there to your right. That is a painting in which Chagall was expressing the joy that his family, friends, and community experienced after a truly evil despot was vanquished from the earth at the end of the second world war. Do you know that painting?"

"Of course I do."

"Good. Take a snapshot of that one and show it to your pals at Phoenix. Tell them I intend to recreate that scene for all the families who have suffered mightily at their hands. Let them know that as I walk out of the courtroom with a verdict in money damages that will shake the very foundation of their company, I will think of that scene and remember that I warned them right here in the middle of nowhere, as you put it, that we will recover enough money for that 'drug addict woman' that she'll be able to purchase an original Chagall if she wants one. Now let me show you the way out that is not quite as direct as me throwing you from the window, but one that will keep you healthy enough to deliver that message for me."

Ron's jaw dropped. He hadn't expected that kind of response. He took a deep breath. "This is a bad idea, Mr. Deketomis."

Deke rose from his chair and opened the doors.

"Deke—I can call you Deke, right? Deke, I get the impression that you have a real tight-knit group here. Any disruption for anyone in that group would cause you serious problems. Is that about right, Deke?"

Whether or not Ron meant that as some kind of threat, it pushed Deke to the tipping point he had struggled against since the first day he had heard the facts of the Trayvon Clapper case. The past came crashing into the room. So much converged that he couldn't control his immediate rage despite his good judgment.

Bucky . . . They killed Bucky . . . They murdered him . . . LIKE AN ANIMAL!

Deke stooped, grabbed the little man around his midsection, and threw him over his shoulder. Ron squealed like a pig, and that gave Deke what could only be called an epiphany. At that moment Deke embraced the guilt that had been simmering.

All my fault . . . all my fault . . .!

Ignoring the screams, flying fists, and kicking feet, Nicholas Deketomis carried the Phoenix thug down the hall. He was unaware of the paralegals and attorneys who stood or sat staring at the spectacle. Deke was somewhere else.

The face of Bucky Carlton loomed in his vision. The dark hair that was a little long and shaggy . . . piercing brown eyes . . .

Michael Carey rushed to grab Ron Jacobi from the precarious position of almost falling to the marble floor head first. Deke's grip on the man's legs and waist was vicelike.

Michael understood it. Rage was something that had kept him alive during his soldiering days. "Deke, I've got this. Let him go, I've got this."

Deke suddenly released Jacobi in a way that might have broken his neck had Michael not had hold of him. The man continued to scream threats of assault and battery as Deke simply continued his walk toward his office. There may have been shouts of "lawsuit," "payback," "my family," and "insane" . . . but none of the words meant a damn thing to Deke.

* * *

1970. Early Summer.

Deke signed the guest registry and looked up at the burly guard.

"You kin to the resident?" the man asked.

"Yes," Deke lied. "He's my cousin."

"It's supposed to be immediate family, kid."

"He has no other family."

"What's in the bag?"

Deke carried a small burlap sack. "Just magazines for Bucky. Newspaper clippings."

The guard rolled his eyes and buzzed the electronically locked door so that Deke could enter Sandbury Housing for Boys. After going through the X-ray machine and having his pockets emptied, he was shown to the visitation room that consisted of several tables and chairs securely fastened to the floor. Just like what he'd seen in prison movies and television shows. Other bubbles of people sat with boys who were incarcerated in the place. Parents or foster parents, maybe lawyers, maybe social workers. Voices were in hushed tones. There were tears on many faces, especially those of the boys.

After a few minutes, Bucky Carlton emerged. He wore no shoes and was dressed in dingy trousers and a shirt. He didn't look too good.

"Hey, buddy, thanks for coming," Bucky said with forced cheer.

"Bucky. It's so good to see you. Are you all right?"

Bucky sat at the table across from Deke. "Sure. I'm okay."

"You're not. I can tell."

"As I told you the last time you came to visit, I'm doing all right. I'm a badass here. They respect me."

It was a wonder that Bucky was still talking to Deke. The plan of Bucky living in empty homes and disappearing into the ranch hand circuit hadn't worked out as Deke had thought it would. Someone had reported to the police that a vacationer's house was occupied. Bucky had been arrested for trespassing. An unsympathetic judge had sentenced the seventeen-year-old to SHB since there were no parents. Even the foster care system was not an option due to Bucky's somewhat awkward age of being on the cusp of an adult. The judge figured that a few months at the facility before Bucky turned eighteen would do the teenager some good.

"Are you eating?" Deke asked.

"Sure! The food isn't bad, and I have a decent place to sleep. I'm tall and have a rodeo cowboy build, so I'm not too worried about any hassles. Some of the other kids here, yeah, they get bullied and beat up . . . but not me. I'm working on being the Big Man on Campus."

"You have to be careful, Bucky."

"Don't worry. I'm still planning to get my high school degree and move on to be a bareback rider on the rodeo circuit. It's my destiny, kid."

"Bucky . . . what if you escaped?"

"What?"

"You could do it. You're outside a lot, aren't you? The sports games. Football, baseball, basketball . . . You could climb that fence. If we set a date and time, hell, I'll drive the pickup truck over and be waiting for you."

Chip Morton had taught Deke to drive. Even though he didn't have a driver's license yet, Jones had allowed him to operate the truck, but only on the cattle ranch.

"You're crazy, Deke. You'd get in more trouble than me!"

"No, I wouldn't. Look, the two of us could make our way to Montana and work on the cattle ranches there. You could break into big time rodeos in the biggest rodeo state in the country! Look, I brought you some stuff."

Deke opened the burlap bag and pulled out the magazines and clippings. "Look here. These are rodeo mags I sent off for. Look at all those gorgeous cowgirls!" He flipped open some of the pages to reveal that indeed, lovely women in shorts and cowboy hats were displayed with horses. "They're in Montana, just waiting for us. They compete in the rodeos there. I've even contacted a couple of the ranches there. They said if we come, they could find work for us."

"No shit?"

"No shit."

"We could be Huckleberry Finn and Tom Sawyer. Run away from this awful state. I'm ready to pick up and leave and try my chances somewhere else. I never knew what I wanted to do with my life until I met you, Bucky. You've inspired me."

"Come on, Deke. Escape from the camp is a really bad idea."

"There's something else. You know the Nealie brothers, right? I've been living with them and their parents, you know. They plan to participate in

an upcoming rodeo near Fort Myers. You could be in it, Bucky! They said if you could get out of here, they'd make sure you'd have a slot."

"Really?"

"Yes! And listen, Bucky." Deke leaned in to whisper. "I might have a place where you can live. It's a really nice family. I've told them about you. Hell, I'd like to live with them myself. The Pearsons. They would maybe take you in."

Bucky leaned back in the chair, his brow furrowed. "Tad Pearson? He's one of the biggest honchos in Arcadia! Really?"

"I'm working on it. But we have to get you out of here first."

Deke could see the wheels spinning in Bucky's head.

"Okay," he said. "Let's ride it to the buzzer."

They made a plan.

* * *

Deke sat in his office, somewhat embarrassed by what had just occurred in the hallway, but he was also unremorseful. He willed himself to calm down. It was clear, though, that he needed to come to terms with some demons.

He almost ignored a knock on the door, but he called for whoever it was to come in.

Cara. She was with Deke's oldest and dearest friend, Mark Prom, managing partner of the firm. There was not a lawyer in the firm who had lived through the challenges, successes, and failures of building the Bergman-Deketomis firm more than Mark. He was the glue that held the company together.

Mark's biggest challenge was ensuring that two of the firm's senior partners acted like mature adults and agreed to play nice. Although Martin Bergman and Deke certainly considered themselves to be friends, the healthy competition that existed between them had, on more than a few occasions, become far from healthy. Martin had hired Deke away from the State Attorney's Office, expecting him to distinguish himself as a national player in courtrooms throughout the country. Deke had delivered, but at times the man who had hired him felt threatened by how far his vision for Deke had progressed.

Mark Prom was considered by most of the staff to be the "Magic Man." He had a snake charmer's ability to redirect wasted energy of jealousy or anger toward building their powerhouse home. A strong bear of a man, Mark carried on his broad shoulders every pending risk, every troublesome secret, and every full-blown catastrophe that inevitably occurred. Deke thought he was one of the most unselfish lawyers he knew, operating in a world where that attribute was rare. Mark was also decisive to a fault. Yes was yes, and no was no. Both Deke and Martin thought that Mark could have been the CEO of the largest multinational corporation in the world, except that Deke liked to joke that the only thing Mark didn't have to make it in that kind of environment was an unethical drive for greed. Their good fortune was that he chose to endure the gremlins that plagued their firm from time to time.

It was apparent to Deke that Cara and Mark were there to deal with gremlins. Cara had one of her "What the hell, Dad?" looks on her face, and Mark displayed "Not again, Deke!" body language.

Sure enough, Mark spoke with an even temper. "So, what was all that about, Deke? Either you have gone batshit crazy, or you have developed some peculiar new negotiation techniques where we pay out money to the very people who are here to pay us money."

Deke sighed. "Nobody was here to pay us money, Mark. They were here to entice me to end my career for thirty pieces of silver. And I am not interested in you taking me to task over why I wanted to launch that little bastard into our parking lot."

"Really, Dad, really?" Cara had her hands on her hips, which indicated she meant business. "We're here to figure out why you just gave your best imitation of an insane UFC fighter, almost maiming a five-foot-nothing guy, and you don't want us asking why?"

"Deke, I've sat in this office more times than I can count when either you or Martin had driven this firm into a place called 'Crazyville,'" Mark continued, "but this little event that the whole firm watched is in a class all its own. So here are the ground rules for the next hour, if that's what it takes. I sit here as a law partner who truly admires and respects you, and Cara sits here not only as the future of this firm, but as a daughter who loves, adores, and supports you no matter what. We need to know what is going on in that disoriented head of yours right now."

Deke's shoulders fell forward, his head lowered, his elbows on the desk.

Mark gently spoke. "Deke, I know there's something bothering you. Cara and I were just discussing it."

"Something that happened a long time ago," Cara added. "When you were young."

"Can you . . . *will* you tell us what it is?"

Deke just shook his head. "No. Not now."

"Dad . . ."

Finally, he did look at them. "They're my demons to deal with."

"Maybe you should go back," Cara said.

"Go back? Where?"

"Arcadia. Your hometown. The demons are there, aren't they?"

"They've always been there," Deke said.

Silence.

Mark quietly stepped out of the room.

Cara waited a moment before saying, "Maybe you should think about it, Dad."

Then she left him alone.

22

After the gathering of the entire Bergman-Deketomis staff in what Mark Prom billed as the Apology Meeting, the energy immediately built toward an all-hands-on-deck attitude around the firm. Deke had disclosed the putrid offer Ron Jacobi had run past him and used it as a war cry. As Diana would often say, "This is a family with a bunch of wonderfully crazy aunts and uncles."

The apology meeting had turned into a vitalizing rally. All those crazy aunts and uncles were focused on Phoenix's demise.

Bribery was a crime that even the Department of Justice was sometimes willing to take a chance on prosecuting. For years, Deke's firm had loaded the DOJ with boxes of files against an array of corporate criminals including tobacco manufacturers, opioid corporate distributors, PFAS manufacturers, and a dozen pharmaceutical producers. The goal was to show the DOJ where all the bodies were buried by giving them the step-by-step trail that always led to rank fraud. And often manslaughter.

The DOJ's predictable course of action when it came to sophisticated white collar crime on massive scales almost always ended with minor slaps on the criminals' hands with paltry fines. Those symbolic fines were generally regarded as simply the cost of doing business for most corporate CEOs. The failure to perp walk men in white shirts dressed in expensive suits was becoming so predictable that courses in elite MBA schools throughout the country were being offered that taught how to commit those crimes.

Nevertheless, Deke's firm continued to provide them with treasure chests of criminal activity, always hoping for more of a bold and courageous change in DOJ leadership. Deke would often tell his team that any effort to actually have the DOJ do their job was typically a long shot, but they were always willing to keep putting cases in front of them.

* * *

Gina and Cara flew to Boston to follow up on leads concerning the connections between Congressman Minds and Phoenix. It was a treasure hunt that would hopefully grab the attention of local, state, or even a federal prosecutor somewhere. With information that both Brian Meyers and Maria Valdez had provided, they had plenty to work with.

Cara had compiled a list of ten people who were ex-employees of Phoenix and two who had previously worked for Bob Minds. At least half of them had been categorized as disgruntled by Cara and the others were total wild cards. Both Gina and Cara had carried out cold call routines in the past. It always began with a simple knock on the door and a hello along with a boatload of luck. Cracks in the opposition's wall would begin to develop.

Gina once achieved a totally unexpected break when a cold call resulted in a disgruntled employee randomly handing over a box of documents that provided a road map to the cover-up scheme devised by the maker of a medicine that was killing pregnant women. That box of documents was the catalyst for the product being removed from the market and potentially saved the lives of hundreds of women and their unborn babies. Gina had explained that it was like gold prospecting: you had to dig through mountains of dirt before the law of averages and good planning allowed you to uncover the goods.

On day one, the two women had a door slammed in their faces by a Bob Minds employee who was apparently far from disgruntled and possibly still working with the congressman in some capacity. The words "bitch" came from behind the door. That was always one of the risks of cold calling. Gina could already visualize the inevitable phone calls that would be made to Minds. Two nosy lawyers were making the rounds asking questions about him. That carried some risks for the two women, and Gina concluded that the event was better left unreported during the midafternoon progress report to Carol and Jake.

By 4:00 p.m., the women had spent time with two Phoenix employees who shared a tremendous amount of information that merely duplicated the stories they already knew about the dysfunctional nature of the organization. In addition, they had learned about the many love trysts between married employees. They had meaningless lists of who all the illicit drug users were, even down to times and places in the women's bathrooms where so-called drug klatches took place. They heard about the HR executive who secretly dressed up as a clown and spent hours in Walmart parking lots juggling, whatever that was about. Not much was useful information.

They checked into the Dagny Hotel. It was Gina's choice because of the wonderful memories that were made there with her ex-trumpet player boyfriend. She had given Cara all the details about the restaurant and the fitness center. Both women had plans to take advantage of all those special niceties. The policy around Bergman-Deketomis was that if lawyers had to leave the comfort of their homes and endure all the nightmares of travel, then they should do it first class.

Fine dining was something that always came to mind when Gina talked about the Dagny Hotel. The five-star Fin Point Restaurant serving expensive wine became the setting that night for the two good friends sharing tales of college and office politics, and then moving on to stories about their past loves, laughable failures, and rare, phenomenal successes with men throughout their lives. Discussions about career expectations and the special challenges a married woman faced as a trial lawyer surfaced by the time of the third glass of wine.

It was then that Cara felt she needed to bring up the elephant that had been in the room, or rather on her mind, for weeks: Zach Morrison, Dunlop and Markle and the offer in Colorado. Cara told Gina all about it.

"Wow, big time, Cara," Gina said. "Congratulations."

"Thanks. I don't know if I'm going to take it, though."

"Why not?"

"Why do you think?"

Gina shook her head. "If it's your father you're concerned about, believe me, he'd eventually get over it. You're right about wanting to spread your wings and try other experiences. Personally, though, I'd hate to lose you. I enjoy working with you, and I think we make a perfect team."

"Well, I enjoy working with you, too! You're actually another factor that plays into it. I feel like I can learn so much more from you than anyone in Colorado."

Gina laughed. "Well, thanks for the compliment, but I'm not so sure that's true." She held up her wine glass. "Look, whatever you decide, I support it. Okay?"

Cara clinked her glass against Gina's. "Okay."

It was a time to ignore the mediocre results of their first day of cold calls and be optimistic that the next day would be different. Cara had scheduled the most promising prospects for day two.

* * *

Bob Minds listened to Skyler's shorthand description of the tense conversation she'd had on the phone with Paul Baker. The gist was that everyone had new and much bigger problems to deal with and that Baker was extremely unhappy.

"Well, then," he told her, "I warned him. And I'm about to make the officious prick a lot more unhappy. The information I got just a few hours ago tells me that there are two lawyers on the prowl right here in my backyard. Lucky for his worthless ass that I at least have people who are still loyal to me. I'm told lawyers already know way too much. "

Skyler sat next to him and listened as he dialed Paul's number. When the Phoenix executive picked up, Bob said, "So, I'm told you're unhappy, Paul. Skyler said she thought I should call and work through your concerns. Did I get that right?"

Paul hadn't had a chance to answer, "Hello?" After Bob's lead-off, he said, "Good evening to you, too, Congressman. You know it's after midnight? But never mind. Concerns? You're describing what's going on as only concerns of mine? I sat through hours of having the absolute hell beaten out of me by lawyers who knew more about the inner workings of my company than I did. It damn well appeared to me that the information he was slamming across my head was stuff that only could have come from those pointy-headed bureaucrats at the ACF. The ones you're supposed to be buying with the half-million dollars we gave you. So yes, I am very unhappy."

"I told you what I would do, and I did it. Whatever kind of inside information you're talking about did not come from the people I own at ACF. The money we paid was simply too good for that to happen. Sounds to me like it's your lawyers you should be talking to instead of me. Destroying and keeping a lid on really bad information is what those corporate lawyer types are supposed to be good at."

Paul responded with every ounce of indignation he could muster. "Bob, this isn't about my lawyers. Don't you see a pattern? Your ideas don't work. How could it possibly have gone any worse than it did with your creepy little friend last week? We give you authority for thirty million dollars to negotiate for us because you say he has some special inside avenue with *the* Nick Deketomis. You talk us into letting this Jacobi guy take care of it instead of actual professionals because of 'special relationships,' as you put it. And yet here we are, still at risk because you blew it again."

"Yeah, and I'm pretty sure if it had worked, you'd be parading in front of your board like some kind of mythical god. Am I right about that?"

"But it *didn't* work! I don't intend to waste any more time with this sophomoric exchange. I actually have problems to solve that you seem unequipped to help me with, so—"

"You got that right, your highness!" Bob yelled into the phone. "I have something else to tell you that might make you even unhappier. Some of those lawyers who you say beat the hell out of you are here in town talking to your people and my people, apparently to tie you and me together with a lot more than just political donations. I made a list identifying the top five ex-employees who are the most likely to cause me serious pain. In fact, we've already talked to two of them and pointed out the risks of them running their mouths. I have plenty of ways to scare the skin off the folks on my list and that's already happening. I'm going to contain all this, and I intend to do that with both honey and sheer terror if need be. It's your list I'm worried about. The one we have already made for you. Your problem is that you aren't deliberate enough. You won't do what I will do, and I can't risk that."

"What are you saying? That I need to employ your baboon tactics by showing up at the houses of former employees or potential witnesses against us and breaking their legs? Is that really what you're talking about, Bob?"

"You got it, pal, and I didn't call you to ask your permission to do what has to be done. I called to ask who you're most afraid of, right here in our fine city, who might pose the biggest threat to you and, by extension, to me. I think we already know the answer, but I want to hear it from you. We've spent hours talking to one of the people who invited those two lawyers into his home. We already know who they're going to talk to next."

Bob heard Paul bluster a bit before the man responded in anger, "Let me tell you something, you damn malefactor. First, there is no 'we' in working through this new problem. I don't need your mobbish goons trying to accomplish anything for me. There is nothing to gain with violence, and I have never asked you to engage in violence on behalf of Phoenix. Nor will I ever. The one person in this city who poses the biggest problem for Phoenix is not the kind of person who would respond to either your honey or your terror. I will handle her intelligently. Are we clear about that? Listen, Bob, it's time for you to step aside."

Bob laughed. "Right, no violence. You don't want any violence." His laugh grew more pronounced. "Sure, Paul, I'm supposed to sit back and let you handle this situation with a genteel conversation between you and someone you obviously know is a real threat. Do you really think we don't already know where both of us are the most exposed?"

"Again, Bob, let me handle this my way. I don't need your little bag man involved any more, and I can promise you it's counterproductive to have any of your other apes, whoever they are, trying to solve our problems with intimidation. I've got this."

"Oh sure, you've got this. Bullshit. You can't even tell me the names of the two lady lawyers going house to house in my backyard, can you? Well, I can. I know where they're staying. I know they're here for three days. I know almost every question they asked on their first day. I know where they're most likely to go next. And I know you don't have one frigging detail yourself. So, don't run off your idiot mouth how you can handle this."

"I'll say it again, Bob. We need a little space between you and me," Paul said with a resigned sigh.

"Space? There is no possible space between me and you, Paul. Your hands are around my neck and my hands are around yours. There is no space. The only question is who has the ability and motivation to squeeze the tightest."

There was silence on the other end.

"Paul?" Bob looked at his phone. The man had hung up. "Son of a—"

"Darling," Skyler said. "Shall I take care of Jessica? You know she lives less than two miles from where we are right now."

Still steaming from the phone conversation, Bob looked at his compatriot and waited for her to continue.

She handed him a small stack of clippings. "Look. Jessica Hammer is all over these articles. She's described as a widowed high society millionaire. She's threatening a shareholders' derivative case against Phoenix. The articles talk about how on several occasions she made statements that the shareholders' suit would shine a bright light on Phoenix's executive management failures like the *Fortune* 500 company losing hundreds of millions for the shareholders because of poorly managed adult prison facilities and children's institutions. Dear Jessica is quoted as saying 'sketchy and possible criminal political activity has the potential to destroy the value of the company forever.' If we don't pay attention to this, you know how it ends. Paul Baker pulls you and me down with him."

Bob barely glanced at the articles before tossing them on the floor of the hotel suite. "Trust me. I know all about this Jessica Hammer. We've had to listen to that socialite bitch run her mouth about the shareholder lawsuit for a year now. I already have donors asking about my involvement. We have to deal with the problem either now or later, so why not now? We potentially take care of a couple of inevitable problems, all at the same time. The big mouth who knows too much, and a potential lawsuit where you and I would likely have to take the stand."

"I'm not taking any stand for anyone," Skyler said with a sniff. "I'm more concerned about the apparent pain tolerance of that bunch of Florida pit bulls. Ron, my dearest friend, offered that Deketomis lawyer the moon, and the crazy son of a bitch tried to break my poor little guy's neck. What kind of lawyers do that?"

Bob cocked his head. "I still don't know what you see in that Ron Jacobi creep. Hell, I wish they *had* broken his neck."

"Oh, he's cute, and you know that. He's better in bed than you might think for such a small guy. And business-wise, he serves his purpose. Look, my bet is that those lawyers are human, just like the rest of us. So, we make another offer. We double the money and at the same time give them a taste of what we're capable of. Not too much blood, but a whole lot of fear and tears. Who knows, they might blink."

Bob smiled at his partner. "You're always so sure of yourself. I love it. How is it that no one in Washington has connected the dots between me and you? We're good, baby, we're good!"

"No, it's nothing to do with being good. To quote Mae West," Skyler said, "when I'm bad, I'm better."

She gave him a rare kiss on the mouth.

* * *

Midas applied and reapplied makeup three times. He had mastered the procedure, but on this particular morning he struggled. Perfectionists carried a heavy weight. Too much primer and foundation covering the few imperfections. Not enough concealer at the cleft of his chin. A little more eyeshadow. He hated her makeup selection, but he had to work with what was available.

There was also the consideration that it couldn't appear to be theatrical makeup. He wasn't about to go on stage and play to an audience of five thousand people. His features didn't need to "read" to someone in the back row. It had to look real. It had to be convincing. He had to become *her*.

Midas had only thirty minutes to look through the huge selection of expensive clothing that was available in the luxurious walk-in closet. Outfits ranged from Chanel to Hermes and Prada. That made him wonder how a woman with such elegant taste could have such a subpar selection of makeup. Not a hint of Tom Ford or even Guerlain. She must have had a connection to a Mary Kay pusher. Perhaps she had been deluded into pushing the stuff herself.

He chose black. No matter what time of day he had to perform, black was always appropriate. The sizes weren't perfect. He preferred eights instead of tens, but with the right choices he made it work. Tight leggings worked perfectly with the long-sleeved mock turtleneck jersey top that was inexpensive at Walmart but cost ten-fold more with the Gucci tag attached to it. It was pricey to be a woman! The understated silver close-toed flats were slightly tight but the flex would work for the short period of time he needed to wear them.

Midas selected a half dozen outfits he intended to keep. There was still plenty of room in the false bottom of his flatbed. He giggled at the idea that the spirit of the fiery tempered woman might find some comfort next to clothing that had at one time made her feel so attractive and alive. In his opinion, she was indeed attractive and there were more than a few similarities between the two of them. She had his high cheek bones and perfectly formed heart shaped lips. Her long, delicate hands and fingers might belong to a concert pianist, and his were the same.

There were a few differences he had to conceal as best he could. The woman stashed in back of his truck had stunning blue eyes, but his were the color of polished onyx. The lightly shaded large-rimmed sunglasses provided cover for that. His jet black hair was shoulder-length and typically worn in a ponytail or a man bun. Her hair was dark brown. One of the several turban headbands hanging neatly organized on her closet wall served as a covering.

The alarm on his watch reminded him that it was 5:00 a.m. It was time for a few finishing touches. He stared at the extensive selection of fingernail polish and exquisite jewelry and decided on the stylish look he was trying to achieve.

What he had done to the woman in the flatbed, who, in another life, he might have befriended, was all for Skyler. Jessica Hammer had been a fighter. Her physique was athletic and fit. Midas respected her. When he had lain next to her on the comfortable and cool satin sheets and watched her sleep, she was so elegant and peaceful. Even the eye covers she wore were expensive silk. They matched her red lingerie. Given the chance, he would have cozied up to her and fallen asleep to the sound of her gentle breathing. But that was a missed opportunity.

It had happened quickly. Midas had intended to smother Jessica with one of her silk pillows. As he had quietly tried to slide off the bed, the woman was on her feet in a millisecond. She had run from the bedroom, heading for her home's front entrance. No useless screams, only focus. Midas had been stunned at how fast and committed she was. Luckily, the master bedroom was on the McMansion's first floor and not up the dramatic marble staircase. It hadn't been a difficult pursuit. He had been able to anticipate her route.

He relished reliving it.

Grab her hair less than twenty feet from the front door.

Drag the fighting woman across the slick marble floor.

Manhandle her into the living room.

She had rallied to the point of knocking over a bookcase that was freestanding in the middle of the room!

Block any attempts to strike him.

Chokehold her.

Appreciate the last couple of minutes of her suffering until she felt her extremities go numb and impossible to control.

Unusually, Midas considered what his victim must have felt, and he was surprised that it made him sad.

She had been a wonderful specimen of a woman whom he would have preferred to befriend over a glass of champagne.

23

It was clear to Gina and Cara that something was noticeably different about how they were being received by the people who had left the congressman's organization and the Phoenix group. The second day of cold calls was disastrous. The folks they thought should be at the top of a disgruntled employees list for both organizations were hiding in their homes. When the lawyers rang doorbells, curtains moved ever so slightly, lights often went off suddenly, and the sounds from televisions or radios abruptly ended. By three o'clock in the afternoon, the women had been unable to speak to anyone remaining on their list. With just three more prospects ahead, the lawyers already felt defeated.

They pulled their rented black SUV into a longish circular driveway. Jessica Hammer's large Tudor-style home was by far the most impressive house they had visited in the two days. A Bentley Bentayga was parked in front.

The lawyers exited their SUV and hurriedly approached the elaborately carved wooden entrance doors. They were surprised when a woman wearing sunglasses, a turban that concealed her hair, a long-sleeved mock turtleneck jersey top, and tight leggings pulled open the huge doors as if she had been preparing to make a quick exit.

"Oh!" she said. "Hello, can I help you with something?"

"Hello, we're here to speak to Jessica Hammer," Gina said, pleasantly. "Are we at the right place?"

"Yes, you're at the right place but at the wrong time. I'm just now leaving for an appointment I need to attend in about fifteen minutes. Whatever you need to speak to me about needs to be quick."

The woman glanced at a watch on her wrist and seemed as if she had no interest in talking to them at all.

"We've seen your statements in the press about the case against Phoenix, and we wanted to talk to you about it if you can spare just a little time."

The woman seemed perturbed. "Are you reporters? Are you from Phoenix? Why should I spend my time talking to you?"

Gina held forth a business card. "We are lawyers working on a case much different from the one you are contemplating against Phoenix. Maybe we have material that might be helpful to you, and you might have material that may be helpful to us."

The woman sighed. "Well, all I hear are mights and maybes, but we can have a seat inside, and we can at least compare notes for just a few minutes. If I'm moved by what you have to say, maybe we can meet again."

She led Gina and Cara into the large living room. With graceful feminine gestures, she motioned for them to have a seat. Cara chose an exquisite antique couch, while Gina sat directly in front of her on one of two wing chairs facing it. The woman didn't remove her sunglasses, nor did she sit to address them.

* * *

Midas had never been asked to beat to bloody hell a person as young as Cara, and that gave him pause. He took an inventory of her features. The fine shoulder-length blonde hair, the mature, kind face—well, none of that dampened his commitment to pummel the young woman to near death. Although he loved the way she carried herself, it was confident beyond her years. He appreciated the way the woman had applied her makeup. Maybe he would check her bag before he left the house and keep her supplies for himself.

Then he caught himself. He had allowed a sliver of sympathy for the woman's apparent young age. That surprised him. Was he having the kind of breakthrough the useless shrinks talked about during his early days of required counseling? This was no time for an epiphany. His mind was clear. Gather as much information as possible about the details the two lawyers were aware of and get them to disclose where they were going with their lawsuit. And then . . .

As he examined Gina in close detail, Midas concluded that battering her would be much easier. There was something about this more seasoned beauty that jazzed him up. He felt sure that she was someone who had emotionally abused plenty of men in her lifetime. Midas had always considered emotional pain much worse than what he was willing to inflict physically. Gina would be first. He'd save Cara for second. Maybe even spend a little more time with her in a one-on-one intimate conversation about her most private secrets.

* * *

The woman addressed Gina. "So you show me yours and then I'll show you mine, sweetheart. We can make this into a little show-and-tell event." She winked seductively but then blinked as if she hadn't meant to do that.

Radars went on red alert for both Gina and Cara at the same time. Cara already felt icky about the woman who was still standing for far too long after they had taken seats. Something was off about her. Cara was torn. Jessica Hammer was mildly attractive, but overwhelmingly eccentric in appearance. On the one hand, Jessica held herself as a perfectly well-adjusted woman. On the other, though, the woman was a totally anomalous character. Her voice was also peculiar. Neither feminine nor masculine. The pace of speaking took wild swings from slow and steady to anxious and erratic. Cara also noticed the presence of too much perfume. That was a social faux pas that Cara ordinarily wouldn't have thought much about, but there was also a peculiar odor of chemical cleaner.

Then, as Cara turned her head to take in more of the living room, her eyes went to the bookshelves. Some of the titles were upside down. A handful of books lay on the floor. The image was not consistent with the overall orderly flow of the house.

Gina continued to speak. "Ms. Hammer, you were quoted in one of the newspaper articles I read as suggesting that the involvement of Phoenix in politics had the capacity to be disastrous for the company. We are interested in why you made such a statement."

"Darling, I can't help but think that maybe you didn't hear me when I said this is a show-and-tell party. You have to show me something first," the woman said with marked attitude and intensity.

Cara eyes dropped to the woman's legs and feet. The skin was slightly bulging out the sides of the shoes. The optics were wrong. That obvious irregularity was different from the meticulous way Jessica Hammer presented herself otherwise. The sunglasses had remained over her eyes. That, plus the head wrap, conjured up an image of a young Gloria Swanson as the washed-up old Hollywood actress Norma Desmond in *Sunset Boulevard*.

Gina said, "All right, I'll tell you that we've been looking at the relationship between the folks at Phoenix and a certain congressman who lives right here in Boston, and we thought maybe you could share what you know about him."

"My dear, when you say you've been 'looking at,' what does that mean? It would be helpful if you were more specific. You can't swing a dead cat by the tail in Boston without hitting a dishonest politician if that is what you have in mind."

Cara said, "We have followed some dollar transactions directly from individuals who work for Phoenix management to Congressman Bob Minds. That has interested us in looking further."

The woman became quiet and gazed intently at Gina. "I'm not really clear about how that would affect any lawsuit except the one I intend to bring. What kind of case are you two ladies working on that might involve a connection between Bob Minds and Phoenix?"

Her voice had croaked into a lower, more idiosyncratic voice.

"Now, who's the one asking all the questions?" Gina asked in a friendly tone. "The case we bring will be a national class action against Phoenix and all its US-based facilities. The Bob Minds part will be the bribery element, which is still against the law in America. Any conduct, legal or illegal, that might have transpired between the congressman and Phoenix is obviously relevant. When we shine a light on Minds, we open any number of ways to go after the Phoenix operations."

Gina knew what she was doing with the "friendly conversation." Mental images of Midas McDonald had already materialized. The woman in front of her slightly resembled him. Only a dozen times in her career, even as a criminal prosecutor, had a fight or flight warning surfaced as strongly as at that moment. It was something she never ignored. The only time Gina had dismissed the alarm, she had ended up held captive for hours in a cellar by a perp with a sawed-off shotgun.

By the time that thought had entered her head, Gina was convinced this person was indeed Midas McDonald. She instinctively remained calm but also knew she had to pull a quick plan together. It was time to face reality. She and Cara had to get out of the web Midas was no doubt spinning.

"I call Bob Minds the Slick Stick among other things," Midas said with a disturbing laugh. The mask had fallen. The voice had become more masculine. He removed the sunglasses, revealing eyes that were as black as bottomless pits.

"I beg your pardon? Slick Stick?" Gina responded coolly with her own nervous chuckle. "You call Congressman Minds the Slick Stick? Why is that, Ms. Hammer?"

"To me, Bob Minds has always been the Slick Stick. He's been carrying on a truly putrid relationship with my sister for years now. With a little luck, the Stick won't be around much longer to physically and spiritually abuse her."

"Your sister?" Gina feigned surprise. "Wow, isn't this a small world. You certainly have my attention enough to reschedule another meeting since you're in such a hurry, Jessica." She gave a quick, time-to-go glance at her watch and then a subtle smile and wink to Cara. She reached to move her large, purse-sized leather document satchel from the floor to her lap. Cara had already done the same, clutching the purse at her side and quietly unlatching the three snaps that held it closed.

"Cara, would you go outside and tell our driver that we'll be out in about five minutes? We can reschedule with Ms. Hammer. We don't want to make her late."

Midas knew there was no driver outside. More importantly, with that lie, he knew it was game-on. "Not so fast, ladies!" Midas flashed his perfect teeth. "We've just started getting to know each other."

* * *

Midas, from the moment Gina and Cara had been led into the Hammer living room, had a fantasy of himself as the sly wolf and the two women as good-natured, naïve bunny rabbits. He believed he was simply playing with his prey. All that changed in an instant.

With the speed of a viper, his fist brutally struck Gina's head directly on the temple. She jerked to the side, slumping over in her chair. Her bag fell from her lap and her arms went limp.

He raised his fist for another powerful blow, but then Midas felt severe pain through his entire body. His legs buckled. His arms felt as if they were on fire. A sudden release of urine saturated the expensive black leggings.

Now he was on the floor. He struggled to remain conscious.

The youngest bunny rabbit was only an inch away from his right eye with whatever it was that had caused him to collapse face up on the floor. He was unable to make sense of what was happening.

But bunny rabbits aren't violent!

He desperately willed his immovable arms to work. He wanted to grab the little bunny and strangle the life out of her, but she pushed her little bunny gadget into his forehead above his right eye and held it there for what seemed like an eternity. For a second he recognized what the rabbit warrior had in her hand. He was conscious long enough to acknowledge the respect he had for the young bunny, even though he knew he was being lit with so much electricity that he might die.

24

It was an hour's drive out of Boston to Palace Gardens in Deerfield, New Hampshire. The beautiful resort offered nature trail walks, peaceful horseback riding through forest roads, and relaxing spa treatments. But there would be nothing beautiful, peaceful, or relaxing about the one-day meeting Bob Minds had arranged. He was losing control of the Phoenix money train, and it was time to continue fishing or cut bait.

There was no particular event that was causing the return of the damn burning reflux pain. In fact, overall Bob was pleased with how some events had turned out. The Douglas murder was seamless. It simply became the sad and tragic tale of a happily married couple killed in a house fire. The Perkins killing was a cold case, thanks to a cooperative sheriff. His harebrained idea to frame the drug addict Clapper's mom caused him to laugh a little to himself. Instead, it worked out all right without that component. As he repeated so often to people, successful men had inventive ideas that didn't always pan out.

But where he'd really lost control was with Paul Baker. Paul was the spigot that turned on the money flow to Bob's bank accounts. Right now, Paul was a scared little bitch whining and whimpering about the stories on newspaper front pages, such as the one that proclaimed that Jessica Hammer was missing. Bob was tired of repeating the same lie to the moron. "No, we had nothing to do with it." "No, we weren't concerned about her." "No, we don't even know where she lives." It was tiresome and a waste of his energy. The default position to all this was "no body, no crime." Too bad that Hammer's body would never be found unless someone did a deep dive into the fifty-gallon barrel of acid where it was still dissolving.

Bob knew that Paul would never be gutsy enough to take care of himself, so it was up to the Minds team to do it for him. Right now, the idiot failed to see the successes. And while the team was working on correcting minor failures, it was indeed time to regroup and keep moving. Not to protect Paul Baker or Phoenix, but to clean up for themselves.

He used his key to open the door to Skyler's luxurious suite.

"Ron, how was your night?" Bob asked, knowing that Skyler had worked extra hard to bring Jacobi back into the fold after the man was thoroughly traumatized by his trip to Florida.

The little Lothario responded with a dreamy contentment, "A night with Skyler is the equivalent of a week in the paradise of the Elysian Fields."

The congressman choked to conceal his laughter at the pitiful scene. Ron sat in a white cushioned chair wearing red silk pajamas. He raised a flowery teacup to his lips and took a couple of tiny sips. Without the coke bottle glasses, his eyes were glassy pinpricks.

"Ron, when you're happy, we're happy. Isn't that right, Skyler?"

Skyler was propped up on a massive canopy bed covered with a cozy, silk comforter decorated with colorful flower patterns. She wore a teddy that was barely there. Raising one of the half dozen oversized pillows as if she might playfully cover her head in shame, she said with a mock little girl voice, "I was bad last night, Bob. Very bad. Was I bad, Ron?"

"Very bad, my dear."

"See? Even Ron says I was bad. But, you know, it was all about making my little lover happy." Then she giggled.

"I hate to break up this little New Hampshire love nest, but I need the two of you and Midas in my suite in about an hour for a planning session. Ron, I recommend you save what strength you have left, if any, and let Skyler get busy getting dressed." Bob turned to leave the suite.

"Bob, sometimes you're just a party pooper," Skyler said as she hopped to the floor and seductively sauntered in front of Ron. She gave him a quick kiss on his forehead. "Time for a shower."

Bob stared and thought to himself, *Elysian Fields indeed.*

An hour later, four of the most morally damaged people in Deerfield had all gathered in Bob's presidential suite.

Midas sat in a large window seat with his legs crossed. The gauze patch on his right eye interfered with his ability to walk with confidence. It spoiled his self-image. Beyond that, he couldn't shake the nagging thought that he was no longer on his game. A persistent voice boomed in his head. He was not as capable as he once was for "thrill work," the pet name for his vocation.

The petite blonde girl had shown such courage, commitment, and raw rage as she tried to kill him. He admired her. Her screams and focused fury as she plunged that stun gun three times into his body, his head, and nearly into his eye was beautiful and pure. He wanted to embrace her and compliment her on a job well done. To tell her that he wished he was normal and that he longed to have a friend like her besides his sister.

He had felt shame when he regained consciousness and managed to awkwardly stumble out of that house. A defeated amateur, undone by a young warrior simply trying to save her friend. It crossed his mind that she might actually be a great lawyer.

Now this. He had to sit quietly and listen to the Slick Stick lay out his next ridiculous plan where Skyler, the little mafia Cupid, Jacobi, and he would take all the risks, while the Stick would keep all the profits.

Bob began the meeting. "I want us to regroup on how we're looking at business. We've been so focused on trying to save Phoenix that we've ignored all the other parts. The Pharma clients bring in big money and so does the oil and gas side. We've added four new exceptional women to our working team. They are fresh and want to make the big money. That's the attitude we all need to take. I'm going to make one more run at saving the Phoenix business, but I'm not optimistic. Paul Baker has turned into a scared little wanker. Skyler, tell us what's on your mind."

Now dressed as if she might be a vice president of a corporation, Skyler said, "One hundred percent agree with you, darling. We need to make sure we correct all the problems that are potentially a threat. We had no way of knowing where the Phoenix case was going to go. We were wrong, and my brother had to take some unnecessary risks down in Florida that, fortunately, have worked out okay. But it took a lot of chits and cash we had to lay out to make it work."

Ron spoke up. "What do you gain by continuing the course with Phoenix? Take it from me that you're never going to be able to call off that rabid team of Florida lawyers. At this point, there is nothing, from what I can see, that pulls you into any criminal risks that Phoenix potentially faces. It's highly unlikely that you'd be affected much by the civil case beyond some possible bad publicity and maybe having to testify at a civil court proceeding. Move on, Bob. Why take any more risk?"

Despite the man's devotion to Skyler, Bob knew that Ron's advice came from two decades of experience evaluating the risks for his extended mob family. His confidence made the rest of the team feel more at ease.

"Skyler, what are the most pressing problems you see hanging out there for us at this point?" Bob asked.

"We are pure as snow without any paper trails that might lead back to Phoenix. I've made certain of that. The money path is a road that leads to nowhere. We're good on our bribe connections. I had a short conversation with two takers who understand their options are either to be prosecuted if they breathe a word, or end up in a shallow grave, compliments of my little lover sitting over there. The lawyers in Florida are truly wild cards in every sense. They are scary smart but also single-focused on their war with Phoenix. Yes, they no doubt figured out it was Midas there waiting to beat them around a little, but there is less than zero proof for them to work with. Midas pulled everything together with a thorough cleanup after he came to. The two lawyers did exactly what I would have done. They got the hell out of the house as quickly as they could without proof of anything. Big screwup, but a big break for us. The Hammer investigation will fritter away over time without a body, no matter what kind of story the lawyers told the po-po. And you know what? The police brass will remember the extra two million in funding you got them last year, Bob, even if they do come around asking questions. So right now, I'm feeling pretty damn good."

"Ron, do we make any more moves on our lawyer friends down in—"

"No!" Midas shouted from across the room where he sat. "They are off limits. No one in this room carries out any kind of threat to anyone in that group. Am I clear enough for all of you?"

No one said a word. Bob was stunned by the outburst. The congressman paused before he spoke. "So, what is that all about, my friend?"

"I'm not your friend," Midas growled. "I'm here only because my sister is, and by the way, my sister understands the importance of following my advice when I give it. You should, too. No one lays a hand on Cara Deketomis or anyone in that law firm. Do we understand each other?"

Skyler indeed understood her brother with every cell in her body, but she had no clue at all why Midas was so adamant about this. However, it was true that she had seen similar reactions from him in the past. The life and death consequences of ignoring his obvious warning was real. Would it be clear to Bob and Ron?

"Got it, little brother," she said. "Loud and clear. Let's move on now."

Midas focused his one good eye on the congressman and hoped the Slick Stick would give him a reason to finally and permanently end Bob Minds's relationship with his sister.

Slightly taken aback by the previous exchange, Ron cleared his throat and said, "One thing to think about, uh, as we say *sayonara* to Phoenix, is that we must continue to develop the natural supply line from their institutions. We would be insane to lose the best quality girls that Skyler develops for our team and the young men who are suited for the work my family relies on. As you think about our recruitment possibilities from those Phoenix facilities, it's important that we keep that gold mine wide open."

Bob already had a plan in mind that would involve one of those quality girls. Despite the outburst from Skyler's brother, nobody was off limits. *I'm in charge here*, Bob thought to himself. He'd already been planning how to push the solidly humiliated Ron Jacobi to organize the dirty work against Deketomis as a last resort. But first he'd try the honey before the sting. The honey had always worked in the past. What Skyler and her freaky brother didn't know wouldn't hurt them.

For two more hours, the four of them focused on the other details involving an inevitable split from Phoenix. It was finally decided that Bob would make one more run at Paul Baker. If it produced nothing, then he would make good on his promise to release a film. An edited video with an unidentifiable nude, buxom woman leading the naked executive around a hotel room with a dog collar. The farther down they could beat Paul mentally and emotionally, the more effective the next warnings would be if they had to go there.

Sayonara.

* * *

The dream woke Deke with a start.

He felt his heart pounding in the dark, but he remained silent so as not to disturb Teri. She was sleeping like an angel.

Dim light from the streetlights on his block filtered in through the window. The familiar shapes in the shadows were all there in the bedroom, and they hadn't changed. Everything was fine. It was just a dream.

He rarely had dreams that frightened him. He supposed he should think of it not as a dream, but more as a nightmare.

The disturbing part was that it was all true.

* * *

1970. Mid-Summer.

Deke sat behind the wheel of the pickup truck, parked three hundred feet away from Sandbury Housing for Boys. He peered out the window through a pair of binoculars that he'd borrowed from the Desmond Ranch.

It was the middle of the afternoon.

He knew he was taking a risk acting as a getaway driver. A big *risk.*

But he had to do it for his friend.

The view from the binoculars revealed the top of the stone fence that surrounded the facility. Both Deke and Bucky thought that the fence was ridiculously easy to climb, and there was no barbed wire at the top like they'd seen in prison movies. Deke wondered why more boys didn't attempt an escape.

Deke looked at his watch. Two on the dot.

Again, through the binoculars . . . nothing was happening at the fence. The plan was that Bucky would be out playing basketball during exercise time. There were so many boys that very few of them actually played the game. The others had to sit on bleachers and watch. It wasn't difficult to slip away, especially for someone who normally kept his head down.

Deke didn't really believe Bucky's claims that he was a Big Man on Campus inside and that he could hold his own against the brutality Deke had heard about. During his visits with Bucky, his friend had told him in whispers about the Little Red House and Fight Night and other horrors that occurred.

Bucky was likely scared to death.

All the more reason for him to escape! Deke had urged Bucky to attempt to flee as soon as possible.

He had finally talked his friend into trying.

Soon they'd be together again.

When it got to be 2:10, Deke's nerves let him know that he was gambling with his future. The actuality of what he was doing suddenly kicked in. Before, it had been merely a fantasy. Help Bucky escape from SHB. Just hop the fence and pick him up in the truck. Take him to the vacation homes area again. Bucky likely wouldn't like that, since it was where he'd earlier been caught and charged with trespassing. But it would be only temporary.

Deke had a lead on a fabulous foster home. He'd done odd jobs for two of the most decent people in Arcadia, where they lived on a small ranch with cattle, horses . . . a swimming pool, tennis court . . . Hell, they had a home right out of Southern Living. *Tad Pearson was one of the most successful businessmen in the county.*

He had spoken to Mr. and Mrs. Pearson about Bucky. They had a small guesthouse they were willing to provide. It sounded idyllic.

Who wouldn't want to live there?

At exactly 2:14, Deke saw hands . . . followed by arms . . . and then a head and shoulders . . . worming over the top of the stone wall. Bucky!

Deke lowered the binoculars and started the pickup.

But then . . . an ALARM SIREN!

Bucky's upper body disappeared in a flash.

Deke felt a cold shiver snake down his spine.

Should he wait? Should he go?

The answer came when he saw Sandbury guards exit the gate and begin to move around the perimeter.

Deke threw the shift into first and took off.

Tears nearly blinded his vision. He made it back to the ranch without discovery, but not without feeling as if he'd personally sent his best friend to the gallows.

25

Gina was told by a board-certified neurologist that she was still suffering from a moderately severe concussion. Rest, avoiding computer work, quiet, low light, and staying away from any levels of sustained excitement would be her world for two weeks. Those warnings kicked around in her still fuzzy head as she sat under bright lights in front of her computer in a noisy room with fully jazzed-up coworkers screaming over one another to be heard. She was concerned that her memory was still unclear about what had occurred at Midas's hands. The order of events was jumbled and incomplete, other than the flashes of Cara dragging her by the arms across the marble floor toward the door, Cara yelling at her to wake up, Cara speeding down a highway while she sat in the back seat, unsure why she was there.

She knew she was not up to it, but Gina would never have sat out the meeting that was taking place at the Bergman-Deketomis law firm. It was rare for Deke to call an all-hands-on-deck meeting regarding the current state of affairs. Two hundred and thirty lawyers, secretaries, paralegals, investigators, and support staff had been shepherded into a cavernous space on the first floor by Diana. Even she didn't know the details of the meeting, and that was rare since Deke referred to Diana as the firm's nerve center. The space was typically used for political gatherings when favored political candidates came to town or for special celebratory events. There was nothing that would be fun at this gathering.

Deke stood at a podium and waited until everyone finally took seats and the raucous conversations ceased. He spoke through a microphone.

"Thank you all for dropping everything and coming this morning. This won't take long, folks, but it's something we need to talk about. Last week there was what we, at least at this point, can only conclude was a well-planned attempt on the lives of Gina Romano and Cara Deketomis. We believe we know who was responsible, but Boston law enforcement has already made it clear to us that they cannot locate this person. The best they can give us is that they believe he has left the country. We don't think he was working alone, but we're told there is no evidence to connect anyone else to the crime. The shorthand to all this is that we're getting almost no cooperation from law enforcement in Boston. We are on our own to keep ourselves safe. Everyone in this room will receive a three-page report detailing what happened in Boston along with a photograph of a man named Midas McDonald. You will also find a couple of variations of that photo where an AI-generated enhancement displays how McDonald might appear dressed as a woman."

There were more than a few nervous laughs from the group, likely generated from an edgy concern. Most of the attendees were aware of incidents that had put the firm's lawyers, investigators, and even secretaries in harm's way. It was not uncommon for Diana's coworkers to jokingly ask if they could buy a life insurance policy on her. This, however, was different. A gathering like this had never taken place at which Deke talked with such intensity and palpable fear for the safety of his employees.

"Folks, I'm asking you to please take this potential threat seriously. If any of you prefer to work from home until my concerns are resolved, you have my blessings. You will find my personal telephone number, along with the numbers of Michael and all our investigation staff, in the material you now have. If something looks out of the ordinary anywhere around this building, please call one of us immediately. Thanks for your time and thank you for the truly incredible work all of you carry out on behalf of people who would often be totally lost without your help. I'd like the Phoenix team to meet with me in my office right after we leave here."

As the group filed out, a quiet buzz of curious and concerned whispers replaced normal conversation. Deke had gotten their attention.

Twenty minutes later, the trial team gathered in Deke's office. Michael had been traveling and conducting interviews with new potential witnesses in three different states and was the last to get the details of the Boston story. Jake had shared with him the seriousness of what the two women had endured, and he could see from the body language what Michael was thinking.

Clue one—Michael had crossed his arms across the front of his midsection. Clue two—he had then leaned back in his chair and run both hands through his thick red hair. Clue three—he had stood and walked around in small circles next to his chair, quietly, without comment. Jake had seen this routine before. The last time it had occurred, Michael had ended up beating two Hulk-like professional bodyguards senseless after they had been instrumental in kidnapping one of his clients.

Michael was the first to speak, addressing Gina and Cara. "Wow, Shield Maiden and Young Amazon Warrior meet Boy George. It all sounds like a great chapter for a book. There are no words that can capture the truth about how impressed and inspired I am by you two." He walked over to the two women who were sitting together, crouched down, and gave them both hugs.

They needed that and appreciated it. Cara's burned and bandaged right hand reached out and wrapped around Michael's neck. She spoke a quiet, "Thank you." Michael then displayed his own right hand where he had the same kind of burn scar on the palm of his hand.

"The business end of that stun gun can sure sizzle when you hold it close and for a long time, but sometimes that's what it takes. What a great show-and-tell you're gonna have. Won't leave much of a scar, but it will be enough for a hell of a story."

Deke watched the touching exchange and knew he needed to move on before he got choked up. He had been struggling with the notion that he had exposed both Gina and his daughter to a danger that could have resulted in their deaths. *I warned you! You wouldn't listen!* But of course he wouldn't say those thoughts aloud. Best to stick to business and move on.

"Let's do a quick review of where we are. Based on that last deposition of Paul Baker, I don't think there is any question that we have enough information to expand the scope of the Sweeton case to a national class case against Phoenix. I'd like to get that class complaint filed this week."

"I'm on it. It will be filed by Thursday," Cara said.

"I think you need to take some time off, Cara, the same as Gina."

"I'm fine, Dad. Really. I'll do the class complaint and then I think it would be good for me to go spend some quality time with Claudia Clapper. I talked to her last week. She is fifty days into rehab, and from where I was sitting, she sounded great. Of course, I can never be sure. The police interviews about the Perkins murder rocked her recovery world just a bit, but she is over that and moving on. I need to find out if my take is just wishful thinking or if it's real. Spend a week with her. Learn her complete life story and get her ready to be put up on the stand in trial."

"I'd feel more comfortable if you stayed put and not be out in the field. I know Claudia's in a safe place, supposedly, but these people, these monsters, they have ways of getting to their enemies."

"Dad, what do I have to do to keep proving my worth? When are you going to trust me? I know you're struggling with some deep, dark secret about your past, but this case is not about you or your past! It's about *all* of us!"

Deke blinked. His inclination was to bark back at his daughter, but he saw the faces of everyone in the room, eyeing him expectantly.

They were on Cara's side.

"Is that what everyone wants? To continue working in the field, despite the dangers?" he asked.

They all resounded with a simultaneous, "*Yes!*"

Cara gave her father a subtle salute and a smile.

He shook his head in defeat. "All right. Fine. But Gina, your job is to follow your doctor's orders for at least the next week. Carol will drive you home after this meeting ends. Okay? Will you give me that?"

From the tone of Deke's no-compromise voice, Gina knew that now wasn't the time to argue the point. Nevertheless, she concluded, "have laptop, will travel." She could help plenty in the unobserved privacy of her home.

Deke continued, jumping right back into the leader role. "Overall, here is my take on where we are. Sometimes no action is the best action.

The things we can control are the pleadings and continuing investigation of the expanded lawsuit against Phoenix. I'm not worried about the Sweeton part of the case. We have enough evidence to more than overpower them in trial. Our attention needs to be on showing a pattern of commonality in the substandard negligent way Phoenix conducts its business at every one of their facilities across the US. My instinct tells me we are almost there. Everything that has happened in the last month is something that we need to regard as noise meant to slow us down. Michael, Carol, Jake . . . let's not allow ourselves to be drawn away from case workup for any kind of 'get even' moment. There is nothing I personally would enjoy more than an independent manhunt and a come-to-Jesus moment with the folks responsible for what happened to our partners. Notwithstanding that, right now we need to remain singularly focused on our emerging national case. There will be opportunities for payback in and out of the courtroom. The three other depositions the judge has granted us are critical. That's where we need to draw blood. Carol, I want you to hire twenty-four-seven security guards around this firm for the next sixty days. Most of you have carry permits, and I'd like you to take advantage of that. Michael, I want you to spend a little time at the range with everyone this week for anyone who wants to go."

Carol responded, "Deke, you need to be aware of the fact that the Boston crime detectives assigned to Gina and Cara's case are absolute clowns. I almost get the impression they don't want answers. When my private investigators up there try to get the slightest bit of information, they're shut down. One of them was almost arrested for asking questions. They say they've seen this before. Someone is spreading around big money in a department that is generally known for its corruption."

"What's the latest story on the Hammer woman?" Deke asked.

"She had no family to push for a broader investigation. The best the idiots up there can say is that there's no body, there's no evidence pointing to who attacked Gina and Cara, and they go as far as suggesting that the whole thing was made up by a bunch of money-grubbing lawyers. Those words were spoken apparently by the number three person heading up the investigation. Everything about what's going on up there sounds as regressive as what we're seeing in Sweeton with that clown car."

As Deke and Carol were speaking, Michael paced the room like a lion planning an attack on unseen prey. He had seen a measured response strategy work in some cases in which violence and threats touched the lives of the staff. Deke's disciplined approach usually worked out, but it felt different this time. Michael had spent too many years as a special ops pararescueman to ever doubt the simple truth that sometimes overpowering a threat required an even more powerful and sustained display of force.

Deke eyed Michael's restlessness but continued talking. "Jake, I need you and Carol to redirect the energy of our Boston investigators to the surveillance of Bob Minds, Skyler Bannock, Paul Baker, and Ron Jacobi. Work out a contract with a limit of two hundred thousand dollars over the next sixty days. All reports need to be reviewed by Michael every twenty-four hours. Jake, I would appreciate you personally going to Boston and overseeing that surveillance operation. Cara, when you're not with Claudia Clapper, how about you and Carol sit down with your AI folks and do a deep dive into that Ron Jacobi fellow? I still have the creeps about that guy."

Michael finally stopped pacing and asked, "Deke, what would you want from me in the next thirty days? I think I've done all the interviews we need, and I've cleared my schedule pretty much for this case."

"You and I will be camped out in the war room for the next couple of weeks diagraming strategy from discovery to trial and potential settlement closure for both Sweeton and our class action."

Everyone in the room, including Michael, knew that was Deke's way of keeping a short leash on his colleague. There was no question in anyone's mind that Michael was already calculating the most direct path to Midas McDonald.

* * *

Paul Baker sat at the foot of his bed in the Boston Raffles hotel suite. At 6:30 that morning, he had appeared in front of a Phoenix management team along with four in-house lawyers. They had informed him that he was officially being placed on a leave of absence pending the investigation that was already underway. The "doggy video," as it had been labeled by Phoenix employees, had been shared on every website that permitted its distribution. Technically, it would be considered mild porn by modern American standards when compared to hardcore material. His face and genitalia were covered to comply with appropriate standards of many sites, but nothing was left to the imagination on the more permissive URLs. Paul's wife and children had viewed the video. The highly respected member of their family was seen with a semi-nude woman issuing doglike obedience commands to him.

Paul was a fighter, though. He had been considered an enforcer on the ice hockey and lacrosse teams on which he had played through his years in school. It was that spirit that had been key to his advancing as a sought-after CEO candidate just five years into his corporate career. As he contemplated the miserable state of his world, his survival instinct briefly emerged. But there were already a few things he was ready to concede as a loss. His wife, his Colorado ski vacation home, at least half of the twenty million dollars he and his wife held in liquid assets, and tons of money he would be paying as future alimony. Maybe in time his son and daughter might forgive him. Paul cared little about what his social friends might conclude. He already regarded most of them as unimportant sycophants who wouldn't pour their cups of latte on him if he were on fire. When he was honest with himself, he despised the parvenus he was forced to endure during summers at the Cape and winters in Aspen.

Nevertheless, there was something that Paul regarded as too important to lose—his career as CEO at Phoenix. His enforcer qualities rose to the surface when he considered his next move in that regard.

He added a plug-in microphone to an external recording device attached to his cell and called a specific person in his organization.

John Spector. Paul's third in command at Phoenix. The one most likely to lay out a trail of criminal corruption by Phoenix.

There were legitimate emails and documents that revealed Spector's footprints back to criminals like the one in the video leading him in a dog collar. In addition to that, a half a dozen other roadmaps led directly to what would be Game Over nightmares for Phoenix, nationally and internationally. And Paul wouldn't stop there. He had the idea of planting new and convincing "Gotcha" documents that he would simply manufacture.

Spector answered on the seventh ring.

"Paul, we've been directed not to have any communication with you," the man said before Paul could speak.

"Well, that's fine, John, for a lot of the folks at Phoenix, but it will be a disaster for you personally if you hang up this phone. Let me get your attention quickly, John, with a 2024 email where you congratulated me for the wonderful new relationship I had just developed with Congressman Bob and that smoking hot hooker that you would like to roll around in the sack with."

"Hold on, Paul, I don't thi—"

"Let me read you the last line here, John. 'Do you think you could arrange one of Skyler's girls to be paired up with me? My wife has become a frigid drag.' Do you remember that email? I bet you thought it would never see the light of day."

"Paul—"

"What you need to understand, John, is that I have a half dozen texts and emails with your name attached that are far worse than that one."

"I don't remember any others on that particular subject," John replied quietly, invoking to Paul the image of a rat scurrying across a carpeted floor.

"Gee, you must have forgotten this one, John. Let me read it to you. It appears right here in my private texts. 'A couple of the guys are wondering if they can meet your girl, Skyler. I guess I ran my mouth too much about the sex machine she set up for me. Senior managers get horny too.' Did I read that right, John? My memory tells me those senior managers were Rick Outland, Joe Thomas, Tom Fidel, and about another four highflyers around our shop. Does that help your memory, John?"

Silence.

"John, are you still there?"

"What do you expect to accomplish with this phone call, Paul? You screwed up. The conclusion is that you're already out of here. There's a mandatory meeting with six key decision-makers tomorrow before this goes to the full board."

"Then your job is easy. Start the politics as soon as I hang up. You know who has the most to lose here. I was with Skyler Bannock twice. You and every one of those whoremongers I just named were with Skyler's concubines dozens of times. By the end of the day, I need every one of those pricks to make damn sure I'm invited to that exclusive meeting tomorrow. No room to fail here, John, for you or for the entire Phoenix Corporation. As you just said to me, back at 'ya—you screwed up, John. Let the boys know Bob Minds's dirty money is just the beginning of where I'm willing to go with this. As you surely must know, I will burn this company down to embers if I must. It needs to be me and those six decision-makers with clear authority to make moves in a room tomorrow. Is that clear enough, John?"

"I'll see what I can do," John whispered.

"I know that you will, Bunky. Isn't that what your girl called you? Bunky?"

Then he ended the call and shut off the recording. For the first time in twenty-four hours, Paul grinned.

26

Deke was midway through his morning walk through the neighborhoods of Spanish Trace, pondering the several cases that were on his plate at the office. At 7:30 in the morning, the sun was already bright, and the Gulf water glistened like sparkling diamonds floating on its moving surface. He loved the ritual of donning sweatpants, T-shirt, tennis shoes, and sunglasses and setting out to get fresh air and a little exercise. His doctor had told him that at his age, it was important to do it. At one time, he had been a gym enthusiast but once he had entered his sixties, Deke had felt out of place in the spaces where twenty- and thirty-somethings dominated the machines and tracks. Besides, walking was more his speed these days. It did the trick.

But while the power walk was supposed to help clear his mind, too, it rarely did. Had he fully dotted all the I's and crossed the T's of that legal document pertaining to the Kaplan case? The preemie baby formula case was heating up; was he ready to dive into it? The Clapper case was quite literally boiling over, ready to explode.

It was the latter matter that occupied a large percentage of his thoughts as of late. He didn't need a psychiatrist's couch to understand that events from his childhood were motivating his drive to cripple Phoenix's operations in the child "protection" business. Deke even visualized those quotation marks around that word when he spoke about it. "Protection" was the last thing those kinds of places did. He knew it from experience.

"Come on, Deke. Escape from the camp is a really bad idea."

Bucky Carlton's voice continued to haunt him, day in and day out. He wanted to shout, "I'm sorry, Bucky! You were right! It *was* a really bad idea!"

But he kept it in. He'd kept it in for over five decades.

And it was tearing him up.

Arcadia . . .

Did he dare return to that place? Was he strong enough to go back and revisit his childhood and teenage years, where he had lived in the homes of decent people who had taken him in without judgement or expectation of any kind of reward? Yes, he had been one of the luckier ones. They were relatively good experiences for him. He had known foster kids in the child protection system for which that was not the case.

And then there was his best friend. Bucky Carlton.

What happened to him was a tragedy and a crime. And it was a millstone around Deke's neck.

He knew very well that until he confronted that demon, he would never rest easy. He owed it to Teri, Cara, and Andy, and to his friends and colleagues at the law firm.

The problem was that he never wanted to step foot in Arcadia again.

"Hey, mister!"

The female voice startled him.

Deke looked over at one of the many vacation home rentals that faced the oceanfront. An attractive blonde woman wearing gym shorts and a tight-fitting tank top stood by a white SUV that was parked in the driveway. The hatch was open, and inside was a large, flat screen television.

Deke stopped walking.

"Could you possibly help me?" the woman called out. "This thing is *really* heavy." She indicated the television and then pointed to the front door of the house, which was open.

Deke figured she was one of the many visitors to Florida who took advantage of the excellent waterfront properties in the area. He noted the address number of the house and filed it away with the name of the street where he stood.

"My husband won't arrive until tomorrow," she called out. "I really need some help, if you don't mind."

The Good Samaritan in Deke kicked in, and he crossed the road to the house.

"Just moving in?" he asked her.

"Yeah." She held out a hand. "I'm Jenny."

He shook it. "Deke. Sure, I'll help you with that."

"Oh, thank you so much. You're a gentleman."

Jenny appeared to be in her mid-thirties and had the looks of a fashion model. There was also quite a bit of bare skin showing. Long legs, prominent cleavage, and an exposed midriff. The woman was barefoot. Blue eyes, shoulder-length platinum blonde hair, high cheekbones. Truly a stunner.

Even though Deke was happily married, he was also a man. He could appreciate beauty and youth. His head could turn. It was natural. However, he was of the same school of thought once expressed by the late actor, Paul Newman. Newman had a long, happy marriage to actress Joanne Woodward. When a reporter once asked him how he handled rumors of infidelity with any of the beautiful starlets and fans who might come on to him, Newman had replied, "I have steak at home. Why should I go out for hamburger?"

Together, Deke and Jenny managed to wiggle the flat screen out of the back of the SUV, and they set it on the driveway.

"Are you able to handle one end?" Deke asked.

"Sure. I just couldn't lift the whole thing by myself," Jenny replied. "The man at the store helped me get it in the car. I didn't know how I was going to get it in the house, though. Luckily, you came along. I appreciate it. Are you ready?"

"I am. Lift with your legs, not your back," Deke advised.

"Oh, I know. My legs are probably my greatest attribute, don't you think?"

That was the first red flag that popped into Deke's mind. Was she flirting with him?

They both squatted and took opposite ends of the television, lifted it off the pavement, and then moved toward the front door. Jenny was on the end walking backward.

"Don't let me trip on anything," she said.

Deke thought it might have been safer for her had she worn shoes, but he didn't say anything.

After a bit of navigating, they got it through the open door and into the foyer of the house.

"Where do you want it?" Deke asked.

"We'll make a left turn into the family room right . . . here."

The space already had furniture—a couch and a couple of comfy chairs and a coffee table.

"Let's just set it on the floor," she said.

Once it was down, Deke stretched his arms and back. He had already worked up a sweat on his walk. He noted that Jenny's skin was glistening with moisture, too.

"When my husband arrives tomorrow, we'll mount it on the wall and hook it up. Thank you *so* much, Deke."

"My pleasure."

"Can I get you some water or something?"

That actually sounded like a good thing. He had forgotten his water bottle that particular morning.

"If you don't mind, that would be nice," he said. "But then I need to get going. Have to get to the office."

She gestured for him to follow her to the kitchen, where a few boxes of vacationing supplies sat on counters, opened but unemptied. "The fridge has a great water dispenser," she said. One of the cupboards already contained glassware she had obviously been stocking. She grabbed a glass, stuck it into the refrigerator's dispenser cubby, and filled it. She handed it to him and then filled a glass for herself.

The water was cool and refreshing. "Thanks," Deke said after downing it. "Well, it was nice meeting you, Jenny, but now I need to go."

"Aw, do you have to?" She put a hand on her hip and struck a pose. "You seem like a really nice guy. Why don't I make some coffee? We can sit and get to know each other for a little while."

Second red flag.

"That's kind of you, Jenny, but I really need to get going."

He began to move out of the kitchen, but she slipped around him and blocked the way. With a maneuver smoother than silk, Jenny wrapped both arms around Deke's neck, her face just inches away from his.

"Come on, Deke, I *know* you don't really want to leave. We can have some fun, what do you say?"

Third red flag, and it was the clincher.

Deke reached up, took hold of her forearms, and gently removed them from his body. "No, Jenny. I'm leaving now."

Then she backed up. "Wait. Don't go." She stood in the archway that separated the kitchen from the hallway and foyer. "Maybe this will change your mind." With that she grabbed hold of her top, pulled it over her head, and tossed it away. She was now fully exposed from the waist up, revealing a perfect female human specimen.

It was all now very clear to Deke what was happening.

He turned his head to eye the cardboard boxes on the counter. One had a hole on the side. Deke grabbed that one, picked it up, and emptied its contents onto the kitchen floor. Pots and pans spilled out with a loud clang . . . along with a camera of some kind. He quickly bent down and picked it up. Deke didn't know how it operated, but he knew it had surely gotten shots of him with a half-naked woman.

Deke reached into his shorts and pulled out his phone.

Jenny, her act now revealed, covered herself with both arms. "What are you doing?"

Deke hit Michael's speed dial. When he answered, Deke said, "Michael, I need you at—" It was a good thing he had earlier noted the address of the house. He spit it out and continued. "Now. As fast as you can. May Day."

When he hung up, he said to the woman, "I just phoned my associate, who is an attorney. I happen to be an attorney, too. Did your employers tell you that?"

Now wide-eyed and frightened, Jenny shook her head.

"Jenny, should I call the police, too?"

"Please, don't."

"Put on your clothes. Maybe we can sit and talk about this situation when my colleague arrives. And maybe you can help us with some information. And maybe . . . just maybe . . . you can walk away from a solicitation and attempted extortion charge that I promise I can make stick."

* * *

It was midafternoon when Deke called into his office the team of Carol, Jake, and Cara. Michael was already there. Gina was at home still recuperating from the injuries she had incurred in Boston. Once everyone was settled in their seats, Deke spoke.

"I had an interesting morning before work. It involves our friends Congressman Bob Minds and his partner in crime, Skyler Bannock. Whether or not anyone from Phoenix is involved remains to be seen, but I doubt it."

"What happened, Dad?" Cara asked.

Deke looked at Michael, who took over the narrative. "It's a little embarrassing for Deke, so I'll speak for him. First, let me assure you that Deke handled himself with absolute propriety, and he's already spoken to Teri about it, too." He acknowledged Cara. "Your mother understands the situation perfectly and agreed that we handled it properly."

"What the hell is going on?" Carol blurted. "Are you going to cut to the chase, or what?"

"This morning while Deke was on his daily exercise walk, he was propositioned by one of Skyler Bannock's ladies of the night, or in this case, lady of the morning."

"What?" Jake coughed.

"Where? How?" Cara gasped.

Michael held up his hands. "Don't get alarmed. Everything is fine. We managed to turn the situation into something that's in our favor." He then went on to tell them exactly what had occurred from the moment the woman stopped Deke on the street to when Michael arrived at the house to run interference.

"Her name is Katharine Dunham, but her 'working' alias is Jenny. Thirty-four years old and a resident of Washington, DC. She had cameras set up in the kitchen, the living room, and the, uhm, bedroom. Of course, Deke never made it there. The plan was to catch Deke in a compromising situation with Jenny and use it to blackmail him and our firm into dropping the lawsuit. Very typical kind of shakedown operation that we're now seeing is the *modus operandi* of this sleazy, corrupt congressman who is a disgrace to our government and nation. Needless to say, we confiscated the cameras. None of the preliminary photos from the kitchen had been uploaded, so Deke is safe from any public embarrassment."

"Oh, my Lord," Carol said. "What happened to Jenny?"

"Well, we sat her down and read the riot act to her. Much of what we said may—or may not—have been totally the truth as to what could have happened to her legally, but it's pretty clear that if we had called the police or FBI, she would have been in a lot of trouble. But we cut a deal with her. She gave us a statement on the camera of my phone along with a hastily written affidavit that it was Congressman Minds who put her up to the job and was paying her. She also stated that she normally worked for Skyler Bannock, but she wasn't certain if Skyler was aware of this particular job. It was Minds who had contacted her, paid an advance fee, and flew her down to Florida. He'd set up the vacation house and everything. Quite a bit of money and quick maneuvering went into this operation, and all just to get a few photos."

"So you let her go?" Carol asked.

"Yes. After we got what we wanted, there was no reason to press charges. She was actually quite remorseful once she realized who Deke was. She didn't know he was an attorney, just thought he was some schmuck who would jump at the chance to have a roll with a woman like her. It's what she usually makes her living doing. She *said* that no man had ever turned her down. Deke did."

"Of course he turned her down," Cara said. "He's my father!"

Everyone had a laugh at that, including Deke.

"Not that I'm defending anything this woman did," Jake said, "but are we sure she's going to be safe now? I mean, what if Minds sics his bulldog, Midas McDonald, on her?"

Deke answered that one. "He wouldn't dare. Minds will know she talked and that we already have her telling her story on camera. If anything happens to her, there's a direct link straight to him. And because *he's* the one who targeted me, then that provides us with an indirect but strong connection between Minds and the Phoenix case. I believe we have enough to tie up that connection for a jury if we actually go to trial and not reach a well-engineered settlement with Phoenix."

"Wow," Cara said. "Congratulations, Dad. I have to say, though, I'm sorry you had to endure all that."

Deke turned a little red in the face and shrugged. "Oh, it wasn't too traumatic . . ."

* * *

"Why in hell did you not tell me about this? Are you mad?"

Skyler Bannock stood over Bob Minds as he sat on the sofa with a drink in his hand. Skyler had been pacing around his Washington, DC, apartment like an angry leopard on the prowl. As soon as she had heard about what had happened in Florida, she had rushed to confront her partner.

"Jenny screwed up," Bob said. "It's her fault."

"Jenny did *not* screw up. *You* did. What's wrong with you? Jenny's one of *my* girls! You don't go sending any of my girls on jobs without my knowing about it! Did you really think this would work on that man Deketomis? He's not your average corporate executive or corrupt political opponent you can extort. Look, Bob, we've been very successful in the operations with my ladies, but I'm the one who plans those operations. I study the target and decide which girl is the most likely to succeed with that target. I set up the situation and the scenario. You have likely exposed us to an unnecessary risk of criminal prosecution, you fool. It's not like we don't already have enough to worry about. And even if there is no threat of an actual prosecution, how would all this look on the House floor when you're brought up in front of the Ethics Committee?"

"That's not going to happen, Skyler. Aw, hell." Bob threw his martini glass across the room, where it shattered against the wall. "We'll have to take care of Jenny. Make sure she shuts up."

"The hell we will. Don't you dare think about it. Jenny did nothing wrong. In fact, I've sent her away with a nice payoff. She's gone. It's not worth pursuing. I'm more concerned about what my *brother* is going to think. Remember his little admonition?"

"Oh, your brother is the least of my concerns." Bob stood and went to the bar to make himself another drink. "Frankly, I'm sick of your crazy brother. He's been useful, but his sudden turnaround with regard to those lawyers in Florida has me more than perturbed. If he weren't your kin . . ."

"Stop right there, Bob. Don't even go there." Skyler eyed the drink he was making and decided to join him. She grabbed a tumbler and poured it full of vodka. She downed half of it and refilled it to the top. Skyler was well aware that Midas had strange tendencies, especially when it came to his female victims. If they proved to be independent sorts who could best him . . . they reminded him of *her*. "Look, I know Midas has issues. He's my stepbrother, you know. Our mother treated him like a pet, but his father treated him like a dog, if you can understand the difference. But I love him, and he loves me. We make a macabre pair of siblings, I admit it. But, don't ever ignore what he has done for us. Some of your dirty work never would have been completed without him. So don't you dare make any kind of half-assed veiled threats about him. Am I being clear enough about that?"

"I know, I know . . . forget I ever mentioned it. The more important thing is to move forward with our plans to bite Paul Baker in the ass and sever our relationship with Phoenix. The further away we can get from them, the better."

"I agree."

With that, there was a slight pause, and then they reluctantly clinked their glasses together.

Fine, Bob thought. So the honey trap didn't work after all. He had tried to settle the matter with Deketomis without bloodshed. He was a true believer in the idea that every organization was only as sustainable as its leader. In his mind, the Deketomis group was no different. The Florida lawyers were vipers who simply would not go away, and it was now time to cut off the head of the snake.

As soon as Skyler left the apartment and before he boarded his private jet back to Boston, Bob would make a call to Ron Jacobi.

27

The investigators Carol hired as a surveillance team had been submitting reports for five days, but Michael's attention focused on something that came from one of their own.

Jake had gotten lucky at Logan International Airport. Ron Jacobi had arrived at the airport in a black SUV driven by an Asian driver. The vehicle parked illegally in a pickup section outside terminal E, which was dedicated specifically for international flights. The driver obviously spent most of his life in gyms that catered to steroid-injected behemoths who made their livings protecting wealthy people and breaking legs when the occasions called for it. Jake had snapped half a dozen photos of Ron and his Frankenstein's monster standing at the loading zone while he talked on the phone, waiting for an arriving passenger.

The man Ron and his driver met wore a leather trench coat, indicating that he came from a cold environment. He had the face of a boxer who had lost too many fights. A leather pork pie hat partially covered bright blond hair cut in a 1980s mullet. Jake noticed that the man, who towered over Ron, failed to shake hands. Jake had caught a few shots of the man's carry-on luggage and the jewelry on both hands, but these would have to be examined more closely at the office. Without delay, the driver loaded the man's bag into the back of the SUV, the three got into the car, and it drove away.

Jake had Carol check the times of all flights that had arrived within fifteen minutes of the pickup. The information was not particularly helpful, but Jake could rule out China, Japan, and Saudi Arabia if he were making big money bets. He leaned more toward the arrivals from Denmark and Germany as points of origin based on the man's European vibe.

From the airport, Jake followed the SUV to a small Italian restaurant in Boston's North End. A sign directly above the main entrance said it all: JACOBI'S. Instead of going through the front door, though, Ron and his guest walked to what appeared to be a private entrance on the side of the freestanding red brick building. They remained inside for less time than it would take to eat a meal. Pork Pie Hat exited carrying a suitcase he hadn't had when he'd entered. Ron and Pork Pie were seen saying goodbye again without handshakes. From there, the SUV drove the newcomer to a small hotel also near Battery Wharf.

Jake parked outside the hotel and waited for several hours until concluding that Pork Pie Hat was in for the night.

Carol and Jake then began working shifts at the hotel. She had been sitting in the lobby for several hours before she decided to ask the female clerk at the front desk if the man she described had checked out.

"Yes, ma'am, I believe he did." The woman looked up the registration. "Yes, he checked out and left at 3:30 this morning."

"Hm. Well, darn. I was supposed to drive him around Boston today," Carol said, wondering how they could have missed the massive man leaving the hotel. "He had hired my tour service." Carol pulled out her phone and pretended to scroll through it. "I have his name here somewhere. Starts with a G, right?" She then casually displayed the folded fifty dollar bill stuck between the fourth and fifth fingers of her right hand.

That, plus Carol's demeanor, put the clerk at ease. "Actually, no, it starts with an M. Mr. Meier."

"Yeah, here it is, Meier. He had a heavy accent on the phone. German? Russian?"

"I believe he was German. I could be wrong, though." The clerk giggled.

"You don't know where he might be headed, do you? I really need this job!"

"I don't, but . . ." The clerk leaned forward and whispered. "He had the personality of a hyena. And he had edges of colorful tattoos peeking through both sleeves and his collar. And his pock-marked face, fingernails that were too long, and horrendous bad breath was a little unbearable. I thought it was odd when he asked to use the back entrance to the hotel. Said that was where a car was picking him up. Looks like someone skated you on this pickup, sweetheart. Probably a good thing."

"Oh, well, then. He sounds like a charmer," Carol said. "Thank you. I'll just delete this appointment." She slapped the fifty dollars on the counter and winked at the clerk.

Leaving the hotel, she immediately got on the phone to Jake to include the information in his report.

Carol and Jake concluded there was a high probability that Ron Jacobi's friend was not in the United States for a quick vacation. Michael agreed. What had always made Michael such a remarkable success in trial was that he was never a believer in coincidences. He never counted on luck. With Carol's new information, he immediately put one investigator at the Pensacola airport, which was the closest to Spanish Trace, and he also assigned one to beat the bushes with three local commercial businesses that provided general aviation services, or Fixed Base Operators, and several car rental companies to see if Meier was possibly going to make an appearance anywhere close to Deke's hometown.

Michael spent hours with the firm's tech group using the Nationview AI software they had in place as a facial recognition system, but they came up with zero leads. Calls made to friends in law enforcement turned up no information about Jacobi's new friend. Michael was ready to resign himself to the reality that, minus a lucky break, Meier would have to be treated as a ghost who might suddenly be loose around town. Was he a threat to the Deketomis team? Michael hated those kinds of questions when it came to the safety of the folks at the firm.

He got his first break through Deke's friend, Tom Sheridan, who owned a local flight operation business. Tom had always been helpful to the firm when information was needed. He confirmed that the ghost had arrived at a Pensacola FBO thirty minutes earlier on a Falcon jet that had originated in New Hampshire. The tail number NJ333 could be traced to a corporation registered through the FAA registry as being owned by Astro Industries in California. The ghost had picked up a two-day FBO rental of a black Toyota Corolla that could be followed with GPS. With the help of Tom Sheridan, the man who had been a ghost an hour earlier was now a big blue dot moving around a screen.

The dot eventually stopped outside the Azalea Fountain Bar and Grill in the late afternoon. In Michael's view, the potential predator had now become the prey.

A half hour later, Michael was comfortably sitting at a table in the Azalea with a plate of chicken wings and a Michelob Lite. The bar at that time was almost empty. The few servers were setting up tables in expectation of the regular happy hour crowd.

Meier was at the dark and quiet end of the bar. He spoke to no one and avoided being spoken to. His well-worn white shirt rolled up to the elbows revealed the tattoos the report had mentioned. His fully developed forearms and biceps couldn't be missed. It was difficult to see the pock-marked face, but Jake had gotten it right when he described features that had beared the brunt of a few bare fists or boxing gloves.

Michael had no intention of calling Deke. Or Mark Prom. Or anyone at the firm who might demand that he get the local authorities involved. Michael had every reason to believe that he was better trained and equipped to handle any potential threat that might develop with the area's new visitor. His intention was to bring about finality to any kind of threat Pork Pie might pose to Deke or anyone else in his family or firm.

He left the bar and parked his car in a position with a clear view of Meier. He had no intention of tailing the man. He had total confidence in Tom Sheridan, who agreed to sit at his GPS surveillance computer until the threat had passed. Sheridan would stay in communication with Michael day and night if required. His loyalty to Deke was the only motivation Tom needed.

The next move the blue dot made would tell Michael everything he needed to know about that night's mission.

* * *

Deke was alone in the war room working and wondering why Michael Carey wasn't answering his phone, when Jeff and Peter rushed in.

"Gentlemen?" he asked, seeing that his two colleagues appeared to be overly excited.

Peter announced, "Deke! It looks like you're back on the Kaplan case! The angry little judge just had her butt handed to her in the twenty-five-page appellate opinion. They actually used these words . . ."

Jeff continued, reading off the document. "'The rulings by this trial court seem to be emerging as a pattern when we consider them together with other appeals that have originated out of her trial court. There is an apparent unwillingness to fully embrace the directives of both the Florida State Constitution and the Federal Constitution. For all the reasons stated in the body of this order, this case should be transferred to a trial judge within the Northern District where that judge does not have connections with lawyers appearing in front of her that might give rise to questions of judicial impropriety.'"

Peter went on, "That is by far the strongest go-to-hell language I've seen in any appellate order in my entire career."

"More importantly, this is so strong that no one from our firm will have to appear in front of Ashworth in any case. We didn't win completely on the gag order question, but the problem with your public statements about the Kaplan family will more than likely never be an issue in front of the newly assigned judge, whoever that might be."

Deke clasped his hands together and shook them in a "champion" gesture. Then he asked, "How about the overall public policy question we raised about the need to disclose confidential corporate information when there's a present risk to consumers? Did we get any help there?"

Jeff answered, "No, they kicked that can down the road but they did say the issue needs to be addressed legislatively, as if that is ever going to happen. Look, Deke, we dodged a bullet here. Had you been permanently removed from this case, both Peter and I were concerned that it would tarnish both you and our firm. We need to declare victory and crank up the machine full tilt again to go after these devilish bastards."

"Don't get me wrong, guys. I'm thrilled about what you're telling me," Deke said. "We live to fight these other issues another day. Thank you from the bottom of my heart for saving my bacon. But can you give me a couple more weeks before I have to totally jump back in? The

Phoenix case is in full scramble right now, and I have a couple of critical moves I need to make."

"All good, Deke," Peter answered. "The Kaplans are already dead men walking. All we need to do is finish digging their shallow graves."

"Great. Oh, by the way, have you guys seen Michael around the office today?"

Both men shook their heads and made their exit. Deke dialed Michael again and contemplated calling his wife, Mona, to make sure all was well. He decided against it. While he knew that Michael could take care of himself and that perhaps he needed a bit of peace and quiet for a day or two, Deke's sixth sense was blinking yellow.

28

The next morning, the blue dot drove by the Deketomis house twice. This told Michael everything he needed to know about the man's intentions. The leash he had on Meier was now comfortably tight. Michael had all the advantages. He knew the hotel the man was using as a home base to store whatever equipment on which he was relying. It was also a place to change clothes if needed. It was doubtful the man would remain in town any longer than necessary after his work was done. More than likely he would drive north from the Florida panhandle and rendezvous with a private jet in either Alabama or Georgia.

Luckily, his target had no way of knowing that Michael was processing this information. It was significant that the man had not driven by the law firm or the homes of other Bergman-Deketomis employees. Just Deke's. Ron Jacobi's plan was apparently to go all the way to the top of the pyramid and cause as much trauma for the firm as possible. Was he driven by the humiliation he had suffered at Deke's hands or by a plan driven by strategic design?

It made no difference to Michael. He knew Meier, if that was his real name, would be a dead man by the end of the night. Jacobi, as well as the people with whom he was associated, would understand what shock and awe looked like.

He had been avoiding calls from Jake, Carol, Diana, and Deke all day. He had left his phone at home so he wouldn't get busted with a phone locator app. Jake and Carol were still at work in the Boston area and had no idea just how close to Jacobi's friend Michael was. Tom

Sheridan and any of the few investigators with a scintilla of knowledge about Jacobi's friend had been asked to keep a lid on what they knew. No discussion to anyone, including Deke.

Secrecy was critical. Michael had indeed thoroughly considered the obvious risks of what he was about to do. When it came to outmaneuvering another predator, the most serious threat to Michael would be potential criminal prosecution if his plan didn't go well. Killing Meier with a sniper rifle would likely guarantee he would be prosecuted. That move would be considered premeditated murder, regardless of the serious threat to Deke. The facts would be clear and simple to present to a grand jury. Michael had stalked a man all day. He had failed to give local law enforcement the opportunity to arrest the man without any loss of life. He had concealed his intentions from everyone involved. He had failed to communicate with anyone for fear that they might interfere with his intent to murder the predator. It would be a pretty tight case against him. In America, even the evilest people shouldn't simply be murdered in cold blood.

What about allowing the police to take over? No, an arrest of the man would be useless because of all the rules of law. The man hadn't done anything. Yet. Meier likely played by no rules. The next predators Jacobi hired would operate the same way.

For several years Michael had been required to end the lives of enemies that disregarded rules. The killing fields for Michael were deserts, mountain ranges, and even city streets in places like Afghanistan, Iraq, and Somalia. But the mission was clear: protect the lives of innocent people. In Michael's mind, what he was planning was no different than that.

The man in the pork pie hat needed killing. Michael was willing to take the risk to send a clear message to Ron Jacobi and whoever else was part of the plan to murder or seriously harm Nick Deketomis.

That message was, *We Can Do That, Too!*

* * *

At 8:15 in the evening, Michael sat in his car parked three blocks away from the Deketomis home. Deke and Michael had long ago arranged for the ability of an app to track Deke's car should one of the inner circle need to do so. Michael studied the screen on his phone and watched as the dot representing Deke's car made its way from the office toward the family home. There was no blue dot following it.

That was because Michael already had eyes on the predator's Toyota. It was parked in front of a neighborhood public park four blocks from Deke's home. Meier sat on a bench in the park. The man was dressed in dark blue slacks and a black pullover. Invisible in the dark. At the same time, he didn't appear overly suspicious if he were to be stopped on the street.

Michael had chosen similar clothing for the same reasons, except his black exercise sweats provided a more plausible explanation. He also carried a runner's strobe light and had a bright fluorescent white shirt underneath his hooded black sweat top to add a little more credibility to what would be his night jogging story.

The app indicated that Deke had pulled into his garage. It was 8:35. Now it was a waiting game. Michael anticipated Meier to make his move sometime after 1:00 a.m.

At 12:45, the former PJ was set up and well-hidden on Deke's home property. The Moon Glow lights that had been installed all around the home cast the entire area with the illumination of a full moon. Michael knew that this could possibly expose him as easily as the predator, so the choices of actions needed to be well considered. If his predictions were correct, the first move the predator would make would be to disable the home security system. Michael had a clear view of the area where that would occur. The next step would be to observe the man as he chose the most exposed place to break in. Michael had a strong instinct where that would be.

He sat quietly and perfectly concealed, armed with a scoped Winchester .223 and a Glock G19 nine millimeter. He considered all the variables. If anything went wrong, Michael could end up in prison at best and dead at worst, but one certainty was that Deke and his wife Teri would wake up alive in the morning.

At 1:45 a.m., Meier made his appearance. He, of course, no longer wore the hat. Instead, his head and face were covered in a black ski mask much like Michael's. His movements displayed a level of easiness and athleticism that Michael expected for such a professional. The man was deliberate, skillful, and quick as he moved across the property to the exact spot Michael had anticipated. It took him less than ten minutes to disarm the door and window security alarm. Michael guessed that the man was willing to take his chances with any other interior security alarms. Even if they went off, he would have time to rain hell inside the Deketomis home.

Michael stealthily darted to the back of the house near the pool. He flattened against a wall in the shadows and watched. He'd been correct that this was where the predator would make his point of entry.

Meier approached the large glass door that accessed the house. Equipped with an effective glass cutter and suction tool, the man silently removed a six-by-six inch section. It took a great deal of willpower for Michael to wait and not attack the guy then and there. But instead he watched as Meier attached a silencer to a short-barreled automatic pistol and then returned his tools to a black bag hanging at his waist.

The predator reached through the hole in the glass to disable the interior secondary lock.

Michael still waited. He wanted the man to actually enter the house. He would kill him inside.

Finally, ten seconds later, Meier made his move. He slid open the glass door.

Michael pushed off the wall and began hurrying toward the back door.

A deafening shotgun blast reverberated in the night air.

Meier hurdled backward, crashing through the closed half of the glass door.

Michael froze in the shadows.

Deke appeared and stood over the predator with the shotgun aimed at the man's head. He gave the lifeless body a powerful kick. Perhaps it was to verify that the intruder was dead. Or maybe it was expressing his hatred for the villain who had come to do harm to him and his family.

Michael knew that he couldn't stay. He swiftly retraced his route back to his car without having to stash his weapons along the way.

Knowing Deke, he was pretty sure that the police hadn't been called when he first became aware that someone was breaking in. Deke was smart and disciplined enough to wait for the opportunity to permanently remove the threat.

As he exited the property, behind the wheel of his car, Michael laughed aloud with triumph. The victory wasn't his, but he was still just as happy about it.

Soon he was gone, as if he'd never been there at all.

29

It was a big story with legs that carried it to the front pages of even mid-sized newspapers, TV, and radio shows.

LAWYER KILLS MURDER SUSPECT HUNTED BY INTERPOL

The folks at Bergman-Deketomis were not accustomed to seeing such overwhelmingly positive publicity about Deke and their firm. Their organization had won huge battles on behalf of American consumers in the tobacco and opioid wars, as well as huge victories against the largest pharma and chemical manufacturers on the planet, but they had never received publicity this significant.

The man Deke had blown in half right at his home was indeed named Meier, but he also had a half dozen other aliases. During his most recent visit to America, he was Claus Meier. In his heyday five years prior, Meier was regarded as one of the more active paid killers, typically connected to only mob hits. According to the reported information, he had disappeared for three years. The articles mentioned that no one from the Deketomis firm had any theories as to why the seasoned killer had shown up in their community to break into the Deketomis home. Nick Deketomis had described it as a total mystery. He joked that he does run an aggressive law firm. "Mobsters wouldn't have any interest in us," he was quoted as saying, "unless they were Wall Street criminals."

* * *

The entire Pensacola-Spanish Trace area was alive with people claiming they had talked to, eaten with, or smoked a cigar with the killer. On the other hand, Tom Sheridan, the owner of the FBO where Claus Meier had landed, played it cool by telling reporters, “He was just another jet arrival. There was nothing particularly interesting about him.”

Meanwhile, in another part of the country, Ron Jacobi sat in a quiet hotel room with the local newspaper in his lap. He had already received a half dozen phone calls asking for details about the botched hit attempt. His extended family was angry that the move had been ordered without their approval. They attacked him for being sloppy, short-sighted, and a threat to the organization. Ron knew there were already meetings taking place at which he was the topic of discussion . . . and he wasn’t invited.

An older uncle, one of the family patriarchs everyone called “Pope,” instructed Ron to begin the process of putting an end to his relationship with Congressman Minds. The powerful family figure connected all the dots, and Ron had to admit he was accurate. Phoenix in bed with Minds was one of the sore points. Pope simply didn’t like that arrangement, but he did have some words of comfort. “There’s no harm in you spending time with or even marrying that beautiful whore, Ronnie,” he had said, “but you can’t carry all the Bob Minds baggage with it.”

Ron had understood his uncle’s message, especially when Pope said that anything going forward had to be cleared with him first. No exceptions.

That had been hours earlier. After taking a couple of sips from his teacup, Ron threw the newspaper on the floor and dialed the old man again.

“Ronnie,” Pope said, “I thought our conversation was over. What is it? Be quick.”

“I heard you loud and clear, Pope,” Ron managed to say with the exuberance of a nephew eager to please. “But I just want to be a little clearer on a couple of things so I can do exactly as you wish. First of all, thank you for a pass to carry on with the woman I truly love. I wanted to make sure I have permission to carry on the business that she oversees. It can be effective for our family. Secondly, I will cut ties with Bob, but I wasn’t sure about how complete that should be.”

"You may not know this, Ronnie, but my wife of forty-five years started out in the same business as the one your friend now runs. I could not have found a more perfect wife, so I understand your devotion. As to the congressman, there's no need to do a thing. He will fade away when we begin drying up his money. He is a nobody who will live the rest of his life as such. Take your lady and walk away. But hear me clearly, Ronnie. No more screwups. I will try to make sure you weather this, but don't make me regret it. I have lunch at the club scheduled, so I'm going now." The old man ended the call.

Ron stared at the phone in his hand. There was something about what his uncle had said and the way he'd said it. *I will try to make sure you weather this.*

He considered a truth that he had been willing to ignore. Pride always surfaced right before the fall.

* * *

Midas McDonald was another person among many who were interested in the Claus Meier story.

I can't believe Bob totally ignored the warning you gave him. Sorry for the disrespect he showed you.

The note had been enclosed with the packet of newspaper clippings about the attempted break-in and murder. Midas's sister was communicating much more than an apology.

It was an approval, a green light, an invitation to come home and take care of business.

No wonder he loved his sister so much! The two stepsiblings had completed each other's sentences as children. He liked to think that they shared the same soul.

* * *

Teri and Deke sat on the cushions at the bow of their thirty-eight-foot center console dive boat, fifteen miles off the coast from the back door of their home. It was a private space that was impossible to duplicate. The

Gulf of Mexico was a slick calm, and it had the appearance of an endless mirror. Schools of baitfish churned the water in places in their efforts to escape unseen larger fish hunting for a late afternoon meal. A pod of four dolphins broke the surface every few minutes, likely chasing their own prey. There was plenty of food all around.

A couple of days on the boat with only the two of them aboard was a medicine that Teri administered for Deke, usually after long trials. Obliterating the body of a professional hit man with a shotgun, Teri figured, was at least as stressful as a two- to three-week battle in a courtroom.

Who valued these respites the most? Deke had told Teri on a regular basis that his private time with her, be it at dinner, having drinks in a cozy corner of one of the area's decades-old honky-tonks, or simply sitting quietly in their home with books in hand was enough medicine for him. Teri knew these weren't empty words. She had seen him heal quickly so many times, right before her eyes. And, sometimes, Teri intensely grilled him during these instances, forcing him to provide answers to probing questions. This, in itself, was a process that they both had found therapeutic.

Deke often shared with her details of what he was planning in a trial or his concerns about the functioning of the firm. His confidence in Teri had originated thirty years earlier when she saved his life. He had been flying into the path of a student pilot who had moved into controlled airspace without notice to either ground or tower controllers. Teri was working in the Pensacola airport tower and directed him to make an immediate turn away from the converging aircraft. Her command to make that quick portside turn cleared his starboard wing from an approaching catastrophe by less than seventy yards. They became close friends after that near miss and were married two years later. In the course of their thirty-three-year marriage, Deke had regularly relied on her analytical input. Today was no different as they reviewed where Deke and the firm had landed after what Teri referred to as "too many weeks of weird."

"I'm just curious, Deke," she said, her sunglasses covering the soulful eyes he knew so well. "What was your reasoning for the narrative you spun? Why this Claus guy would show up at our home wanting to kill you. Never mind what happened with that woman who accosted you in our neighborhood, but wouldn't it be safer to let law enforcement know that Phoenix or that congressman might be behind both that and this more serious attempt on your life?"

Deke held up a finger, something he did to make a point. "It's what they expect me to do. Right now I've left the door open for Phoenix to negotiate with me. If I blow this thing up, Phoenix would basically be unable to do that. I'm banking that they don't want a huge civil case, which is the thing that we, as a firm, do and are good at. They also want to be sure they're out of the woods on potential criminal indictments if I should demand a criminal probe. Also, Teri, between me, you, and those four dolphins over there, I legitimately don't have enough evidence against Phoenix to convince a DOJ prosecutor to go after them. We have plenty for a civil trial. Involving the DOJ would also add months, even years, to these proceedings. What I do have is the advantage of them *believing* that I have enough evidence and could release it today, tomorrow, or a month from now. It's a strategy I like to call the 'night sweat threats.' Where in the middle of the night you start projecting your very worst fears that most of the time are wildly unreasonable. I predict I'll be getting a call from their legitimate negotiators within the next week. Closure is what they need now, not criminal edge controversy. They will *want* to settle, and I'm confident I can get exactly what we want from them, like better facilities and qualified employees."

"What about that congressman? Isn't he still a threat? What you told me about the murders of those poor people in Sweeton tells me they aren't afraid of violence and that really concerns me about Cara's safety. She's caught up in the middle of all this. No one saw the attack on Gina and Cara coming, and there is no way to know if it can happen again."

"Cara took it upon herself to go to Colorado to be with Claudia. She'll be there for at least the next couple of weeks. As far as the congressman is concerned, if he's behind this, he overplayed his hand. Any relationship he had with Phoenix, I'm guessing, is history. If I had disclosed all the information we had on the congressman and his little flying monkey, Jacobi, Skyler and that whole bunch might have begun making immunity deals with the DOJ. The first thing they would have done in exchange for a plea deal would be to throw Phoenix under the bus. Then the door would be completely shut as far as being able to carry on settlement talks with Phoenix."

"So, *sweetheart*, you're telling me you're trying to save Phoenix just so you can keep your case against them alive? Really? That's what I'm hearing? *Sweetheart?*" Teri sometimes enjoyed being playfully sarcastic.

Deke simply grinned but took her comments to be rhetorical. They continued to cruise on the water and eventually Deke grew silent. Teri could see that something had shifted in his mood. The *thing* that had been bothering him so much lately was back.

"Hey," she said.

"What?"

"Isn't it about time you tell me what's going on with you? You haven't been the same since this case cropped up. Cara's noticed it, as you know. I'm sure Andy would if he were here. *I* most certainly notice it. When I've asked you about it before, you always say, 'Not now.' Talk to me, Deke. I'm your wife. I love you."

The boat rocked on the waves and Deke remained quiet, lost in thought. Finally, he sighed and said, "For thirty years, I've spent the vast majority of my time exposing and beating down some of the most calloused, dishonest human beings crawling on this planet. They were predictably always capable of rationalizing truly horrible conduct to make themselves feel better. That little creep I was fully prepared to cause physical injury to right there in my office made me feel dirty, and at the same time he made me ask myself if I was different from him on any given day. He resurrected ghosts that sometimes remind me that the damn exalted place I prefer to occupy is purely illusory. At the end of the day, I am no better than that morally empty, pathetic hustler."

"Oh, Deke," she responded, "I know you had a rough childhood. Most of the time, though, you've told us that it was positive."

"It *was* positive, aside from the fact that I had no parents. Well, not really. My father became the invisible man early on, and then my mother split as I was turning fourteen. Luckily, there were some families that took me in without me having to go to one of those awful places that I'm trying to bring down. I almost *did* have to go!"

"What do you mean?"

"It was shortly after my mother left. I was staying temporarily with a family. The Nealies. First there were the Mortons, and then the Nealies. They owned a big citrus farm. They had two boys a little older than me. We were friends but not real close. Anyway, there was a sheriff in Arcadia, not a nice man, not a man with any kind of integrity. Sheriff Crane. His son was a year or two older than me, and I'd known him from here and there around town. He always picked on me. Ty. Maybe it was short for Tyler, I don't know. One day, Ty went too far. We got into a fight and, well, I clobbered him. Left him on the ground in the park. His dad, Sheriff Crane, arrested me. He threatened to send me to Sandbury Housing for Boys because I had no parents. The Nealies couldn't help me. But then another couple, an older couple who had no children, stepped up. They were a prominent family in town, owned another big citrus farm, probably the biggest in the county, and they had some political influence in the community. They took me in and saved me from the reform school fate."

"Gosh, Deke, how come you've never told me that?" Teri asked.

He shrugged. "Sometimes we push away painful memories."

"But there's something else, isn't there? Something about Bucky Carlton?"

He nodded.

"Deke, I think you need to go back to Arcadia."

He closed his eyes as if that was a suggestion he was dreading.

She continued. "Whatever it is that's back there, you need to go face it. Come to grips with it. I'll come with you, if you want me to, but it's definitely something you need to do." Deke continued to remain silent. "Honey, you've always told me I was wise beyond my years. Well, that's my wisdom for today. Please. Confront your demons head-on. Go back to Arcadia. Just for a visit."

"To tell you the truth," he began, "I have been thinking about it. I've been avoiding it, well, for decades. You're right. I have to go back and face some truths."

Teri placed a hand on his. "Honey, you know I'm good with it. It won't be anything that's dangerous?"

"No, it won't be dangerous. Not physically, anyway. As for what it will do to me emotionally, I can't say."

She paused before speaking. "Deke, do what you need to do."

He nodded.

More silence, and then he slowed the boat until it came to a stop on the water.

"What are you doing?" she asked.

He gave her a grin, indicating that her support and the push to get him to do what he needed to accomplish had swept away the dark clouds. "How about we go skinny dipping with those dolphins? They seem to really like us, *sweetheart*!"

She laughed. "Wow, okay, that's a sudden twist in the plot." She gave him one of her looks. "You know how I like dolphins."

"What do you say?"

"Does this answer your question?" Teri pulled off her red bikini for a dip in the Gulf. "So tell me, how do I measure up to that, uhm, *woman*?"

"There's no contest," Deke said.

Her man was usually right more often than he was wrong.

30

The flight on the Airbus A380 from Brazil to Boston was in Midas's opinion the best first-class accommodations on commercial airline travel he had been offered in years. The nine-and-a-half-hour flight from São Paulo included medium quality champagne, two fairly decent meals, and two gorgeous flight attendants who spent a comfortable amount of time flirting with him. It would take some adjusting for the cultural downgrade from the remarkable Guarujá Beach area he now called home to the unsightly streets and architecture of urban New England. Driving through the city, he referred to it as a vast sewer pipe. Nothing had changed his attitude about the ridiculous place some locals referred to as Beantown. He wanted to be winging his way out of town as soon as possible.

The only positive to being there was that Midas would be cleaning up the nasty place a little bit. If the so-called Pilgrims and Patriots of Boston only knew how he was spending a part of his coveted personal time trying to improve their lives, they would no doubt throw a parade down Boylston Street in honor of Midas the Avenger. Unfortunately, the important improvement he was donating to the city, and the state of Massachusetts for that matter, would not be something he could disclose, even with his sister, until he was back at the beach in Brazil and sipping on a cold Cachaça.

Midas typically hated quick turnaround trips, but this one was an exception. No visits to favorite haunts. Not even a hello to his sister. If things worked out as planned, he would be headed back to Brazil by nine that evening.

The Esplanade, an area beside the Charles River, included a three-mile jogging circuit within the park that was one of the more popular locations for joggers and health-conscious Bostonians who preferred outdoor exercise, everything from cycling to tai chi. Midas had used the scenic spot for six-mile runs when he was forced to spend time in the city. Today, though, his plans involved a much shorter run. He would need to concentrate more on speed than distance. Sunday morning was also not his first choice as a time to blast through three miles as fast as he could. But Midas was not a complainer. At least he was happy that few people were running the route early on a Sunday morning.

As he began his first lap, he noticed a few cyclists and people practicing yoga scattered along the pathway. He passed an overweight man dressed in a set of grey sweats and wearing a red kerchief tied around his head. Midas laughed to himself, thinking that was the most disturbing optic of the entire beautiful surroundings.

Finally, halfway through Midas's second lap, he closed the distance on the Slick Stick. The congressman was moving at a moderate speed that exposed his preference for leisurely laziness over real exercise. Midas knew that the politician often bragged about the well-maintained esplanade, as if he personally had been responsible for it. Nothing was further from the truth, but that was typical of Bob Minds. Nevertheless, it wasn't uncommon for the regular Sunday morning serious runners to give the man a quick pat on the back as they jogged past him on the pathway.

Midas was preparing a pat of his own.

He assessed distance, speed, and potential witnesses that might be too close for him to pull off his plan without complications.

It was down to the twenty seconds he was waiting for. Midas approached Bob with a 4.4 forty-yard sprint.

A quick reach of the arm.

The needle jammed into the exposed neck quickly and expertly.

Bob reacted as if he were swatting away a bee.

The variability of how the Novichok toxin had the potential to kill depended on the dose that was delivered as well as the weight, conditioning, and overall health of the victim. Physically, Bob Minds wasn't out of shape. Nevertheless, the high dose Midas had just administered with a 1.5 inch eighteen-gauge needle was enough to down a bear.

The nerve agent had a long history of success with Russian assassins ending the lives of pesky political opponents. Midas put plenty of distance between himself and the Stick before glancing back to see the erratic seizures the congressman was having.

Midas was proud to add one more statistic to Novichok's reputation.

* * *

By the time Bob Minds was rushed to the Massachusetts General Hospital emergency room, he was experiencing convulsions, paralysis, and difficulty breathing. This could not be improved with oxygen because of the massive amount of fluid secretions that were filling his lungs. His blood pressure readings made major swings. His extremities were as rigid as heavy iron piping. ER doctors were unable to save the man they barely recognized due to the horribly contorted face. They were unaware that this was their congressman who was swiftly dying before their eyes. Even administering atropine and diazepam as an antidote for the toxin commonly referred to simply as VX was useless.

Bob Minds was DOA the instant the poison hit the congressman's blood stream—it just took a half hour for him to cross the finish line.

Reporters were already outside the hospital. Blood and gore narratives surfaced within a matter of hours. Hours later, law enforcement officials, including the FBI, were still trying to make sense of the fuzzy statements given by wannabe witnesses. Some of the stories were simply preposterous.

Three Mexican men had held the congressman down and poured something down his throat!

Two men had screamed at the congressman in Russian before they sat on his body and sprayed him with an aerosol can!

A homeless old lady had tripped him and then poured a liquid from a soda can into his mouth!

Only one report, from an Asian woman practicing tai chi, described a thin, fast-running person with a long ponytail and wearing a fashionable orange running outfit, who had come into close contact with the politician. "I wasn't sure if it was a man or woman at first, but the person was remarkably graceful, like a gazelle!" the woman proclaimed, something that would have flattered Midas.

MSNBC had their usual talking heads out in full glory blaming Russia and China for an attack on an American congressman on US soil. Politicians of every party and description were reporting on Fox News and CNN that the incident was a clear declaration of war that needed to be answered speedily.

Midas caught probably the most bizarre take on the incident minutes before he boarded his plane back to Brazil. The report suggested that a cabal of both Democrat and Republican war hawks had ordered Minds's death because he was preparing to dramatically cut the funding for the military budget. Midas had laughed so loudly that the hot redhead who had been eyeing him for an hour smiled and asked if he would share what he found to be so funny with her.

A spin mentioning Skyler Bannock also made it to air as breaking news. A witness had seen her entering the hospital shortly after the announcement that Minds had been rushed to Massachusetts General. But the tale was just a tease. There might have been a bigger story in the media had journalists known that Skyler had indeed appeared, but she had also abruptly disappeared after leaving the congressman's side in the emergency room. No one saw that she had been escorted out of the hospital by two men in colorful sport coats to a grey van with blacked-out windows.

* * *

Skyler sat comfortably in a cushioned wingback chair next to an unusually quiet Ron Jacobi. The eyes of big men dressed in excessively gaudy clothes and dispersed around the room fully focused their eyes on her. The putrid smells of cigar smoke and garlic were thick in the air of the old Victorian home. It was indeed an impressive, if kitschy, place. Dark blue velvet-covered chairs stood beside heavy carved wood side tables and freestanding bookshelves. The ceiling was completely covered with hand painted cherubs and life-sized angels staring menacingly down at the very chair Skyler was now occupying.

The silence was almost deafening, save for the Frank Sinatra tunes faintly playing through the speaker system elsewhere in the building.

Ron and the other brutish men all stood when the elderly man with hair as white as milk stepped into the room. No one really knew his age except the few in his immediate family that were still alive. Six feet tall with perfect posture. Smooth olive skin. Clean shaven. Skyler figured he'd had a partial facelift. The bright emerald-green eyes should have been those of a happy man, but they always projected anger.

One of the men picked up the heaviest chair and, grunting, placed it directly in front of Skyler and Ron. It was a routine that everyone in the room, including Ron, had seen before, but Skyler had never had the pleasure.

Only when Pope took a seat did the others follow suit.

He cleared his throat, took his time lighting a cigar, and finally spoke. "Ms. Bannock, I'm so sorry to hear about what must have been a horrible death for your friend."

After a beat, Skyler realized she should say something. "Oh, thank you."

Pope nodded in acknowledgment that this was the correct response. "Over the years, as you are no doubt aware, my family and I have donated huge amounts of money and created votes for his campaigns. Although you and I have never met, I do know quite a lot about you. If things go well this afternoon with our little talk, perhaps we can have dinner together and we can discuss your interesting life in more detail. Right now, though, we need to have a question and answer session about the death of your, er, business colleague."

Skyler had been in more than her fair share of situations in which she found herself alone with johns, trapped in a locked room at their expensive condos or high priced hotel rooms. She always had an almost mystical ability to talk them away from the cliff edge.

This situation, however, felt different. The level of terror surging through her spine was not generated by just another perverted john. She knew without being told who this man was and what he was capable of.

She knew that the scary angels on the ceiling above were there to comfort Pope, not her. A glance at Ron had revealed his petrified expression that concerned her even more. Usually he was in full control of events occurring around him. This time, Pope was in charge. And, although she could barely speak, Skyler believed that at this moment, *she* was more capable of handling Pope than Ron.

"I'm pleased to meet you, Mr. Jacobi," she said as calmly as possible.

"Please call me Flavio. You may know that I am called 'Pope,' but I allow certain people to address me as Flavio, the name my mother gave me."

She'd had no idea that was his real name. "Thank you, Flavio. I certainly hope we can have an extended discussion over dinner. But, with respect, I'm not sure why I have been invited into your beautiful home on this, the very day I have lost my business partner. I'm certain that if you could share with me something about that, then I believe I'd be better equipped to answer all your questions." She then intentionally crossed her bare legs and allowed one high heel to dangle just enough. Every man in the room noticed.

"Well, Ms. Bannock, let me start this way. I know all about the wonderful times you and my favorite nephew have had over the years. I've watched all that develop with strong admiration for you and your business partner. In Italy, they have a term for how you both might be described. The term is *truffatori*. Do you know that word?"

"No, sir, I do not."

"In a sense, in English it might mean "hustlers.' Plural. And please don't be insulted by that because, as I said, I truly respect the abilities you have shown. You, in particular. The feminine form of a *truffatore* is *truffatrice*. I like the sound of that, don't you?"

"It sounds . . . sexy," Skyler answered with a smile.

Ron, sitting nervously near Skyler, had an inkling where Pope was heading with this, and it had something to do with the death of Bob Minds. Ron was also pretty sure who had done the deed. Midas McDonald's warning to leave the Deketomis family and firm alone had been disobeyed. Skyler's brother had carried out the hit as revenge. Unfortunately, Pope would have a hard time believing that neither he nor Skyler had any hand in it, so he kept quiet and allowed Skyler to remain at the helm. He was well aware that she knew how to read a room.

"Flavio, I'm only guessing about this," she said, "but is it your belief that for some reason your nephew and I had something to do with the death of the congressman? Because I can see how you'd think we might benefit, big time. I can understand how the two of us, now having complete control over what I call my 'working girls,' would benefit your nephew's business. I mean, with all the things he has to accomplish with politicians, judges, prosecutors, and law enforcement. Men who, well, like working girls. Especially highly trained loyal women who for years have gotten remarkable results when remarkable results were needed. Most people might even look at the team I've assembled and conclude it would take years to duplicate. I can also see how you might have considered how easy it would be to shift that entire operation away from focusing on pharma, oil and gas, and Wall Street connections . . . and maybe slide *that* business over to areas you and Ron might benefit from. Is that what you're thinking, Flavio? Are you thinking we had my partner murdered so that your nephew and I could take total control of a hugely profitable enterprise that has taken years to build? Is that it?"

Skyler crossed her legs again and then delivered the slyest, most seductive smile she could conjure.

The seconds ticked by, but eventually Pope smiled and laughed aloud.

The broad is sexy and *smart!*

A perfect business move trumped the need to deal with minor skirmishes every time.

He could also see that she had masked her fear of him well. He admired that.

She also reminded him of the woman with whom he fell in love forty years before.

"Ronnie, you have sat there quiet as a mime. I want to hear from you." Pope wasn't certain that his nephew fully understood what his mistress had just accomplished.

But Ron surprised his uncle. He knew Skyler well and was very aware of what she had just delivered completely on the fly. "Uncle Flavio, what happened to Bob Minds today will never be connected to Skyler and myself. Not in a million years. But the possibilities surrounding the business that Skyler single-handedly built and was sharing with her useless partner are endless. There's nothing typical about what Skyler has built. These are a quality of girls that are far from normal. Granted, they make a monumental amount of money, they live extraordinary lives, but they accomplish extraordinary things. I have watched it first-hand. Each girl is assigned just one person, maybe two in very unusual circumstances. The industries that use Skyler's services have never had a clue about how her legitimate PR firm accomplishes what they do. No questions are asked and no details are disclosed. It is a business that has operated without problems for six years now. A typical pharma company, for example, is paying for what they think are legitimate public relations services that consistently deliver stellar results."

Skyler added, "The results they're looking for, Flavio, involve stealing competitors' secrets or influencing regulators and politicians. The extras for us are even bigger when we occasionally create extortion films and recordings in the operators' luxurious apartments with scenes so salacious that it would shame even most porn sites. To give you an example of the success of this business, last year it generated eleven million dollars. It could possibly double this year. The other part of the success is that the operators stay with us because of the security we offer, the splits in profits we share, and the incredibly pampered, cushy lives they lead. The targets also lavish them with limitless extras. What they make from targets is theirs. Some of them have been with the same target for years, and they're happy to follow orders strictly prohibiting them from having relationships with any other males. We give them some leeway when it comes to other, uhm, female relationships."

Flavio was well aware that Skyler and his nephew were working him like pros, building visuals he could easily understand and maybe improve upon with the power of his organization. They had gone from hoping they could make it out of the room alive to recruiting him as a business partner in less than thirty minutes.

"Enough, enough, I get it," he said. "But let me make sure you understand something as clearly as possible. If there is even the slightest hint that this hit can be traced to either one of you, I will see to it that both of you will . . . regret it. If you thought what happened to Congressman Minds was disturbing? Well . . . This family cannot take the risk."

"We understand, Uncle Flavio," Ron said.

"Of course, Flavio," Skylar echoed.

With that, Pope stood and held out his arms. "Princess, welcome to our family for now. You intrigue me far too much for me to want to harm you. Ron here can attest to the fact that I take matters in hand before the sun sets on any day that I ever believe you've betrayed me or posed a threat to this family. Now, let's relax and the three of us can drink champagne and smoke cigars. What kind of cigar would you prefer, Princess, bold or mild?"

31

Paul Baker propped his feet on the edge of his thirty-thousand-dollar desk, designed and built by Aston Martin, and reclined in his Vitra Grand executive work chair.

He felt pretty good.

Four of the executives he had extorted days before sat in front of him. A young man who until today had been a five-year staff lawyer serving the company's in-house counsel sat further back near the door of the huge office. The company's chief counsel, who had held that position for ten years, had been fired that very day.

"This is Cleanup Day, boys," Paul announced, "and I want to make certain everyone in this room is prepared to sign the documents that will give me full authority to do that cleaning." He swung his feet to the floor, stood, and went over to the conference table in the center of the space. He motioned them all to join him.

Well-organized stacks of documents with yellow and red stickies attached near signature lines sat on the table next to neatly lined pens. The group of men approached the table silently and with body language that obviously indicated they wanted out of the room as quickly as possible.

"Lewis," Paul addressed the young lawyer, "I'm appointing you as interim counsel for Phoenix. At least for today, since your boss did not fully understand the direction the company is now heading with regard to its substantial legal problems. I will need for you to first sign the proposed settlement authority papers laying out the guidelines for our strategy on closure with the Bergman-Deketomis law firm. Naturally, I will need each one of the four pertinent executives here to sign right below your name. The documents are lined up in order around the table. Easy peasy. Let's get to it."

The five men followed Lewis, a "kid" still in his twenties who was just as astonished to be the company's new in-house counsel as everyone else in the room. He signed his name, struggling to appear disinterested in the words contained in the documents.

They all knew the details of how Paul Baker had returned from the dead with threats of becoming the vehicle that would end the life of Phoenix if no serious compromises were made. Paul, days before, had laid out details well supported by documents of potential prosecutions that were sure to follow if he remained true to his word. The fallout could be disastrous. Probabilities of divorces, individual prosecutions for bribery, losses of jobs, and years of rebuilding to raise the company from the ashes.

"Hey, the name of our company is Phoenix, you know, the mythical bird that rises from total destruction to rejoin the land of the living!" he had said with relished irony.

The executives would later speak of the obvious confidence and indifference Paul had displayed as he listed his demands. Reckless abandon was by far the best description of his attitude. It was clear to everyone in the room that Paul was committed to his plan to destroy the company regardless of the inevitable criminal prosecution he would face.

At the top of his demands was that he would retain his position as CEO of the US arm of the company. To assure his security in that position, he would be entitled to a new five-year contract with salary and bonuses exceeding eight-million dollars a year. All the executives implicated in any wrongdoing that he exposed would also keep their jobs and be entitled to contract extensions. The special gift to those executives was Paul's attempt at rebuilding and assuring long term loyalty, but the subtext was that they were all put on notice. Any attempt to disclose the smallest detail of any uglies that had transpired would obliterate their future careers in corporate top management anywhere in the United States. They knew he could do it, too.

Finally, Paul was willing to spend a great deal of money to make Phoenix's legal problems with the Bergman-Deketomis law firm disappear, and this shocked his small audience until the men understood that a settlement of the lawsuit was the only way to go. Too much dirt would come out at a civil trial. The DOJ could possibly get involved after that. No, Phoenix would have to "pay, pay, pay, and make it go away." The further expenditures to completely reorganize national operations policies, which would most certainly be a component of the settlement, would also be extensive.

Luckily, the four executives and the in-house lawyer signing papers had been taught at their schools to never allow their moral compass and courage to get in the way of ambition. In their minds, cheating, lying, and furtherance of corruption might have a cost to somebody but that cost would rarely be passed on to them.

Personally, though, Paul considered Cleanup Day to be about the risks he faced if the Deketomis firm continued to expose Phoenix. His goal was to settle existing or future legal claims with Nicholas Deketomis so that he could close a dangerously troublesome chapter in Phoenix's—and his own—corporate history books. The only question in his mind was when he would set the meeting.

Paul went back to his recliner as the men signed the papers. The feet returned to the top of the desk. This was a perfect day for the enforcer who had turned desperation into victory. Maybe someday he could lecture a class at Yale, bragging about what he had accomplished, but he knew those kinds of lessons were best taught at exclusive gentleman's clubs over drinks.

* * *

Cara Deketomis and Claudia Clapper sat in front of the twenty-foot high picture window that revealed a stunning late afternoon view of the Snow Mass mountain, the playground of one of Colorado's many ski resorts. It was the kind of place Cara had spent a good many winters cruising along slopes on her snowboard, and something Claudia had never seen until Deke had arranged her stay at a successful drug rehab in the state.

A scenic vacation for Claudia as a child was a rare day at a sketchy public swimming pool in one of the many blighted, crime-ridden urban hellholes her mother had dragged her to in order to follow just another violent, deadbeat man.

Cara had grown up with the comfort of caring parents, three meals every day, a home that looked and felt like the set of a Disney movie, transportation to school and soccer practice, excellent education from preschool to law school, a reason to feel confidence, hope, and a well-developed vision of her future.

By contrast, Claudia had a childhood with her only parent being Kiki Clapper, who exposed Claudia to every conceivable sad, scary, stressful, and insufferable situation the selfish alcoholic mother could possibly be a part of.

In the many hours that Cara had spent talking with Claudia, she had zero sympathy for her takeaway of Kiki Clapper. Kiki had been raised in a Middle American home that had produced two other girls who were well-educated, both successful in their careers as nurses, and living well-adjusted lives. She'd had the opportunity for a wonderful life.

What was particularly galling to Cara was that Claudia's grandparents and aunts had on several occasions offered to take on the responsibility of raising the child that Kiki was unequipped and unwilling to raise. One of the aunts went as far as asking the court to assign custody to her. To avoid allowing that to happen, Kiki went on the lam and disappeared with Claudia. This happened repeatedly, and they usually ended up in some version of hell.

"Claudia," Kiki would tell her, "The hateful police officers want to kill Burt so we have to keep moving around." Burt was a horrible man with whom they were living in a camper truck, one of Kiki's many bad choices. Living in the camper was "perfectly fine" with Kiki, and she had tried to convince eight-year-old Claudia that she should "simply ignore Burt" when he reached over in the night to touch her because "he liked her."

Cara had such a difficult time listening to the dozens of similar stories that she often excused herself for a bathroom break. Cara didn't like clients to see her sobbing. Deke had explained many times why it was critical to project strength and control with emotionally weak clients. He had warned her that stories she might hear from people who were relying on her to be powerful and strong would change the way she regarded her fellow man. They would change *her*, too. But the resentment Cara felt toward Kiki Clapper was probably not the kind of change her father had meant.

The young lawyer had been right to take on Claudia's rehabilitation. Her father had been dubious, as had most everyone else at the firm. Cara had seen something here that could be saved. Claudia's disturbing life stories might never be testimony a jury would be permitted to hear unless a moronic defense lawyer opened the door for them at trial. Cara saw a few potential avenues to use, especially Claudia's mental anguish at the loss of Trayvon. If defense attacks broached how Claudia was a drug-addicted mother, Cara had mapped out what she liked to call her "lying-in-wait strategy." If the defense went there, then the tales of Claudia's life could be told and would help jurors understand exactly why the woman might not have been America's best mother. Closing statements could remind jurors that life did not always have a Hallmark ending.

"Claudia," Cara said, "I'm betting that one of the important issues the counselors here will do is to help you understand that your addiction is just a symptom of serious baggage you've had to carry around most of your life. That could be something we may or may not have to talk about in trial. What do think about that?"

"For the first three weeks I was in this place, I really couldn't think of nothin'," Claudia said. "I was hurtin' all over. I swear to you, my hair, my eyeballs, hell, even my fingernails, were beating me down with pain I never thought I could live through. All I wanted was another fix. I don't even have no memory of when I figured out I was alive. But yes, I've heard all that from the head doctors and that's what they spend most their time spouting at me about."

Cara often studied Claudia's physical appearance during pauses in conversation. There were no more angry red blotches on her arms and face. She had voluntarily removed the ring piercings in her nose, ears, and eyebrows. The natural color of dirty blonde was emerging though green and pink patches of hair coloring that had been a branding for her. The teeth that had endured the ravages of meth were still salvageable and could be improved before trial. Cara recognized there were miles to go before putting Claudia on the stand, but she was getting there. The goal was to present the woman so that jurors would not blame Claudia for the death of her child.

"Claudia, does it offend you that I've been talking to you about what we have to do with your physical appearance to get you ready to testify in front of a jury at trial?"

"I won't lie. When you started talking to me about the way I looked, I was close to telling you to kiss my skinny ass, but I get it. I'm good with that. I ain't never gonna look like your sweetie pie beautiful ass, but I just might surprise you when the time comes."

They both had a good laugh at that, and then Cara said, "Okay. Here's the tougher question. Can I get you to voluntarily stay here until we get that skinny ass of yours to work through all that baggage your counselors say is the key to your recovery?"

"Darlin', this is the nicest damn place I've ever lived. Got my own bed to myself where the sheets feel like cool silk. Got the best food I've ever put in my mouth, three times a day. Snacks if I want 'em. Couple of good lookin' male nurse types who won't give me as much as a glance right now, but they soon will be! Got this view out my window every day. Go on hikes. Hell, they even have me ridin' horses. So yes, I will stay here even if they decide I need a damn exorcism."

Claudia almost went from those manic words to soulful tears as she reached out and took Cara's hands. "I need to go to a session now. Cara, my dear Cara, will you please tell your daddy that no one walking this earth has done as much for me as you are doing, and there ain't no damn way on earth I'm gonna let you down. Please tell him that, Cara."

Claudia then stood, gave Cara a little wave, and walked away.

The timing was perfect because Cara had already lost the fight trying to follow her dad's advice of showing nothing but strength and control.

Outside, sitting behind the wheel of her rental car, Cara pulled herself together for the next meeting on her schedule.

Being in Colorado, it made sense to see Zach Morrison. He was waiting for her at his hotel.

It was time to deliver her "Yes" or "No" decision on joining his firm.

32

It had been almost fifty years since the last time Deke walked down Oak Street, the major road that passed directly through downtown Arcadia, Florida. Except for the short two-hour visit when he'd driven through the community with Teri a few years earlier, this was really the first time he'd stepped foot in Arcadia since he was a teenager.

The population of the city had grown to more than ten thousand people. They made their livings working in and around citrus and cattle. The city referred to itself as "The Home of the All-Florida Championship Rodeo," and some of the most well-known rodeo riders in the country competed in Arcadia.

The early settlers to the area initially called the small 1883 settlement "Waldron's Landing" and sometimes referred to it as "Tater Hill Bluff." Deke had called it home for most of his childhood. As he walked, memories of growing up there surfaced a notch higher each time he passed a stranger. They said hello and often hesitated for a second or two to maybe help with directions or engage in a small conversation, something that might make one feel more welcome. After being gone from the city for so long, now they were all new faces to Deke, just as his was likely one to them. Age had a hand in redesigning a population, for better or worse. Had Arcadia been this friendly long ago when he was there?

It crossed Deke's mind that if anyone asked him why he was in town, he could not have given them a reason they would understand. He wasn't even certain he fully understood. Indeed, he was strolling through Arcadia without any specific direction or purpose.

Teri had encouraged that he revisit the place. After their outing on the boat, they discussed it further. She had spent a good five minutes explaining how and why he might benefit from returning to his hometown. Once Cara found out about the possible trip, she put on the pressure for him to do it, too. His wife and daughter's go-to wording several times was that "it might be helpful or beneficial."

The thing was that they knew Deke was hurting. Whatever it was in the past that was tearing his soul apart lay back in Arcadia. He needed to go back and face the monster in order to make peace with himself. And then, perhaps, he would reveal to his family what it had all been about.

Deke occasionally commented how he felt as if he had turned his back on the town that helped raise him, and that he was never sure why. It was a meaningless excuse for him to suggest he had simply become too busy with his career and family. But some of his most valuable friendships had developed in Arcadia, and this was something Deke always valued. Nevertheless, if he were truthful, he would admit that he had spent no time staying in touch with the folks he always declared were so important to him.

Yet, here he was. After nearly fifty years of self-imposed isolation, he had flown more than two hours south from Spanish Trace to Punta Gorda, and then driven forty minutes north to Arcadia, the town where good and decent people had helped him become the person he was today.

Ironically, he might have used the words *wasteful* or *ridiculous* to better describe how he felt about his self-inflicted seclusion.

Eventually, Deke stepped into one of Arcadia's oldest cafés, a restaurant that had served only breakfast and lunch for decades. He had memories of countless excursions from school to the welcoming little place where Arcadians crowded the tables from six in the morning to 2:30 in the afternoon. Conversations about football, deer hunting, church, politics, bountiful citrus crops, and local rodeo riders created a cacophony so clamorous that the ability to read lips was a must.

Deke noticed a quick, quiet hush that came over the lunch crowd, much like in a Western movie in which some kind of foreign varmint of a character walked through the swinging doors of a frontier saloon.

He quickly concluded that it was because he was overly dressed in an expensive sport coat, shirt, and slacks that contrasted with the strapped overall jeans, cowboy hats, Caterpillar caps, and Brogan work boots. But things returned to normal in a flash.

Then, as he took a seat at an empty two top corner table, amidst the loud conversations, he heard the name 'Deke.'

The elderly waitress might have waited tables at the café from the day it had opened, but he didn't recognize her. She handed him a menu with the specials of the day neatly handwritten, Xeroxed, and clipped to the top of the first page.

"Sweetheart, can I start you off with a water and a glass of tea?"

Deke read the name on the tag shaped like a large sunflower. "That would be perfect, Joline. And I'd appreciate it if you would hold the sugar on that."

The aging but still classically beautiful woman gave him a smile and commented how "extra special" the daily special was that day. "Fried pork chops and mashed potatoes with gravy and fried okra. It's my favorite, darlin'."

"With that endorsement, that's exactly what I'll have."

She went away and Deke scanned the faces in the crowd, thinking that among the fifty or sixty people in the room, just by law of averages, he had to have long ago known or had some interaction with one or two of them. Some customers occasionally looked over the edges of their coffee cups and drinks to stealthily stare his way, while others made attempts to make him feel comfortable with smiles or a quick, polite wave-hello.

Deke again teased out the question—why was he here? He had generally prided himself with his ability to remain self-aware, to fully understand his motivations, regrets, expectations, and intentions. But as he sat waiting for the pork chops that he really didn't want at Weekman Café, his internal alarms were telling him to make a quick exit for home.

But before he could make a move, a man with a big smile approached his table, his right hand out for a handshake. Deke didn't initially recognize him as he stood to shake.

"Deke, is that you?"

He was slightly taller than Deke and had broad shoulders with the muscular build of men much younger than he appeared. He wore a brown John Deere cap, was dressed in a tan pearl snap work shirt rolled up to his elbows, Levi jeans, and black lace-up boots. His face had the kind of deep lines of too much sun exposure, and his black hair was greying at the temples.

Deke's brain was in overdrive until the very old but noticeable scar across the man's right forearm triggered both the man's name and how he had earned the scar.

"Danny McCourt. Either my old eyes are playing games or I'm shaking hands with Danny McCourt."

"Yep, it's me."

After the handshake, Danny grabbed Deke around the shoulder, pulled him closer for a quick hug, and slapped him on his back twice. Other patrons in the restaurant turned and smiled at the two. The local guy they respected had just given his approval of the stranger dressed like a tax collector.

"Danny, will you join me for lunch?"

"Are you kidding me? I'll spend as much time as you have for me today if you can stand me for very long. I've been up since four-thirty repairing fences, gates, and branding fat cows. My day is as good as done."

Deke chuckled. "Seems like my hometown hasn't changed all that much since I headed out of here, so let me congratulate you for that."

"No, bigger and better has never been on the agenda for Arcadia, but most people I know around here are good with that. We're in the middle of nowhere, but it's somewhere to me." He took the opposite seat at the table when Deke gestured to it.

In just a few seconds, Deke ascertained from the way the eyes in the room followed Danny that he was something of a big man in that small town. That was no surprise. Danny was a big man both in size and character, and he would have been such in any place he chose to call home.

"Deke, what do you think about the two of us taking a tour around town and letting me show you some of our success stories that we're proud of? Like I said, my workday is over and my truck can handle some of the roads around here that would break the axles of anything you might be driving. Plus, I'd love to hear the backstories of some of your big cases we read about, even in the *Arcadia Gazette*."

At first, Deke felt ashamed. Danny was offering as much kindness as he could to a man who had chosen to turn his back on the people who had done so much collectively to raise him. Older versions of folks like Danny were decent people who had provided him with homes when he was without a place to live. They had provided him with jobs that paid him far more than his worth as a kid. They had even scraped up enough money to create a scholarship to help pay for his first year at the University of Florida. Doctors and dentists had given him free medical care.

If he were being honest, he knew he had rejected them not because they had done anything wrong, but because it was his way of rationalizing and excusing himself for what he had done to Bucky Carlton. Someone who was decent, just like Danny. In fact, Danny was exactly the kind of man his best friend would have grown to be.

Deke had made himself an outsider to his hometown by choice. His simpleminded arrogance had allowed him to conclude that these people were somehow responsible for his own selfish actions that had caused Bucky's death. For forty years, Deke had been incapable of coming to terms with how intentionally wrong he was. These were *wonderful* people.

Danny had posed the question and his eyebrows were still raised. He was waiting for Deke's answer.

"Sure, Danny. I'd love to drive around with you," Deke said.

By one o'clock, they were loaded up in Danny's well-used diesel pickup. "How about we drive by the Nealies' old place?" his old friend suggested. "The city declared it, along with about half a dozen old homes around here, as a 'cultural heritage site.' I bet you're gonna remember your time with the Nealies. Y'all were a damn wild bunch from what I recall. Both those Nealie boys have set the world on fire with the way they've helped grow the citrus industry down in South America. They both made a boatload of money and built a whole new teaching facility for the FFA students at the high school. It's now regarded as one of the best in the state of Florida.

"Is that so?"

"Last time I saw them was at our twenty-five-year high school reunion. They probably asked about you, like most everybody else."

"They were two and three years ahead of me," Deke said. "So were you, if I remember correctly."

Danny creased his brow. "Is that so? Yeah, I guess you're right. But you always seemed older than you was. Doesn't mean folks weren't asking about you at *our* reunion. Old man Nealie lived to be ninety-five. They found him sitting on his ancient Caterpillar tractor with a cigar in his mouth, dead as a rock. The engine was still runnin'. Tough old son of a bitch. Probably helped you and those boys understand tough, I'll bet. I missed you at his funeral. I think the whole damn city showed up."

Deke certainly had memories of the Nealies. He had lived with them for several months until the incident with the sheriff's son. The Nealie boys had also been instrumental in convincing Deke to push Bucky into attempting his escape from Sandbury. It wasn't the Nealies' fault, though. They meant well.

Danny continued his drive down wide dirt roads where his friends fifty years earlier had raced trucks, tractors, motorcycles, and any other thing with wheels. Deke halfway listened to stories about the times they had camped out in woodlots along pasture roads or swam in ice-cold water in the gentle downstream currents of Peace River. He was torn between nostalgic joy and an uncomfortable feeling of guilt as Danny helped him remember the special childhood they had both lived. Memories he had shoved aside while he built a life far from the realities of Arcadia, Florida. These were truths of what his hometown was really like rather than the invented lies that had for so long comforted him in his commitment to never look back. The truth was that the people of Arcadia had been incredibly *good* to him, and it was his own guilt that had painted a false portrait over the place.

"Deke, you really are missing something if you haven't seen what used to be that broken down excuse for a rodeo arena we loved so much. It's now one of the premier rodeo arenas in the Southeast. It packs in fifteen thousand visitors twice a year, and we are still continuing to add on. It's just ten minutes from here. I'd love to show you, and don't think

I'm trying to hit you up for a donation 'cause I'm not, but they put me in charge of a big money raise to add on room to build a school for young rodeo riders who want into the big leagues."

Those words touched Deke. "Nothing would make me happier, Danny, and I'm sorry I haven't been around enough to do my part to help you with projects like that. I regret not being here to give back a little."

"Don't worry, pal. That's not gonna change a thing about how folks around here remember you. You don't need forgiveness for one darn thing. Oh, let's drive by the Pearsons' old place. I'll bet you want to see that."

Deke turned his head squarely to the passenger door window as if he had suddenly seen something of great interest. He didn't want his friend to know what was really happening.

"Wow, I almost forgot what this country road dust does to my eyes, Danny."

* * *

1970. Late Summer.

The same ritual as before.

The burly guard made Deke go through an X-ray machine and empty his pockets. When it was determined that he wasn't there to pass drugs, contraband, or any other prohibited items to one of the "residents," he was allowed inside.

Bucky looked even worse than the last time Deke had visited. Dark circles were visible beneath his eyes. The hair was unkempt. His skin was pale.

"Did they hurt you for trying to escape?"

Bucky didn't answer immediately. Finally, he said, "I'm okay."

"Geez, Bucky. I'm so sorry."

There was silence for twenty seconds. Then Bucky said, "It's not your fault, Deke."

"No, man, I am *sorry. I'm sorry that it didn't go the way we thought. The way that* I *thought. I planned the whole thing."*

"Stop it. It was a good plan. I was careless. Too many of the other boys saw me. I was dumb. I caused this to happen. Not you. Not your fault, bud."

"I'm not sure about that, Bucky . . ."

"I mean it, Deke. Stop blaming yourself."

"Bucky . . ."

"Don't look so down. I'll survive in here until I'm eighteen. It's just a few months." Bucky narrowed his eyes at Deke. "Hey, do you have a black eye?"

"Oh. Yeah. I got into a fight with Ty Crane. I beat his ass."

"I'm glad to hear it. Ty Crane deserved to have several of his asses beaten."

That made the two boys chuckle a bit.

"His dad almost sent me in here with you," Deke said.

"Well, as much as I'd like to have you by my side, you do not want to be in here, Deke. No way."

Deke nodded. "I know. I'm so sorry, Bucky."

"Stop saying that. It won't be much longer, and I'll be out." He raised his eyebrows. "Unless you've found a friendly home that will make an appeal to take me in."

Deke's eyes went to the tabletop, unable to face his friend. "I haven't found anything, Bucky."

Bucky sighed. "Oh, well. Keep looking, I guess. Keep trying."

"I will."

After they said goodbye, Deke left Sandbury Housing for Boys with a heavy heart. The guilt that was boring a hole in his chest was almost unbearable. He only felt somewhat better when he made a resolve to visit Bucky at least once a week until he got out. Deke owed it to him.

In the meantime, the fifteen-year-old went to the new home where he'd been living since the incident with Ty Crane.

With the kind Mr. and Mrs. Pearson. That perfect family. The one that got him out of trouble with the sheriff and was now providing Deke with the best home life he had ever known.

He never saw Bucky alive again.

33

Cara was at the house with Teri when Deke came through the front door, carrying his travel bag. It was nearly ten o'clock in the evening.

Teri stopped him in the foyer and gave him a hug and kiss. "Welcome back. Was the flight okay?"

"It was fine."

Cara stepped up and also embraced her father. "How was your trip, Dad?"

"Good, good. Let's go inside. Teri, do you have any more of that sauvignon blanc we were drinking the other night?"

Teri raised her eyebrows. "No, but I have a good cab I picked up today. I'll open that, all right?"

"Sure. Give me fifteen minutes to freshen up, and I'll meet you at the kitchen table."

So it was going to be one of those family talks.

Cara had received a message from her mother earlier that day. "Your father wants to talk to us when he gets back from Arcadia tonight. Can you be at the house?"

Absolutely. Cara was well aware, as was Teri, that her father's sojourn to his hometown was intended to be therapeutic and revealing. Perhaps now they would get some answers as to why the man they both loved had been in so much torment over the past few months.

She also had something to tell her parents, too.

Right on time, Deke came in to the kitchen and joined his family. Teri poured him a glass of the red wine, and he took a few sips.

"Arcadia hasn't changed much," he said. "It's pretty much as I remembered it. The people are the same down-home folks that live in a small town. I ran into at least a couple of guys I knew back then. One of them took me for a nostalgia tour around town in his truck. It was a very nice gesture on his part."

"That's great," Teri responded, still waiting for the shoe to drop.

Deke took a breath and went on. "I realize that you both have been concerned about me. My colleagues at the firm are, too. I'll probably have to repeat this little repartee with them tomorrow. So tonight will be good practice. I'm sorry Andy isn't here, too. When I next see him, I'll have to go through it all again."

"Deke . . ."

He held up a hand. "I want to do this, hon. It's time." He took another sip of wine and began. "When I was fourteen and fifteen, I had a best friend named Bucky Carlton."

"You showed me his grave there," Teri said. "I remember. I know he meant a lot to you."

"Right. But you don't know the whole story, dear. I never told you."

"Okay."

Deke nodded and continued. "He was a couple of years older than me, but we hit it off like gangbusters. Very talented kid who was good with horses and cattle and was on his way to being a true rodeo star. Unfortunately, like me, he became a kid who was on his own. I moved between homes with anyone who would take me in until I landed in one of the best situations I could have ever dreamed of having."

"The Pearsons," Teri said.

"Right."

"You've spoken about them often," Cara said.

"Bucky wasn't so lucky. His mother had died in a car accident, and his father was missing in action. Before the state could put its claws into him, I thought I could use the experience I had finding places to live to help him out." He sighed. "I guess the headline is that I was smart enough to know that I was putting Bucky in danger. I knew all the stories about how a boys' reform school worked. I was well aware of the dangers Bucky faced with the half-ass way I handled things after his mother died. If I'm honest with myself, I even remember thinking how excited and focused I was to try and beat the whole bureaucratic state-run system that I was always having to avoid myself. Hell, I made it into a game. But I knew the risks. In doing all that—"

"Deke, stop right there," Teri said. "Let's start from the beginning. No hiding. No memory avoidance. Tell me the story about you and Bucky without all the edits."

Deke cleared this throat, took another sip of wine, and nodded.

He then related the entire tale. How the attempt to hide Bucky in an empty vacation home had gained the boy a trespassing charge and landed him in Sandbury Housing for Boys. How Deke had convinced him to escape. Bucky was caught. In the interim, Deke had gone to live with the Pearsons, the family he had initially proposed to Bucky as a possible unofficial foster family. And then his best friend was killed at Fight Night in the camp.

"Bucky had repeatedly told me that he would be fine in the institution. He had made it clear to me that he could easily survive for a year. Because of his size and rodeo cowboy build, I wasn't much worried about any serious physical risks many of the other kids had to face. Bucky had one goal in mind that he had told me repeatedly. That was to get his high school degree and move on to become an accomplished bareback rider on the rodeo circuit. I believed he could do it, too."

Another sip of wine. "I remember . . . well, in a way I felt envy and jealousy that Bucky could see his future so clearly and with a truly achievable plan. It was Bucky's self-confidence that always inspired me. It was a sense of security that I almost never felt myself as I moved from family to family without any kind of safety net. Bucky had optimism about the future as he constantly adjusted to ways to simply survive."

"Dad, I understand you wanting him to try and escape," Cara said.

"It was nothing short of selfish hubris, Cara. I can try to dress it up with some high ground kind of reasoning where I was there to purely help one of my dearest friends. That I was there with a purely honorable all-for-Bucky intention. It was also as much about wanting my friend back with me in my world, surviving together, beating that whole dysfunctional scary life into which we were thrown. Without my friend,

I would have no one who could ever relate to *my* world. I felt isolated and I wanted that friend back. In my mind, we were a team that was stronger together."

Deke then hung his head. "The truth is that I was directly responsible for his death. I didn't kill him, but I might as well have. You see, I've been lying to myself about it. I've hidden the most important fact from everyone. I'd had a place for Bucky to live, and then I lied to him about it. I hid it from him because I wanted to have that place to live for myself and eventually did. *I took Bucky's spot at the Pearsons.* And I never told him the truth. He probably thought that home was still waiting for him, and that's why he ended up fighting for his life the day that animal broke his neck."

Tears formed in his eyes. "The Pearsons were so good to me. They helped me get my college scholarships and gave me the tools to become what I am today. But it could have been Bucky!"

Teri leaned in to him. After a moment, she spoke in a soft, comforting tone. "Deke, as you think about this tragedy, the space you occupy today is far different from the one you did at fifteen and when Bucky was seventeen. You are now living a long way from that survival mode you woke up with every day. So, I see why in this near perfect world you suddenly can examine the past with a different, more objective judgment. The key word is 'objective.' Today you have the luxury of looking back and critically analyzing every choice you made as a child grasping for survival. Your memory doesn't do you any favors when it comes to scrutinizing the choices you made. Hell, Deke, it's a bloody miracle you're even here today. So, if this is all about you trying to be honest with yourself, be honest about that simple fact as well."

Coming from most people those words would not have had a fraction of the impact as they did coming from his bride's mouth. Deke had told Teri many times that she was the wiser of the two of them. He believed that was absolutely true.

Cara took the hand closer to hers. "Dad, you don't need to forgive yourself. You have to forgive a fifteen-year-old child who was only trying to survive. Can you do that, Dad? If not for you, then can you do it for our family?"

Teri took his other hand.

Deke just looked at his wife and daughter.

"Maybe now is a good time to tell you something important," Cara said.

"What's that?" Deke asked, his voice cracking a bit.

"I turned down Zach's offer to join his firm in Colorado."

Deke's eyes widened. "You did?"

"I decided that I can learn so much more about the business from people like Gina and Michael and, well . . . you. At first I thought I wanted to get out from under the Deketomis name. But now I can see it's a badge of honor. It's a feature. I'm staying, Dad."

After a beat of silence, Deke embraced his daughter.

Nothing else needed to be said.

34

Paul Baker sat alone in the luxury of the same hotel room in which he had met with Bob Minds and Skyler Bannock so many times. A ten-foot Herman Miller conference table now sat in the middle of the suite's living room. A legal pad with an expensive Baccarat pen and a Waterford crystal drinking glass were on the table in front of each seat. The dining room just beyond the conference table had been decorated with arrangements of plants and flowers ranging from colorful varieties of orchids to long-stem white, yellow, and red roses. An arrangement of low-cut Asiatic lilies had been placed in a silver pot sat in the middle of the dining table. Exquisite place settings, handmade by one of Paul's favorite local artists, and polished silver flatware accompanied each setting.

Paul was committed to not leaving the room until he had solid closure to the legal nightmare the Bergman-Deketomis firm had unleashed on what was truly now his company for five more years. At least. Everything was on the line for Baker.

A young man stood at the suite's double doors to greet Deke, Gina, and Michael as they entered. He led the team to the dining table and asked if he could pour them a glass of wine from the extensive selections that were propped label-up in several silver champagne tubs arranged around the table.

"Maybe we'll pass on the wine until we see where this is going today," Deke answered.

Michael rolled his eyes and smiled at Gina as she made her way around the room, checking out the extensive floral arrangements. He took in the elaborate decor and said, "Guys, if I kick off before the two of you, I want a room set up exactly like this for my End of Life Celebration. In fact, I want you to double up on the orchids."

"Be nice," Deke said.

Michael joked, "You sure you don't want me to pour you a little bit of that Cristal to chill you out a few degrees, my friend?"

Paul Baker made his entrance from a side door adjacent to the master bedroom. "Actually, I would recommend the Prestige Cuvée if you really want to chill down," he announced as he extended his hand first to Deke and then to the other two. "My team was told to make you feel comfortable, but I must admit when I saw the end result of that request, a Catholic wake came to mind. Forgive us for going overboard, but at Phoenix we were more than pleased when you agreed to meet me after that last settlement encounter you had. All I can do is, again, apologize for that and ask you to take my word. That was not an event planned nor approved by Phoenix management."

Deke nodded his head. "All three of us are much appreciative of the chance to take a legitimate shot at closure to the Phoenix litigation, and I suppose I should officially apologize for the way I handled the messenger, regardless of who was sending the message. It was not my best day at a negotiation table. Besides, you're way too tall for me to carry you around on my shoulders, so I hope the effort to talk will be less tense."

Paul laughed a little too boisterously. "It's also my hope that no one gets carried out of this meeting. In fact, I'm optimistic to the point that we can spend some time over a late afternoon lunch or early dinner, depending on what time we finish up. Since you're foregoing a glass of wine to start out, let's jump to the chase. Please make yourselves comfortable around the conference table." Paul led them to the room next to the dining area. "Deke, have a seat here if you would." He pulled out the chair at the head of the table, and then he took a chair on a side across from Michael and Gina.

It was what Paul often referred to as his "controlled surrender seating arrangement" that signaled to the other side that there would be no ridiculous posturing of strength or power on his part and to let the person at the head of the table know he was there to get a deal done.

"Deke, the white paper sitting in front of us was my attempt at a first move toward settlement of all cases you now have pending against Phoenix. I was hoping the three of you could take a little time and read it through, and then we could have an open and sincere conversation about your reactions. While you review that document, I hope you will excuse me so I can make a few calls that are pressing. I assure you no one will overhear your private discussions, and, in fact, you're welcome to use a room across the hall that we've rented for you if a prolonged discussion by the three of you becomes necessary."

It was one of the more unusual settings in which Deke had negotiated when it came to serious settlement discussions, but it was apparent that whatever Paul Baker had in mind was something he felt would end the legal battles.

As Paul left the room, Gina went back to the dining room table and gathered three wine glasses and a bottle of Australian-produced chardonnay. She brought them back to the others and filled the glasses halfway. "The least we can do is drink a bottle of these people's expensive wines as we make our way through their settlement proposal, ya think?"

"What's this really all about, Deke?" Michael asked, gesturing at the entire suite. "I'm thinking you've seen this kind of road show before, but I haven't. These folks look way too confident that we're going to cave even before depositions or any relevant discovery has begun."

"As a point of information for the two of you who are far less refined than *moi*," Gina said, "these pens on the table are easily worth about a thousand dollars apiece. Those crystal glasses in front of you are somewhere in the range of six or seven hundred dollars each. Just the wine in this room alone is worth in excess of six-thousand dollars. And, by the way, I could set up a weekend vacation in Paris for the cost of the flatware and silver bowls laid out in that other room. So what's the message here?"

Deke pointed his index finger upward like a schoolmaster. "The message right now is to start reading so we can figure out whether there's going to be a celebration dinner today, or if it's a day when Phoenix wasted far too much money trying to impress us." He lowered his hand and began turning pages. "I would prefer that we all simply make notes as we go, and let's hold our comments until we've finished reading the document. Let's see if we land in basically the same place with our opinions."

Michael took his copy to what he deemed might be the most comfortable wingback chair in the room. Gina carried hers, along with a glass of wine, and made herself comfortable between large pillows on a sprawling couch.

After thirty minutes, Deke noted that the others appeared to be finished reading. "So, it's not that I don't trust what Mr. Baker said about no one listening to our conversations, but how about you jot down your overall reactions on the back of that last page and hand it to me?"

Michael handed his page to Deke first. It read: *Not sure what is up with this, but this is an incredible first move. 150 million is not enough, but my bet is we can double that if we hang in here today. The rest of the terms like reorganization and overhauling the reform schools are exactly what we started out wanting. Do not walk away, Deke. Sell, sell, sell.*

Deke again showed nothing but an outward appearance of indifference, even though he was already feeling near-jubilant about what he had read in the document.

Gina then placed her written response in front of Deke without a word. It read: *There is more to this story to cause them to make this move but . . . so what! The money is still too low for both the Trayvon claim and the national case that we would absolutely win. Just close the gap on the money. 250 mil is a reasonable target. The terms they laid out to completely revamp their operations are better than we would ever achieve in a court battle. Be patient today. I can't wait to see what they're going to serve us for dinner!*

Deke asked both of them to look over his shoulder and read what he wrote. They did so and saw these words: *I need both of you to leave the room for about an hour. Maybe take a walk around downtown or whatever you choose. I need some one-on-one time with Baker. The two of you leaving will be a concern to him. Much appreciated.*

"Okay, Deke," Michael said. "Say, Gina, it's a nice day outside. Want to go for a walk and clear our heads?"

"Sure, Michael. Some fresh air would be nice," she answered with a wink.

The two lawyers left the suite. Deke stood and began pacing around the room. Surely someone had been watching them. About five minutes later, Paul made his grand reentry.

"Bad choice of wine, substandard hors d'oeuvres, something I said?" he asked. "Surely your partners weren't offended by my offer."

Deke clasped his hands together. "Actually, we all saw that you brought us here in good faith. Let's sit."

The two men sat at the table across from each other, and Deke continued.

"There's nothing particularly offensive about your offer. We're glad that you anticipated the kinds of changes we would demand in completely revamping your facility operations nationally. The changes you are agreeing to will improve the quality of life for the kids who have to call your institutions home. You've added strict hiring requirements, training requirements, mandatory immediate dismissal of employees for even the hint of bad conduct. Thanks for that, Paul, but know that it changes nothing without strict enforcement. So, we have a couple of ways we can ensure that if we can get closer to a deal today."

"What brings us closer, Deke?"

"With all the details you've covered in this proposal, there is one that I'm certain you know will not work. One-hundred-and-fifty million will not come close to settling all the claims that would result from us focusing state by state on all the carnage you've caused, both physical and mental, from the way your company has conducted business since you opened your doors."

Baker spoke up quickly. "I'm sure we could find another twenty-five million to help with that."

"Paul, both you and I know that sounds like sympathy money. We don't want sympathy money. We want Phoenix to set up a claims facility that handles all the potential past claims that are directly related to your business operations. We want that claims facility to be in operation for six years. During that time, three impartial judges will review claims and decide on the viability of each one. If at the end of six years, if the four-hundred-million dollar fund has not been used, the remainder is returned to Phoenix. It's a built-in motivation part of the settlement that puts pressure on Phoenix to live by improved standards. You do well with those standards and you get money back."

"Four hundred million?"

"That sounds reasonable to me, Paul."

"Two important questions. Can we pay the funding over a period of three years? And what about your attorneys' fees?"

"Begin with the first payment of two-hundred-and fifty million. The first claim will be the Trayvon claim for twenty-five million. If you can do that, I'm pretty sure all your shareholders will be thrilled to know that there is some certainty and predictability in what all this potential litigation will cost. Let's get this first part of our offer finalized and that last part about attorneys' fees we can negotiate over dinner in this little paradise you put together. It will be a big number, Paul, but I'm thinking all of this—as you have figured out—will change your life, in particular, for the better. Can I call my partners and tell them that we're going to have an early dinner?"

Paul smiled at how seamlessly Deke had delivered that last nuanced threat. "Even that comment about my personal interests, which I hope will not be repeated, there is little doubt that these changes will help us build a more sustainable company. Also, there is no need to call your partners. I have someone behind them right now who can deliver the message in person."

The relief apparent on his face seemed out of place for a CEO who had just committed his company to a multimillion dollar settlement, but both men knew that Paul Baker had clearly just saved himself and his entire company.

35

The timeless rock anthem, "Black Betty," shook the ground around the open-air party venue as the lead singer of the hottest band in North Florida set the space on fire with their cover rendition. The partygoers could have closed their eyes and believed that Myke Scavone and his band Ram Jam were performing live. The UltraViolets were not only known for their original music but were also the go-to rock band within a hundred miles of Pensacola when there was something to celebrate.

It was just such an occasion for Deke's firm.

As he, Teri, and Michael clinked beer bottles together, Michael asked the boss how he felt.

"Michael, to be honest, at the top of the list is that I can move on from a sense of constant fear for the safety of the team. I can legitimately tell Teri here that Cara and the rest of us are no longer in harm's way."

"Amen."

"And, look, I'm more than grateful about what we accomplished. We made huge inroads into how the largest institutional children's housing corporation in the country will conduct business when it comes to the protection of the kids they house. A national fund of four-hundred-million dollars to compensate child victims of abuse in the Phoenix facilities will more than cover the potential bill for claims for many years ahead."

"Deke," Michael said, "CEOs will always continue to do some damn ugly things way beyond our time on this earth, but I'm genuinely proud to be a part of the machine you have built to push back while we can."

High-fives reverberated through the air between spinning and jumping moves on the dance floor while the core trial team raised toasts to each other and retold stories in a huddled group in the loudest voices they could over the vintage rock and roll blaring through speakers on the opposite side of the room. Mark Prom and Gina waved Deke, Teri, and Michael over to join them.

Gina commented in her outside voice, "This team is always talking about how some projects are magic and some are tragic. There was no magic involved in this one, my friends," Gina managed to say. "Beatdowns, near death experiences, murders, dangerous psychopaths, impossible odds . . . No magic was involved here, just vision, hard work, and commitment. It's our brand and it works."

It was difficult for anyone in the group to adequately express the true quality of emotions they had all felt during the tense and sometimes terrifying months that were now manifesting in a celebration, but Mark gave it his best shot. "Look, I'm not in the trenches with this team every day, but I've managed this law firm mad house for a couple of decades now. What comes to mind is what *The Guardian* reported about what you people do. I think their quote was that without oddballs like you, the practice of law would be relegated to eight-hundred-thousand lawyers defending big corporations, trying slip and falls and auto crash cases, divorcing people, and drawing up wills. And by damn, that is mostly true. I put this little celebration together quickly so we could all say thank you for what you put on the line in this legal horror story. So, use the rest of this week to rest, take some personal time, and let's jump back in next week and get to work on our next oddball case."

Deke reflected on Mark's words. A legal horror story indeed. The echo of guilt had been deafening. Now it was silent.

Michael then held up an envelope he'd had in his pocket. "Before we're sent back to the cellar, Deke, the team put together a little gift for you. They say, 'you can't go home again,' and yet you did it. Teri told us about your trip back to Arcadia. She directed our interest to that new rodeo ground they built down there. Here's a little something that might allow you to put a name of your choice on at least a part of that new project. We all pitched in to make that happen."

Deke took the envelope. Written on the outside was the message: *In the words of a great sage, there is always one more thing you can do.*

This had special meaning to everyone in the group, for it was something Deke had told them countless times when they felt as if they were in a corner without a next step in trial. A message to start fresh, create a new beginning in the way they analyzed situations, avoid self-pity, and above all, keep moving.

Deke thanked them without opening the envelope. "When I see this team together, I realize that I move around on the shoulders of giants every time I walk into a courtroom. I know I am blessed."

After a brief thank you speech to the partying crowd, Deke and Teri made their exit. On the way home, Teri's curiosity overwhelmed her patience. "Deke, if you're not going to open that envelope right now, I will."

He handed it to her. Inside was a check for $200,000 with a note.

We all thought it would be a great idea for you to match this amount and create a school for emerging rodeo riders. Maybe put Bucky Carlton's name on that school. Just a thought. Your Brothers and Sisters in Arms.